"If you'd behaved better," Angelo said, "you might not be in this predicament."

Surely Angelo wasn't suggesting they might still be together? Not when Gemma knew the kind of man he was. A playboy. A man who traded one beautiful woman for another, as soon as her sell-by date was over.

Her lip curled. "You mean if I were still your mistress? Putting up with your demands, your – "

"I thought you'd forgotten everything. So how do you remember how demanding I was?" His tone held a sensual rasp, belied by his shrewd gaze. He reached out and put a finger under her chin. He put enough pressure to tilt her head up, so that he could stare down into her eyes.

The sudden flare of heat that followed in the wake of the touch of that one finger shocked her. No. He was the last man on earth to whom she could afford to be attracted.

A spoiled playboy who'd had a fortune handed to him on a plate. A dilettante who destroyed without compunction.

"You tempt me to prove you a liar," he said.

Rich Man's Vengeful Seduction
by Laura Wright

ଓ✕✦ଓ

"Are you trying to get rid of me, Tess?" Damien asked.

"My partners are on their way over here and they know – "

"Nothing about me?" Damien finished for her, a flash of venomous pleasure lighting his eyes.

"They know nothing about my life before we started the company."

He considered this for a moment, then nodded. "All right. I'll see you tomorrow, Tess."

She looked up. "What?"

"I'll be at your office tomorrow at one."

"No!"

Damien leaned in close to Tess's ear, the heat from his breath making her hair stand on end and her heart twist painfully. This she remembered and, long ago, this she had loved.

"I'm not here to reminisce about old times," he uttered darkly. "I'm here to collect on a debt that was never paid."

Available in October 2008
from Mills & Boon® Desire™

Iron Cowboy
by Diana Palmer
&
Seduced by the Rich Man
by Maureen Child

ᓱ✕ᓰ

Millionaire's Wedding Revenge
by Anna DePalo
&
Stranded with the Tempting Stranger
by Brenda Jackson

ᓱ✕ᓰ

The Apollonides Mistress Scandal
by Tessa Radley
&
Rich Man's Vengeful Seduction
by Laura Wright

The Apollonides
Mistress Scandal
TESSA RADLEY

Rich Man's
Vengeful Seduction
LAURA WRIGHT

MILLS & BOON®

Pure reading pleasure™

*First published in Great Britain 2008
by Harlequin Mills & Boon Limited,
Eton House, 18-24 Paradise Road, Richmond, Surrey TW9 1SR*

The publisher acknowledges the copyright holders of the
individual works as follows:

The Apollonides Mistress Scandal © Tessa Radley 2007
Rich Man's Vengeful Seduction © Laura Wright 2007

ISBN: 978 0 263 85917 1

51-1008

*Printed and bound in Spain
by Litografía Rosés S.A., Barcelona*

THE APOLLONIDES
MISTRESS SCANDAL

by
Tessa Radley

Dear Reader,

As a teenager I read romances that I discovered in the garage…and later in the library and bookshops. There were all sorts of stories. Reunion stories, stranded at sea stories, secret baby stories…some of them seemed quite far-fetched to me. But it didn't matter how unrealistic a story might be, I finished it to discover the happy ending.

In those days I used to horse ride a lot. I'm told one day I fell off a horse – I don't remember. Or rather I remember getting onto the nag early that morning. It had been giving me a little bit of trouble and I was supposed to sort it out – well, three hours later I was in hospital, lights out. I came round the next morning with a killer headache. The funny part of it all is that the guy who saw me fall off and who called my mum, summoned help and did all the things a hero should is now my husband – and I don't remember the first time we ever met.

Every time I fell off a horse afterwards, I waited for the jolt to bring my memory back, like in romances I'd read – it never did. But I still got my happy ending!

I hope you enjoy *The Apollonides Mistress Scandal*. Please visit me at my website www.tessaradley.com to find out more about my new books. I always love hearing from readers!

Take care,

Tessa

TESSA RADLEY

loves travelling, reading and watching the world around her. As a teenager Tessa wanted to be an intrepid foreign correspondent. But after completing a bachelor of arts and marrying her sweetheart, she became fascinated with law and ended up studying further and practising as an attorney in a city law firm.

A six-month break travelling through Australia with her family reawoke the yen to write. And life as a writer suits her perfectly; travelling and reading count as research and as for analysing the world…well, she can think *what if* all day long. When she's not reading, travelling or thinking about writing she's spending time with her husband, her two sons – or her zany and wonderful friends. You can contact Tessa through her website www.tessaradley.com.

ACKNOWLEDGEMENTS

To the readers on the eHarlequin.com 10,000 Book Challenge boards. You blew my annual book budget in about a month! :-) But I thank each one of you for the great recommendations and lots of fun.

To Melissa Jeglinski, my thanks for valued advice and thanks to Karen Solem for always being there for me. And Abby, Karina and Sandra, what would I do without you?

To my family –
Tony, Alex and Andrew,
you guys are simply the best!

One

Gemma Allen was back.

Forcing himself to snap out of the shock that held him rigid, Angelo Apollonides strode across the pale sand towards the woman who had betrayed him.

His staff had not lied. The nasty truth was that his beautiful former mistress stood on *his* beach, on *his* island admiring one of *his* sleek, double-hulled catamarans. And Angelo intended to find out precisely why she had chosen to return.

"What are you doing here?" Angelo fought to keep his voice even, to keep the string of ugly curses from escaping. "I never expected to see you again. Particularly not here on Strathmos."

She turned, her tawny eyes wide and startled. The first week of November had passed, the evenings on

Strathmos had begun to cool. The sea wind caught at Gemma's dark red hair, whipping it across her face, hiding her expression for a beat of time. When she brushed it back, she'd recovered her equilibrium and her eyes were wary.

"Angelo." Gemma's voice was cool, composed. A world away from the alarm that had flickered in her eyes only seconds before. "How are you?"

"Forget the pleasantries. You have nerve showing up at the Palace of Poseidon." Angelo pressed his mouth into a tight, forbidding line. "I couldn't believe it when I was told you are performing in the Electra Theatre."

She shrugged. "It's a free world. I can work where I want."

"Anywhere except on Strathmos. This is my world, run by my rules." The island was more than his world; it was his home. The resort had been created from his dreams. Today he'd returned after a hectic month away to find that Gemma had already been working here for over a week.

"Do you really want to be faced with an unfair-dismissal action?" Her wariness had been replaced with attitude.

Angelo froze. He was known to be a fair employer, hard but just. He didn't need the headache of an industrial action—and there was a good chance she'd succeed. Frustrated, he stared at the face that had grown more beautiful in the years since they'd been apart. Her hair was longer…wilder, her eyes glowed brighter and as for her mouth…that lush red mouth taunted him with fighting words. He jerked his attention away from her provocative mouth and gave her slender body an insultingly slow once-over. "Singer is certainly a step up from exotic dancer."

"It's been three years. Things change," she pointed out.

"*I* haven't changed." He widened his stance and put his hands on his hips.

"No, you haven't changed one little bit," she agreed.

He assessed her through slitted eyes, not liking the bite in her tone. "So what do you want, Gemma? A second chance?"

An emotion he couldn't decipher flitted across her stunning features. Gemma gave a brittle laugh. "A second chance? With you? You must be mad!"

He frowned, not liking the fact that he couldn't read her any longer. "Why are you here?"

"I'm here to work…it's a free world." With a sweeping hand she gestured to the blue stretch of the Aegean Sea beyond the beach where the catamarans rested. "You—or rather your minions—gave me the job. The money was too good to pass up."

"Aah. Money."

"Don't scorn the lack of it so easily." Her eyes were flashing now. "Just because you inherited an empire of resorts that stretch across the Greek isles before you turned twenty-one doesn't give you the right to look down your nose at me. I need the money."

Angelo felt himself bristle. Her tongue had developed a razor-sharp edge since their last unforgettable encounter. "I worked damn hard to build a chain of family hotels into world-class resorts. And you never objected to the funds it gave you access to in the past."

He felt her withdraw, even before her eyes went blank. Then she murmured, "If the recent tabloids are to be believed, you're so far removed from us ordinary working mortals, you might as well inhabit Mount Olympus."

"You should know better than to believe everything you read in the newspapers," he snapped, shuddering at the memory of the latest batch of headlines about his breakup with Melina.

"Really?" She raised an eyebrow. "You're not the playboy they portray you to be? You don't wear a different rising starlet or supermodel on your arm every month?"

He glared at her, his frustration increasing to a rising inferno, fanned by her sharp words. "The media exposure is advantageous to both the women and myself."

"So it's all about glamour? About creating an illusion about the rich and famous, then? Nothing more?"

His brows jerked together. "Why are you so interested—unless you do want a chance to get back into my bed?"

She snorted. "I don't want you back."

His mouth slanted. "Didn't anyone tell you that you should be nice to the boss? Three years ago you would've never dared speak to me as you just did."

"Three years ago, I was a silly little goose."

She shifted and her tank top rode up, revealing a strip of tanned midriff. Every male instinct went on alert. "But you don't deny that you are interested?" Angelo moved closer.

Gemma glanced at her watch. "I can't deny you're a fascinating man."

The bite was back. He gave a surprised laugh. "You don't want me back…but you're interested enough to admit you find me fascinating? What message are you trying to send me?"

For an instant she looked rattled. He noticed that goose bumps had risen on her arms. "Are you cold?"

"No." She rubbed her arms briskly, not meeting his eyes.

He touched her arm where the fine hairs stood on end. Gently. With a fingertip. "If you are not cold, then what is this?"

She jerked away. Her gaze swung up to meet his. He read bewilderment…and something more. A stark, turbulent emotion. Fear?

Gemma stepped away. "Excuse me." The smile she gave him didn't reach the eyes that were stretched wide. "But I need to go. It's nearly time for the show. I've got to get ready. Maybe you can come watch." She flung the invitation over her shoulder. As she brushed past him, Angelo let the weight of his hand land on her arm, stilling her.

She turned. This time, he was certain of the emotion that darkened her eyes from tawny to a deep sherry-brown.

It *was* fear. Powerful and totally overwhelming. He inspected her. From close-up he took in her darkened eyes, the taut tension in her face, the tiny shivers that rippled across her skin. He could smell the saltiness of the sea in her hair and feel the cool edge of the wind on her skin.

Why was she here? She'd implied she needed money. Was that the only reason? Or, despite her denial, did she hope to rekindle the burnt-out embers of their affair?

"Let me go." Her voice was toneless. Pointedly, she stared at his long, tanned fingers lying against her skin.

He removed them, taking his time and watching intently as she hauled in a steadying breath.

The nagging wind tugged at her wayward hair as she gave a hurried glance at her watch and scooped up the sandals lying in the sand. "I suppose I should say it's been nice seeing you—"

"But you'd be lying."

"I didn't say that." She stilled. There was chagrin in her eyes. "Don't put words in my mouth."

Her mouth. His gaze dropped to her rosy lips. Full and lush. The sudden surge of desire was unexpected. It left him reeling. He clenched his fists. How could he want Gemma Allen? After everything she'd done?

How the hell could he have forgotten how sexy she was? The lush bee-stung lips, the sinuous curves of her sleek body, the cloud of dark red hair…how could he have let those details slide from his consciousness?

Reluctant to examine the discovery that he still desired her, he said softly between his teeth. "From exotic dancer into singer…I want to see this transformation. I'll be at your show."

Half an hour later, wearing only lacy briefs and a silky black halter-neck slip, Gemma sat alone in front of the mirror in the dressing room she shared with Lucie LaVie, a likeable comedienne who did a very funny routine in the bar adjacent to the Electra Theatre.

Meeting Angelo on the beach so unexpectedly had been a shock. Dammit, she hadn't even known he was back. She'd been on Strathmos for just over a week, waiting for him, half-dreading their first encounter. She'd planned to be prepared…to be dressed to the nines…to show him what he was missing when they met again. Instead she'd been wearing shorts, no make-up and her legs had been covered in sand. She certainly hadn't expected the curious numbness that had enveloped her.

Staring into the mirror, Gemma couldn't help wondering what Angelo would make of the transformation. The heavy stage makeup gave her skin an unnatural perfection, blotting out the light sprinkle of freckles across her nose and cheeks. Eyeliner accentuated her tawny eyes and dark ruby lipstick added lushness to her lips that gave her an in-your-face sensuality.

Angelo liked his women beautiful and flamboyant. His most recent mistresses had all been actresses or famous models. And, according to the recent tabloids she'd studied, he still showed no sign of settling down. She examined herself in the mirror. She looked beautiful…flamboyant. And Angelo would be out there tonight watching her.

Her plan had to—

A rap on the door broke into her desperate thoughts. "Ten minutes to showtime, Gemma."

"Won't be long," she called back, and ran her fingers through her hair in an effort to tame the wild auburn curls. She couldn't remember the last time a man's fingers had stroked through them. A vivid image of Angelo's hand on her arm, his long fingers and buffed square nails, flashed into her mind and she swore softly.

An instant later the door burst open and Angelo entered with all the force and energy of a hurricane.

"Hey. You can't come in here!" After the initial shock, Gemma resisted the urge to cross her hands over her breasts. Despite the skimpy fabric and the low dip in the front, the slip covered all the strategic places.

Angelo shut the door and, folding his arms, leaned against it. "There's nothing to see that I haven't seen before."

Right. Gemma swallowed. Then she let her gaze run over him. He looked magnificent. The white dinner jacket must've been tailored to fit his tall body. Under the lights, his hair gleamed like old gold and his startling turquoise eyes blazed. He looked assured, wealthy, powerful.

And this was the man she intended to teach a lesson he'd never forget.

"What do you want?"

"Join me in the theatre for a drink after the show."

Gemma hid her exultation. It had been worth coming all the way to Strathmos. A few years ago he would've impressed her—with his Greek-god looks and the sheer force of his personality. But these days she didn't go for the domineering masterful type.

She dared not give in too quickly. She didn't want to lose his interest. Nor could she let herself forget for one moment why she was doing this.

"Don't you think you should wait outside until I am dressed?" Gemma waited a beat then added delicately, "Boss…"

Angelo's brows jerked into a frown at her disparaging tone and Gemma felt a fierce rush of pleasure. Of course, he was accustomed to admiration…adulation… women falling all over him. But not her.

"You—" He broke off and sucked in a deep breath. Then in a soft, dangerous tone, he said, "Do not presume on our past relationship."

"I would never do that." In the mirror, she slanted him a small smile. "I came to Palace of Poseidon to sing."

"Precisely." He didn't smile back. His eyes were bright and ruthless. "Or were you lying earlier? Perhaps you *were* hoping I'd want you back in my bed?"

Annoyance swarmed through Gemma. Quickly, she veiled her gaze before he glimpsed her ire. "I never imagined you'd want that. And nor do I. I've told you that already." Gemma drew a steadying breath. She had to be very careful; she could mess it all up with one careless mistake.

"I thought you might be hankering after the style to which you'd become accustomed."

God, he was arrogant. Gemma spun around on the plastic stool and glared up at Angelo. He was so tall, he positively loomed over her. "You make me sound like a sycophant. I worked for you, as well."

"You consider sharing my bed for half a year work?" The look he gave her stripped her naked of the silky slip and told exactly how little respect Angelo had for her.

Again, she fought the urge to cover her breasts, to check that the silky material didn't reveal the outline of her dark nipples. Supremely self-conscious now, she rose and crossed to the corner of the room where a small closet held several outfits.

Gemma peeled the dress she intended wearing tonight off its hanger. Keeping her back firmly to Angelo, she slid on the sleek crimson tube covered with winking sequins that should have clashed terribly with her hair but didn't.

The electrifying quality of the silence behind her flustered her. Gemma swivelled. The expression in Angelo's eyes made her breath catch. She became aware that the dress hugged her curves like a lover, that the neckline was low, provocative. That she and Angelo were totally alone.

Hurriedly she said, "My career has always been important to me." And fame had been important, too, she supposed.

"If you say so." He gave her a strange, intent look. "I say that changed once you got what you wanted…"

"And what do you think I wanted?" Then wished the words unsaid as tension sparked in the air between them. Suddenly Gemma didn't want to know the answer.

A frown drew his surprisingly dark brows together. "A man wealthy enough to pander to your every whim. A gold card with no ceiling…clothes, jewellery…" His gaze dropped pointedly to the gold ring set with a large showy topaz on the little finger of her left hand. "You chose that after we visited Monaco for a weekend. Remember?"

"I'm afraid I don't." She grabbed a pair of gloves out the closet and, with an ease born of practice, pulled on the long, black lace gloves embroidered with dark red roses and covered the ring. Outside the door, Mark Lyme, the manager of the entertainment centre called her name. Gemma moved towards the door. "I must go, I'm due on stage."

"Wait, you're not running out on this conversation." Angelo flung his hands out wide. "Of course you remember. That night we attended the Rose Ball, and you wanted to go partying afterwards. You flirted with every man who glanced your way."

Men? She hesitated. *What men?* "No—"

"Were there so many men that you cannot remember the one from the other?" Angelo's eyes glittered.

"I don't remember—"

"Oh, please, don't feed me that. You're wearing that ring *I* bought and paid for. Did I buy you so much jewellery that you can no longer remember the occasion of each purchase? I'm sure you remember every moment of the time we spent in bed afterwards."

Gemma's stomach turned. Outside, Mark called again. Gemma wrenched open the dressing-room door. "That's just it," she cut in before Angelo could interrupt again. "I don't remember. Nothing about that night at the Rose Ball. Nothing about you. Nothing about our time together. I've lost my memory."

Gemma bolted out onto the dimly lit stage, the vision of Angelo's stunned expression imprinted on her mind. She stared blindly out at the audience. She had to get a grip. She had to thrust the disturbing scene in the dressing room with Angelo out of her mind.

The chatter stilled and the cutlery stopped clinking. By now most of the patrons had finished their meal. Being Friday night, the supper theatre was packed. Gemma paused. Clouds from the smoke machine swirled around her, coloured by red and blue lighting and adding to the moodiness.

For a moment the familiar nervousness swept her. Then she embraced it and stepped forward to the waiting crowd. This was a space she cherished, a special place where her voice and mind and body all flowed into the music.

It was at the close of the second song that she spotted Angelo through the feathers of smoke. He sat alone at a table, casually propped against the wall, his arm along the back of the chair. The narrowed gaze focused on her revealed nothing. And the table in front of him was empty of food or drink.

Gemma quaked at the prospect of joining him for the drink he'd invited her for. The memory of how her skin had prickled when he'd touched her and the blind fear that had followed, swept over her.

Ripping her attention away from him, Gemma worked to make the crowd smile…and sigh. As her voice died after the final held note of the last song there was a moment's silence, then clapping thundered through the theatre. Gemma blew them two-handed kisses and sank into a bow, her unruly hair sweeping forward. She straightened and flicked her hair back and the clapping evolved into stamps and whistles.

"All right, one more, an Andrew Lloyd Webber composition, a personal favourite," she agreed. Her voice reverberated and the cacophony subsided. "If you've ever lost a loved one, this one is for you."

Gemma launched into "Memory." Her voice cut through the theatre, sharp and pure. She barely noticed that the audience seemed to hold its collective breath and when she reached the last line she let the final notes slide into silence.

This time the crowd went mad.

Smiling, Gemma waved to them. But she couldn't stop her gaze seeking Angelo's. The lyrics lingered in her mind. *A new day.* For a long moment their eyes held, the connection taut, and her smile faded.

There would be no new day for them. The past lay between them like an unassailable barrier.

Gemma was trembling with reaction by the time she reached the dressing room. She felt as if she'd been two rounds with Rocky Balboa. Lucie had returned from her act and lay sprawled along the length of the two-seater couch, dressed in funky street clothes that suited her spiky blonde hair and wide eyes.

"Boss wants to see you," she said, tossing a slip of paper into the trash basket as Gemma sat down.

"Mark?"

"No, the big fish, Angelo Apollonides." Lucie's green eyes were curious. "A reminder that you're to join him for a drink at his table. You didn't say anything about that invitation."

Gemma should have known that he wouldn't let her get away. That he'd want to know more about the bomb-shell she'd dropped before she had rushed out.

"It happened just before the show." Gemma wasn't confessing that Angelo had been here, in the dressing room. And she'd never told Lucie anything—thankfully no one had commented on the past affair. Perhaps most of the entertainment staff had only been there less than two years. "I'm too dog-tired to cope with Mr. Apollo-nides," Gemma muttered. The fatigue was not physical. It went soul-deep. She felt raw and emotionally drained. And she couldn't face Angelo right now.

The memory of how she'd reacted to his touch had spooked her. The last thing she needed was to feel desire for Angelo Apollonides. She needed time to come to terms with that unexpected complication. When she confronted Angelo it would be in her space, on her terms, not in the dark smoky intimacy of the supper theatre.

At Lucie's look of blatant disbelief, Gemma added, "And you can tell him that I'm passing for now." Rejection would do Angelo the world of good. Make him more eager to see her again.

"Gemma, you're being stupid. In the eight months I've been working on Strathmos he's never once invited an employee for a drink. And you refuse?" Lucie jumped up and started pacing the small space. "I just don't get you. He didn't even bring a woman with him to Strathmos this time, rumour has it that he ended it with—" she named a well-known model "—last month. Why not try your luck?"

Gemma didn't answer. She picked up a bottle of makeup remover and a packet of face wipes and started to clean her face with quick, practised moves. Soon Angelo would come looking for her, and she had no intention of being here.

After a moment Lucie gave a snort of disgust and stalked out of the room, muttering something about being the messenger of bad tidings and that some people had all the luck.

But Gemma knew Angelo's demand to join him had nothing to do with luck. His reaction on the beach had made it clear he was less than happy about her appearance on Strathmos.

She had to play this very, very carefully. For a year she'd been trying to get close to him. She'd finally been granted a four-week chance when the performer who was originally booked had pulled out. Gemma's agent had scrambled for the booking. With only eighteen days

left to discover what she wanted and find a way to make
Angelo pay for the grief he'd caused her, she couldn't
chicken out just because her senses had been set on fire
by the touch of a single finger.

Two

Gemma had stood him up!

And she hadn't even bothered to tell him herself, she'd sent a messenger to deliver the unwelcome news. The anger that had simmered within Angelo since he'd that discovered Gemma was on Strathmos, living and working in *his* resort, took on a new edge.

Gemma claimed that she'd lost her memory. How had that happened and what did it have to do with him? And why had she returned to Strathmos?

Angelo found himself glaring in the direction where the maddeningly capricious Gemma had vanished from the stage, while the bare skin of her back and that provocative red dress remained imprinted on his vision. He hated the sneaky realisation that he hadn't stopped thinking about her since he'd arrived back on

Strathmos. And now she'd deliberately left him cooling his heels.

Angelo rose to his feet, abandoning the bottle of Bollinger he'd ordered—Gemma had always had a taste for champagne—and, jaw set, stalked out to find her.

She was not in the dressing room. But a comprehensive scan took in the red dress hanging in the closet. Clearly, she'd already been and gone. Nor was she to be found in the row of bars and coffee shops that flanked the theatre. Angelo barely slowed his long strides as Mark Lyme hurried over. Two minutes later, with the next potential crisis averted, he exited the entertainment complex, searching for Gemma's distinctive dark flame hair under the lamps in the wide paved piazza.

About to veer off to where the staff units were located, he spotted a lone figure walking towards the deserted beach. Hunching his shoulders against the rising wind, Angelo quickened his pace. With her give-away hair, not even the fact that she wore jeans and a bulky sweater could hide that it was Gemma.

He came up behind her. "If I give an employee an order I expect it to be obeyed." The deceptive softness of his tone didn't hide his anger—or his frustration.

Gemma's shoulders tensed and she came to a halt. Then she turned. In the dim light of the lanterns that lined the promenade, he saw her eyebrow arch. "I thought it was an invitation," she said with soft irony. "One that I never accepted."

"Or refused."

She considered him, her head on one side. "Give me one good reason why I should have joined you."

He blinked. Women usually thronged to his side.

Hell, he didn't need to issue invitations. Women gate-crashed celebrity functions to meet him. "Because I wanted to speak to you."

"What about?" Her tension was tangible.

"Your memory loss."

"Not true. You invited me for a drink before you knew about that."

She had him there. What he really wanted to know was why she had come back to Strathmos. It had to be about more than money. His gut told him it had something to do with her amnesia. He wasn't about to admit that what pricked his ego was the fact that she didn't remember him. Or was it a ploy? Was her amnesia nothing more than a sham designed to avoid facing up to her treachery three years ago? Or a last-ditch effort to recapture his interest? At last he said, "You've forgotten carrying on with every male under the age of eighty at the Rose Ball? You don't remember about me…us?"

She closed her eyes at the sheer incredulity in his voice. "Is that so hard to accept?" she asked warily. "I have amnesia."

"How convenient."

Gemma opened her eyes and met his narrowed gaze. She tried to speak but her voice wouldn't work. So she simply shrugged and let her arms fall uselessly by her side.

"What kind of amnesia?"

"Does it matter?" The sick feeling in the pit of her stomach tightened. Couldn't he see how much she hated this? "Fact is, I can't remember anything about what happened here three years ago. It's just…one vast blank."

"It certainly explains how you have the gall to come back."

She let that barb go. "It's not easy being here. But I need to find out about my life. What it was like… well…before." She slid him a sideways look. The anger had faded, but his eyes still glittered with suspicion. "It's really strange, because I remember lots of stuff before I met you. Most of it, I think. And I know what happened…afterwards. It's the time in the middle that's gone."

He loomed over her. "How did it happen? Did you fall? Did you hit your head? What do the doctors say about the prognosis? Will you ever get that part of your memory back?"

"I don't know. I don't want to talk about it." Gemma's voice sounded thin and thready even to her own ears. "It upsets me."

Angelo gave a harsh sigh. "I suppose I can understand that. It must be scary."

Not as scary as Angelo. Even when he was being nice—like now, when his eyes were full of sympathy— there was a taut purpose to his body, an air of danger and tension. Gemma shuddered. Nice wouldn't last. Not with Angelo Apollonides. He hadn't transformed a string of family resorts into modern extravaganzas built for year-round entertainment by being a nice, sympathetic kind of guy. He was tough, decisive and ruthless. A man who worked hard—and played harder. A Greek success legend.

His gaze was direct. "Have dinner with me."

The unexpected request startled her. She chewed her lip. It was what she ought to do.

"Is it such a difficult decision? Do I scare you so much?" His hands came down on her shoulders and the touch scorched straight through her lamb's-wool sweater.

She went very still. "You don't scare me at all," Gemma said with false bravado.

His hands tightened. "Prove it by having dinner with me."

A dare. How infantile. She froze under his touch. A hint of stubble darkened his jaw and the hard line of his mouth had relaxed into a sensual curve. The dark intensity of his gaze and the way her flesh reacted to his touch told her that he was way out of her league. She wasn't ready to have dinner with him, to be the sole focus of his attention. He was so much more than she'd expected. But she had no choice. Not if she wanted to learn what she needed. "Not tonight. It's been a long day. And it's late."

He was about to say something, to argue, when his cell phone trilled. He mouthed an apology and turned away, talking rapidly in Greek, and Gemma realised she'd lost his attention.

Gemma wanted to kick something—preferably herself—and she wished desperately she'd accepted his invitation. Even though the prickles of excitement his touch had generated terrified her.

He hit a button and slid the phone into his pants pocket. "Tomorrow night?"

Relief overwhelmed her. She hadn't blown it. She drew a deep, shuddering breath. "Okay, I'll have dinner with you."

"So how did we meet?" The following evening Gemma sat across from Angelo in a secluded corner of the Golden

Fleece restaurant, her half-eaten meal of grilled calamari garnished with sliced lemon in front of her.

"At the film festival in Cannes." Angelo set down his knife. His plate was empty. "I thought you were an actress."

That would explain some of it. Angelo had never been linked with a dancer previously.

"Oh? What happened next?" She speared another tube of calamari and popped it into her mouth.

"You were beautiful—and funny. I enjoyed your company so I invited you to spend a weekend at Poseidon's Cavern." He named one of the famous resorts that he owned. "You accepted. And, when business called, you came back to Strathmos with me—it's where I live, after all." He gave her a grin that transformed his face, the harsh line of his mouth softening into a passionate curve.

Gemma set her knife and fork together and shifted in her chair, uncomfortable with the notion that it had been so easy for him. "And then I got a job in the resort? Right?"

"Do you want desert?"

"No, thanks."

"Coffee?"

She shook her head, impatient for his answer to her questions.

He came around and pulled out her chair. Close to her ear he murmured, "There was so much more glamour in being the boss's girlfriend than working." His voice was loaded with cynicism. "And you'd led me to believe you were taking a break from stage work. I had no idea you were an exotic dancer until about a month later."

"Oh." Gemma rose and shot him a wary glance. "I never wanted to…leave?"

He gave a hard-edged grin. "Why should you have? You had it all. Great resorts to live in, an unending credit line and good sex."

That was supposed to be funny? Gemma had never felt less like laughing in her life. She walked quickly ahead, not noticing the attractive man with long dark hair who waved to her. She smouldered silently until they exited the restaurant.

"So I no longer had a career—" She squawked in shock as Angelo pulled her into an alcove behind an immense bronze statue of Hephaestus. The sconce of fire that burned in the statue's raised hand cast leaping shadows against the walls. Gemma opened her mouth to protest.

"If you mean, you no longer danced half naked in an upmarket bar, then no, you no longer had a career. Instead you had me." In the close confines of the alcove his face had changed, toughened. He looked hard and ruthless and suddenly Gemma could see exactly why he was such a successful businessman and commanded so much respect. She had to take care not to provoke him.

"I had you." Gemma struggled to keep the anger at his arrogance out of her voice. "And what did you get out of this deal?"

"A beautiful woman in my bed."

"I don't suppose it occurred to you I might've wanted more?"

"More?"

"A career—"

He gave a snort. "You scored by being my live-in

lover. Travel to different resorts. A-list parties. No need to work. Believe me, it was better for you my way."

His way. Gemma had a feeling that most things ended up his way. The alternative would be for his kept mistress to hit the highway. "Did you love *me?*"

"Love you?" His head went back and she could see she'd surprised him.

"Yes, did you love me?" She pressed. "With all this good sex, did you feel anything for me at all?"

"Look, Gemma, this wasn't about love. It was about two consenting adults who met and enjoyed time together." He spread his hands sideways. "Hell, we were hardly Romeo and Juliet."

"If we had been Romeo and Juliet, you'd have been dead by the end," Gemma said through gritted teeth.

"Hey," he objected, "what are you getting so worked up about? All I meant was that we weren't young lovers, dizzy from an attack of first-time love."

"Did *I* love *you?*"

He gave an astonished laugh. "What's the fixation with love? You certainly never told me you loved me. But then you weren't in it for love. And nor was I."

Gemma bit her lip, thinking furiously. "I can't believe I would've lived the kind of life you've painted for any other reason than because I loved you more than anything in the world. It's so against everything I believe in."

"Well, you showed no sign of loving me…and if that's what you believe now, then you've changed."

She stilled. "Maybe I have."

His eyes darkened. "Gemma." He stretched out a hand and stroked her arm. "You should—"

"What am I doing?" She dropped her face into her hands, then raked her fingers back through her hair.

"Trying to regain your memory? Maybe this will help you remember." There was a huskiness to his voice that caught her attention.

Slowly she raised her head. He was close, far closer than she'd realised and in the flickering light his gaze was intent. Her heart started to pound. She swallowed and the sudden ringing silence stretched between them.

"Yes?" The sound was little more than a croak. But Angelo understood. It meant yes to so much more. Even to that which she most feared.

The instant his lips brushed hers Gemma knew her life would never be the same again. Every preconception she had of what it might've been like to be kissed by him vanished.

It was fire and light. Energy and emotion. Then his tongue touched hers and sparks shot through her. Adrenaline. And something magical.

She held her breath, didn't move in case the magic vanished. Then his tongue swept her mouth and the fire leapt inside her. Gemma groaned, closed her eyes and abandoned herself to the wonder.

When his fingers stroked the naked skin of her shoulder, every nerve ending went crazy. Frissons rippled down her spine and a reckless want followed. She moved closer, pressing herself up against him, until she felt the unmistakable ridge of his erection through the soft silk of her dress. It was a shock…a sign of how out of control this had become…but it was also incredibly satisfying.

Whatever the past held, Angelo wanted her. Now.

She sighed into his mouth, he deepened the kiss and

his breathing grew ragged. His hand closed on her shoulder and he pulled her against him.

At last he raised his head. "Do you remember that?"

Gemma stared at him, then regretfully shook her head.

He put her away from him, his hands shaking a little. "*Thiavlo*. I think we both need to cool down. Let's visit the casino—you always enjoyed that."

"Okay," she managed as he led her out from behind the inscrutable Hephaestus. Her knees shook. She had never felt less like gambling in her life.

Large double doors opened into the Apollo Club, the casino reserved for A-list clientele. Crystal chandeliers hung from the domed ceiling painted with beasts and heroes from myths Gemma knew well. The ambience in the room warned her that the stakes would be frighteningly high.

Angelo led her to a table with a group of men in tuxedos and two women—a blonde and a brunette—in evening gowns, jewels glittering at their necks and wrists. No voices hummed in here. Only the clatter of chips broke the solemn silence.

Murmuring an order, Angelo placed a wad of notes on the table. An elegant croupier in a long black dress slid several stacks of chips across the baize. Angelo passed the stacks to her, and Gemma realised he'd spent a small fortune for her to fritter away. She started to feel ill. "I can't gamble that kind of money."

The look he gave her was more than a little pointed. "It never troubled you in the past."

Gemma bit her lip. "What if I lose it all?"

Angelo shrugged. "Then I'll buy more."

And what would he expect from her then? Sex? Obviously that had happened in the past. Something within her shrivelled at the thought.

"No!" She shoved the chips back at him. "I might have forgotten how to do this, forgotten the rules."

"Try and we'll see."

"Angelo, I don't want to do this."

His gaze held hers. After a long moment he said, "All right. We'll see if we can penetrate that memory another way. Keep these—" he separated a small heap of chips "—in case you decide you want to play later."

She shook her head and pushed the chips away. "I don't feel like gambling tonight."

"Would you like to go for a drink?"

She nodded. This close she could see the laugh lines around his eyes, the glitter in his compelling eyes. He stilled in the act of gathering the chips and stared down at her.

"Gemma?"

With a start, she looked away, breaking the tenuous thread that linked them, and turned her head, searching for the source of the call that cut through the hush of the huge room.

"I *thought* it was you." The guy coming towards her was darkly tanned with Gallic features and carefully styled shaggy black hair. Gemma stared at him blankly.

The blonde at their table squealed in delight and grabbed his arm. He bent to kiss her cheek. Her much older companion didn't look happy.

The hand cupping Gemma's elbow tensed. "Did you invite him?" Angelo murmured in her ear.

"Invite him?" She swung around to cast Angelo a frown. "What are you talking about? I don't even know—" She broke off.

"Who he is," Angelo finished smoothly, and started to laugh, but Gemma noticed his eyes were devoid of humour. "I don't think Jean-Paul will appreciate being forgotten so soon."

"Who is he?" Gemma hissed.

"Jean-Paul Moreau." From Angelo's air of expectancy Gemma suspected the name was supposed to mean something to her. It didn't.

She lifted her shoulders and let them drop. "So…" she prompted.

"Your lover." Some ugly emotion flashed over Angelo's face then his features turned wooden. "The man I threw naked out of my—our—bed three years ago."

Three

Gemma stared.

Angelo's shocking revelation was the last thing she'd expected. Yet, judging by his narrow-eyed expression, he clearly believed it to be true.

She tested the discovery against her own belief. No, she couldn't accept it. Angelo must've made some awful mistake.

But before she could question him further, a mist of designer aftershave surrounded her. Then came a whisper of "*Cherie,* you are more beautiful than ever," and male lips nudged her cheek.

"Hello—" she tried frantically to remember his name "—Jean-Paul."

"I thought you were ignoring me, *cherie.* You stared straight through me earlier. I'm glad to know you remember your old friends."

Beside her Angelo snorted. Gemma shot him a warning look. She didn't want Jean-Paul knowing about the amnesia.

At least not yet.

Coming face-to-face with a man Angelo considered her lover had taken her aback. Much as she disliked Angelo, he had no reason to lie to her about the past. She needed to learn more.

With an extravagant flourish Jean-Paul produced a roll of euro notes from inside his jacket and signalled to the croupier. When the chips came, he slipped one pile across to Gemma. "For you, *cherie.*"

The smile Jean-Paul gave her was disconcertingly intimate. The secretive smile of a man to a woman he knew very, very well.

Gemma could sense Angelo's silent tension. Her stomach rolled over. "Thanks," she said stiltedly. Realising that she sounded terse she pointed to the unused chips on the table that Angelo had been in the process of gathering up before Jean-Paul's arrival. "But I have enough—and we're going for a drink."

Jean-Paul's gaze swept over her, explicit, knowing. Leaning towards her, he whispered, "*Cherie,* you're not the kind of woman ever to have enough. Here—" he slid a handful of chips towards her "—have a bet on me."

"Enough!" Angelo said harshly. A tanned arm hooked around Gemma's waist from behind, his other hand pushed his chips towards the croupier. "The lady doesn't want your chips." Against the length of her spine Gemma could feel Angelo's body through the thin silk of her dress. It was at once comforting and vaguely threatening. His arm lay coiled around her, under her breasts like a hard band, and awareness of his strength, his power, shivered through her.

It was the sudden ratcheting tension in his body that made her realise that Jean-Paul had moved. Within Angelo's hold, she twisted around on her stool. The two men faced each other like duelling adversaries.

Jean-Paul's gaze shifted from Angelo to Gemma and his mouth twisted. "It's like that, is it? *Cherie,* don't be fooled. Apollonides is the same man as three years ago. Work will always be his first mistress. Will that be enough for you this time around? Or will you come searching for warm arms, words of lo—"

"I said *enough.*" Even Jean-Paul heard the suppressed violence in the whip-crack sound and took a hasty step back. "You go too far, Moreau. If I catch you near Gemma I will have you thrown off the island. Do you understand?"

A Gallic shrug and Jean-Paul smiled. "Keep cool, man. It doesn't mean a thing—it never did." But there was a wariness in his dark eyes that hadn't been there seconds before.

The last thing Gemma wanted was a scene. Already they were attracting the glances of people alerted by the bristling men and hissed words. The two women at their table were staring openly, while the croupier called for bets with a touch of desperation.

"Angelo—"

The arm tightened, cutting off her protest. "Gemma, you will not encourage this man. Moreau, you will keep your distance from Gemma. I've told you both before, I don't share my woman. Understand that." Releasing his hold on her, Angelo moved between her and Jean-Paul and with a hard glance at her, he added, "Both of you."

Then, in a swift movement, he swept the euro notes off the table and nodded at the croupier. "Come, Gemma. Let's go."

Without a glance in Jean-Paul's direction, Gemma slid from the stool.

The hand that came down on her shoulder was possessive, a warning. *His woman.* Angelo had warned Jean-Paul—and her—that he had no intention of sharing his woman, clearly not for the first time. Did that mean he still considered her his woman?

A frisson of dark emotion speared her. Gemma wasn't sure what to make of his claim and kept silent as they left the gaming room.

By the time they exited the elevator a floor down and walked out the hotel into the starry night, the anger inside Angelo was still simmering. Maintaining a terse silence, he strode along the path lit by decorative Victorian-style lamps. He was aware of the anxious glances Gemma kept casting him as she hurried along beside him, her high heels clicking against the terra-cotta flagstones.

"I'm sorry about what happened."

He shrugged. "It had to happen sooner or later. And it's only a matter of time before it happens again…before another man rises from the ashes of your past."

"I don't remember him," she said quickly.

Too quickly? "Meaning, you won't remember the others, either?" He shot her a derisive smile. "Poor bastard. I can almost feel pity for him."

Yet he had to admit he found it immensely satisfying that she didn't remember the Frenchman. Especially after…

Hell!

"I knew about Jean-Paul, saw you both in my bed with my own eyes." His tone took on a dark edge. "I can give you details of how you were straddling him, your knees around his hips, your bare breasts bouncing and the satin sheets—*my* satin sheets—crumpled around you. Your skin like a pearl against—"

"Stop." Gemma came to a jarring halt. "I don't want to hear this." Her head bent, she stared at the shadowy footpath and tension hunched her bare shoulders. She shivered as a sharp gust of sea-wind cut through the night.

"If I tell you what I saw, what I can still see so clearly, it might help you remember." He knew his bitterness was showing. But he wanted to hurt her, cut to the heart of her. Humiliate her as he'd been humiliated. "How many more men like Jean-Paul will there be? Men that I don't know of? Men that you don't remember?"

Gemma shivered again.

Angered by her lack of response, he said, "Tell me, Gemma, how many more?"

"I don't know," she said in a very small voice.

"Look at me." His hands closed on her shoulders. Her skin was like ice. He swung her round and her eyes snapped open revealing her bewilderment as she stumbled on her high heels.

"Careful!" He tightened his grip and couldn't help noticing how soft her skin felt.

She ducked away. Her heel gave and she almost fell.

With an exasperated imprecation he yanked her upright. "Are you okay?"

"No thanks to you." She wrenched herself free. "If

you hadn't grabbed me like some Neanderthal I'd have been fine."

"Neanderthal?" He didn't know whether to laugh or to swear at the crack. *"Neanderthal?"*

Gemma's heart sank as she absorbed his outrage. Then she stiffened as her own indignation kicked in. It *was* his doing that she'd nearly fallen. He'd spun her round. Ever since Jean-Paul's arrival he'd been acting like a jealous jerk. She didn't have to put up with it.

Tossing back her hair, she lifted her chin. "Yes. Neanderthal. You know—some primitive three-hundred pound gorilla type." Her heart was galloping as she stared at him defiantly, waiting for his response.

For a moment he simply stood there. Then he gurgled something that sounded like *gorilla* and his arms shot out.

She gave a squeak. And then it was too late.

He had her in a hard hold, his fingers imprinted on her shoulders, and his lips slanted across hers, grinding down against the softness cooled by the night breeze. She wriggled and murmured a protest.

He raised his head, and she gulped a much-needed breath. "So I'm a gorilla, am I?"

Hastily she shook her head. A mad urge to laugh bubbled through Gemma. Then his mouth was back, open and hungry on hers, and all coherent thought left her. His tongue stroked the soft, tender skin inside her cheeks. Heat sliced through her, a restless yearning started to build. The desire he'd ignited when he'd kissed her in the alcove returned in full force. Gemma's head spun. What the hell was happening to her?

His arms tightened, drawing her up against him. He was already aroused.

The realisation sent a wave of reckless euphoria coursing through her. Her bones softened, and in her lower body the heat started to spread. Her hips seemed to have developed a life of their own and moved in slow circles against him. Angelo groaned.

His hot breath rushed into her mouth and the intimacy turned her knees to liquid. Gemma staggered backward, her heels digging into the turf, and Angelo followed, his thighs moving against hers in an erotic dance, their mouths devouring each other.

The roughness of a tree trunk stopped Gemma backing up. Angelo didn't pause until he had her plastered against the trunk, his body reamed up against hers in the dark space under the wide canopy of branches, his hands twisted in the tangled mass of her hair. Her nipples pebbled, aching under the press of his body. Here, in the silent darkness, the golden glow of the lamplight seemed far away.

The pressure on her mouth gave a little and then the tip of his tongue started to outline her lips, slowly, deliberately, his hands holding her head, positioning her for maximum impact.

It was teasing, frustrating. She wanted him to kiss her. Intimately. *"More."* The demand was torn from her. She butted her hips forward, finding the length of his erection and started to rock back and forth. She wanted more of his mouth, more of his touch…more… of the intense want ripping through her.

But he kept the tongue strokes light and toying and she writhed against him.

When Angelo finally lifted his head, Gemma moaned a protest. In the stillness of the night the sound of their breathing was hoarse and ragged. His fingers fiddled at her nape and a moment later she felt the straps of her halter dress and the bra beneath give.

A warm hand slipped under the fabric and stroked the bare flesh of her breast. His fingers brushed the nub; sensation shot through her and she gasped, arching against the tree. He repeated the motion. She tensed as a rush of heat pooled beneath her panties.

"Ghhh." The sound that escaped her was foreign, incomprehensible even to her own ears. Rising on tiptoe, Gemma rocked harder, rubbing herself against his solid flesh, concentrating on that sensitive part of her—the part that touched him, aroused him, despite the rasp of the fabric that separated them. Then his leg moved, bracing his weight, so that the hardness in the front of his trousers fitted in the space between her legs.

Her eyes tightly closed, her head flung back, Gemma focused on the fingertips massaging her nipple, on the sensation spreading out hotter and hotter from the junction between her legs.

She started to pant and the desperate heat climbed higher…higher…within her. She rocked faster still, rubbing against him, and he responded, his hips moving back and forth, the friction building—building until Gemma knew that she was poised on the lip of the void.

The taunting, teasing touch on her nipples tightened. And when his tongue entered her mouth in wild, consuming thrusts a bolt of electric sensation shot through Gemma.

Turned on beyond belief, Gemma gasped, a wild, keening sound. Her body tightened, the sensitive point at the apex of her legs caught fire and the convulsions began.

She sagged against the tree, spent and dizzy, her pulse pumping furiously through her head. Her legs had turned to water, and she suspected that had the tree not supported her she would've collapsed.

Angelo lifted his head and withdrew his hand from her breast. Her body cooled as he stepped away, his expression unfathomable in the criss-cross shadows of the branches.

"Maybe that will help you remember!"

God, how she hated him. At his awful words she fumbled for the straps behind her neck, but her fingers were shaking so much she couldn't tie them. Finally, with an impatient mutter Angelo stepped forward. But this time he kept his body from touching hers, and unexpectedly Gemma ached for the loss. The pull of the straps tightening as he knotted them was unbearably intimate and Gemma searched desperately for something to say to break the ghastly, growing silence.

What was there to say to the man who'd pleasured her so thoroughly without taking the time to remove her dress or her panties? Hell, despite her dislike and distrust, she'd let him do what he wanted, touch where he wanted without a murmur.

She shuddered with shame.

Telling herself she despised him didn't help. She'd driven him on, rubbing herself against him like… Oh, God! She flushed at the memory of what she'd done… her lack of restraint. Fully clad, Angelo had touched her with only with his mouth and the fingertips of one hand and brought her more ecstasy than she could ever remember experiencing.

She wanted to run. To hide. Before her composure gave way.

"I'll find my way from here. You don't have to come any farther." Then she closed her eyes as she replayed her own words and waited for him to point out that he hadn't come. Yet.

"I will walk you to your unit." His voice was colder than winter. "The sooner your contract ends and you leave Strathmos, the better for both of us."

"I'll leave tomorrow," Gemma blurted out, her eyes stinging. "Leave me alone. I don't want your company."

Once inside her unit, Gemma flipped the kettle on with hands that trembled, and blinked away the tears that blurred her vision. Feeling utterly wretched, she craved a mug of camomile tea to soothe her shattered nerves while the aftershocks of their terrifyingly passionate encounter quaked through her.

She couldn't stay.

She would leave Strathmos tomorrow, catch the first ferry out—even if it meant breaking her contract and putting her professional reputation on the line. She could not do this.

Never had it crossed her mind that she would melt under Angelo Apollonides's touch, press her body up against his, encourage his kisses. He was a suave playboy. No one knew better than she.

Oh, God. How had she gotten herself into this fix? Distraught, Gemma speared her shaky fingers through her hair.

She needed to get a grip. Fighting for control, she tried to think analytically about what had happened out there, under the cold stars. Okay, so she'd provoked him. Intentionally. But she hadn't expected him to react so fiercely, to move so quickly. His cool eyes, his mocking smile, his legion of beautiful cookie-cutter lovers had indicated Angelo wasn't a man given to impulse. That devastating kiss—and what had followed—stunned her.

He was far more dangerous than she'd ever known.

When the kettle clicked off, she reached into the cupboard for a mug and poured boiling water over the teabag. *Why had she risked all the ground she'd made by provoking him?* What had she hoped to gain? What was it about Angelo that made her itch to disconcert him? To prove to him she wasn't the woman he thought he was?

Cradling the mug between her hands, she propped her elbows on the bench top. The photo at the end of the bench top mocked her.

Setting her tea down, she picked up the photo. It looked like such an idyllic family. Mum and Dad flanking their smiling, all-grown-up daughter against a backdrop of lovingly tended rosebushes. Tears pricked again. Gemma craved a dose of her mother's kind common sense. Checking her watch she calculated that in New Zealand it would be morning. She picked up the handset from the wall and punched in the familiar number of her childhood home.

"Hello?"

Despite the distance her mother's voice was clear and familiar.

Gemma swallowed the lump in her throat. "It's me, Mum."

"Sweetheart, I'm so glad you've called. I've been worried sick about you!"

"I should've called sooner." Gemma had known her parents were worried. She'd been avoiding their concern. "But you know I had to come."

"Yes." Her mother's voice held a touch of resignation. "Has it helped?"

The grief counsellor had supported Gemma's determination in the face of her parents' objections. Closure came in strange ways. And that's what this trip was about, closure. "I don't know. Mum, I'm so confused." Gemma thought of Angelo's effect on her, how he only had to touch her to send her up in flames and gulped. "Sometimes I feel like I'm losing my mind." But tomorrow that would end. She would leave…and never see Angelo Apollonides again. It was for the best— even if it meant she'd never know the truth…

"How is Dad?"

"Fine."

"No, I mean, how is he handling my coming to Strathmos? He was very upset when I left."

Her mother sighed. "He's worried. And it's opened up the memories about your sister's death. He's afraid of what might happen to you."

"Tell him I'm fine…and I love him."

"He's gone back to therapy. The doctor says he's over the worst of the depression. For him, like you, the hardest part was not knowing why Mandy died."

"Double trouble, that's what Dad used to call us." Staring at the photo, Gemma searched the face of her twin for answers. Mandy had died, unhappy and lost. But no one knew why. Only Angelo could provide the answers that would let her father—and Gemma herself—find a little peace.

Closure.

That's what they all needed.

And that was why she could not tell Angelo to go to hell and walk away. Cold seeped in, chilling her all the way to her soul.

She could not leave tomorrow.

"Oh, *sweetheart*. Come home."

"I can't." Her lips barely moved. "I have to find out what happened to Mandy. For all our sakes. Then we can get on with our lives."

"Oh, Gemma. Your sister wouldn't want you to suffer like this, she'd want you to remember the special times you had together."

"I know. But I need to understand what happened to her…what this bastard did to her and why she reacted like she did. Dad and you need to know, too."

"Your father and I don't want you meddling with this man." Her mother's voice was anxious. "He's wealthy, powerful. He could hurt you."

Like he hurt Mandy.

Gemma knew what her mother was thinking. But the words remained unspoken.

"Mum…" Gemma's voice trailed away. She thought of what had just happened between her and Angelo. If her parents knew about that…they'd be on the next flight out to rescue her.

"Have you spoken to him? What did he say?"

Reluctant to admit that she hadn't confronted Angelo about Mandy's death, and even more loath for her mother to discover that Angelo believed she was Mandy, Gemma spoke in a rush. "I wanted to find out what kind of man he is first."

"And what kind of man is he?"

Compelling. Passionate. "It's difficult to explain."

"Gemma, be careful." The sigh came over the miles. "You're not Mandy. Chasing after trouble was her speciality, not yours. You were always the sensible one, Gemma."

Her mother was right, Mandy had always been a little…wild. Taking Gemma's passport and credit card to Strathmos and assuming Gemma's identity was only one of the pranks Mandy had played.

Oh, Mandy, what happened on Strathmos?

Gemma couldn't help thinking about the familiarity in the Frenchman's tone earlier, his easy kiss. She remembered Angelo's hard gaze, the coiled tension in his muscled body. She remembered the taste of his mouth—hot and seductive against hers—the thrill of his body pressing into hers and her pleasure as she came apart under his touch.

Once again confusion and turmoil wrestled within her. God! How could she teach the bastard the lesson he deserved if she desired him?

And how could she face him again?

Gemma squeezed her eyes shut. How on earth could she have reacted like that to the man who had destroyed her sister?

Four

Gemma tossed and turned for most of the night. Several times she jerked awake from confusing dreams of what had happened in her sister's life. Beneath it all festered an uneasiness about the disturbing passion that had flared between herself and Angelo. Just before dawn the pitter-patter of rain against the window pane lulled her into a restless sleep.

In the morning she clambered out of bed, crossed to the window and hitched the curtain back. No sun peeked through the cloud cover. The trees outside swayed in the wind. But at least the rain had subsided. With her morning free of rehearsals and her next show scheduled for later that evening, Gemma decided to make for the beach to go windsurfing. That was one place where wet and wind wouldn't matter. And it would certainly shake the dark mood that gripped her and take her mind off Mandy, Jean-Paul and… Angelo.

Pulling on a sleek black maillot, she called reception to check that no storms were forecasted, then grabbed her wet suit out of the cupboard and trod into a pair of ancient sneakers. A couple of bananas, a bottle of water and a towel, and she was ready to go.

The beach was deserted. To Gemma's relief, there were no whitecaps on the water. A gust of wind tugged at her hair as she hauled a windsurfing board out of the stack. Dragging the board into the sea, she waded calf-deep into the water and waited with both hands on the boom. When a puff of wind came, she pushed the mast straight up and stepped onto the centre of the board. Shifting her feet, Gemma adjusted the sail and, looking upwind, she turned the board to the open sea.

The sail filled and she took off, the wind rushing past her ears. She barely noticed the rain and her worries evaporated as she raced across the water.

She welcomed the freedom.

A couple of hours later Gemma became aware of another windsurfer on the water, coming towards her through the rain. Leaning her mast back, the nose of her board started to turn upwind across the face of the wind, away from the intruder. But the other windsurfer gained on her, trespassing on her solitude.

A quick glance at her watch showed that she still had lots of time before her show. It wasn't often that she had the sea to herself. Why would she go in simply because someone was crowding her? There was a whole sea for the two of them. If she tacked away, perhaps the other windsurfer would get the hint.

But the larger black-and-white sail continued to bear down on her. Glaring at him—it was undoubtedly a male figure—Gemma's annoyance grew when she recognised the windsurfer.

Angelo.

Setting a course upwind, Gemma decided to force him to yield to her. A glint of white as his teeth flashed. *He knew what she was up to.*

Determined to get ahead, she started to work every ounce of speed out of her rig. The board responded willingly and elation swept through her.

Then she saw that Angelo had taken up her challenge.

For a moment she thought that they might collide. She faltered, her board wobbled and her nerve almost gave in, before he gave way, falling back to sail in her wake. Her sail shivering under the pressure of the wind, she skimmed across the water, while her heart beat rapidly at the near miss—and the euphoria that came from racing the wind...and besting Angelo.

Angelo stared after Gemma not sure whether to whistle in admiration or holler at her recklessness. She was going full tilt, not giving an inch. He pointed his board to a destination upwind of where she was headed, and he set off after her.

The breeze blew on his face, lighter on the inside near the shore. He came down the line he'd planned, unfazed by the rain, tacking with speed and closing his distance on Gemma.

She turned, glancing over her shoulder as he gained on her. He could see the determination in her stance. This was no beginner. She was going to give him a good run.

They battled it out downwind. Her jaw was set. She wasn't giving an inch. She wanted to win. Despite the rain, her hair streamed behind her like a bright banner, a lithe graceful figure in tune with the elements.

Never had he wanted her as much as he did at the moment. She looked elemental and a little elusive. Not the sure thing he'd always considered her.

Working furiously, Angelo finally notched ahead and threw a triumphant smile over his shoulder, confident that the race was done.

The next instant the wind dropped and the rain eased. Both boards slowed. Angelo bit back a curse at being deprived of a clear victory. He dropped down to straddle the board and, glancing sideways, saw that Gemma had dropped onto her stomach and was already paddling with her arms and making for the shore.

Pacing himself, he kept abreast of her, his powerful arms stroking through the water. But she didn't look at him, she kept her gaze firmly ahead.

In the shallows, keeping her face averted, Gemma leapt off the board, dragging it in behind her, intensely conscious of Angelo following close behind.

Flutters of apprehension started deep in her stomach, and the battle of the last half hour between them was forgotten as the memory of what had happened between them last night rose in her mind.

She didn't know how she was going to face him.

The attendant, now at his post, came running to take the board. She gave a brief, abstracted smile of thanks. Her saturated sneakers squishing with water, she hurried to where she'd dropped her towel and water bottle earlier. Collapsing onto a damp wooden bench, she uncapped the bottle and took a long sip, her heart banging against her ribs as Angelo approached.

He stopped beside her. She stilled, then took another sip, pretending to ignore him, while every nerve ending quivered warily at his closeness.

"You never told me you could windsurf."

The rasp of the zip sounded loud in the silence. Gemma was achingly aware of his peeling off his wet suit and slinging it over the back of the bench. Underneath he wore a pair of boardshorts that rode low on his hips. The unwelcome memory of last night clear in her mind, Gemma tried not to notice that his stomach was taut and tanned, the defined muscles revealing that he worked out regularly—or led a very active lifestyle.

Gemma whipped her gaze away and shrugged. "I don't know why I didn't tell you. I would've thought I had." Why had Mandy not told him? Especially as it was clear it was something Angelo excelled at. Her parents had paid for lessons for both her and Mandy to learn to windsurf down at Buckland's Beach, near their childhood home. Mandy had been more interested in flirting with the youths in the class than learning to sail. Deciding to distract him with flattery Gemma added, "You're good. Those were some great moves out there."

But Angelo didn't bite. "So, when are you leaving?"

Gemma drew a deep, shuddering breath. "I'm not." His expression never altered, but she sensed his sudden tension.

"Last night you said you were going, why have you changed your mind?"

Even though his tone remained even, his eyes told a different story. Her gaze fell before his challenging stare, landing on his legs. His thighs were solid, the skin darkened to a deep bronze by the Greek sun. She felt herself flush and quickly looked away over the sea. She didn't want this awful awareness of this man. "Because my reputation would be mud in entertainment circles if I walked away from my contract."

"I would see to it that didn't happen."

He wanted her gone that much? Gemma swallowed, then said baldly, "I can't go, I need the money."

A coolness entered his voice. "Is this where I'm supposed to offer to pay you to leave?"

"No!" Gemma jerked her head up to stare at him, horrified by the conclusion he'd drawn. "But I've got a contract and I'm entitled to payment for doing my job. I need it."

"What do you need the money for?" Angelo dropped down beside her and his arm stretched along the back of the bench, so that it rested behind her head.

She thought furiously. "Medical expenses," she said at last, trying to ignore his arm. It wasn't easy. "From the…er…car accident." She swallowed again and stared out over the sea.

"That's what caused your amnesia?"

Damn. What to say now?

The silence stretched. He was waiting for her reply. Gemma discovered she wasn't crazy about lying to him. Strange, because she'd never thought it would worry her in the least. Not after what he'd done.

"Witnesses say it was a hit and run," she expanded, sticking to the story she'd originally planned. "Luckily when I came round in hospital I remembered who I was. But I don't remember anything about you, about Strathmos…or anything that happened for a while after I left Strathmos."

"So you're suffering from retrograde amnesia. You lost the events immediately before the accident."

Retrograde amnesia? Gemma blinked. "Uh…yes." His interest took her aback. She gave him a weak smile. "Have you been doing research?"

"A little. Did you experience any memory loss after the accident?"

This time she was prepared. "Yes. There was some anterograde amnesia. I remember waking up in hospital. I don't remember the accident itself—or getting to the hospital. The specialists did say that the events I could no longer recall before the accident might return as time passed. But to date they haven't. I lost several weeks of my life." She delivered the explanation as she'd prepared it.

"Was there any other damage?" His fingers brushed her shoulder. Despite the thick protection of the Neoprene wet suit, Gemma felt as though she'd been scorched.

"No, I was fortunate," she said a trifle huskily as shivers coursed through her.

"Nothing lucky about it," he said abruptly. "Such an accident should never have happened. Did the police catch the perpetrator?"

"No." Gemma fidgeted. She hadn't expected his concern and outrage on her behalf. She folded her arms across her stomach, feeling terrible. Then she recalled her father's depression, her mother's tears after Mandy's unnecessary death. Instantly her heart hardened. "Now can you understand why I need money?"

"What will you do when you finish here?"

"My agent is looking for something for me." There had been offers, but Gemma hadn't been in a hurry to take another booking. She hadn't been sure how long she needed on Strathmos to learn the truth.

"So long as you know that your contract to sing here will not be extended. I don't want you here."

Gemma gulped. That was pretty direct. It also meant that she had less than three weeks to find out the truth. "I understand."

Two days passed without catching sight of Angelo. On Wednesday morning Gemma lounged beside the resort's heated outdoor pool, soaking up the mild early morning sunshine. She'd heard that Angelo sometimes swam laps after breakfast before the resort guests started to congregate.

Huge sheets of glass shut out the unpredictable autumn wind without obscuring the view of the Aegean. In the centre of the pool a marble quartet of golden winged horses danced under the spray that jetted from three tall fountains. Through half-closed eyes, Gemma could almost imagine the mythical beasts thundering across the heavens, steered by the sun god.

A young poolside waiter had just delivered a tall glass topped with a pink umbrella and a row of cherries on a swizzle stick when a familiar voice shattered the fantasy.

"So this is where you've been hiding."

Tensing, Gemma wished she was wearing more than

the tiny bikini with the skimpy bandana top. Hidden behind sunglasses, she said, "Don't you have more important things to do than look for me?"

Angelo waved his hand dismissively. "You told me you are here for the money. Right?"

"Y-es," she stretched the word out, waiting, wondering why his eyes had turned as hard as stone.

He dropped down on the lounger beside hers; only a low glass-topped table on which her drink stood separated them. Uncomfortably conscious of his closeness, Gemma pushed her sunglasses firmly up her nose, grateful for the protection they offered from his icy scrutiny.

"I've just learned you wanted this contract badly enough to take a drop in pay." His voice was edged in steel. "I want to know why. How could you afford to do that with the medical expenses you cried about only a couple of days ago?"

Raising her shoulder, Gemma dropped it with false aplomb. "I took the drop because I was desperate for money. I needed an income—I haven't been getting regular work."

His gaze glittered with suspicion. "You once told me that one of the joys of being an exotic dancer is that there's always work. So if you were short of work why sing? Why not dance?"

Gemma forced herself not to shudder. She'd never understood why Mandy danced or how she put up with the hoards of leering men—even if the money was good. "Uh—I don't do that anymore. I love singing." That, at least, was true. "And singing pays more when I get the right spots, which I'm getting more often. I'm on the rise."

"What's this?"

Something in his sharp tone turned her head. He was scowling at the glass the waiter had brought. She frowned, puzzled at his ferocity.

"You can't drink before you sing."

"Not even fruit juice?" she asked tartly. He looked unconvinced, so Gemma picked the glass up and thrust it at him. "Here, sniff it."

"Very clever." At her baffled frown, he added. "Given that your preferred drink is vodka, sniffing won't help much. Not with the overpowering flavour of pineapple."

Of course! Mandy had always been partial to vodka. "My only vice," Gemma said at last.

"*Only* vice?" His smile was sharklike. Setting the glass down, he leaned closer.

This close up his eyes were mesmerizing. The vibrant turquoise irises were surrounded by a row of lashes too long for a man. Dark brows arched over the top. No question about it, Angelo Apollonides was the most gorgeous male she had ever set eyes on. Pity he was not her type.

"It's the only one I can think of right now," she said carelessly. "If I thought about it very hard, I might discover one or two more."

His mouth flattened. "Try. I'm sure you will find there are more vices that you will remember. Like lying."

Gemma's breath left her in a rush.

"When did I lie?" Did he know? She gave him a searching look as adrenaline started to pump through her. *God.* What would he do if he discovered—

"When I discovered you'd taken a drop in pay, I thought you lied to me. That you had another agenda. Don't ever lie to me."

She almost collapsed from relief. So she glared at him. "I'm *not* lying. I do need money. My credit card is a little over-extended." The thirty-thousand dollar debt merited a bigger description than *little*.

"Too much shopping and partying?"

If he only knew. While Mandy had been a party animal, Gemma preferred spending her spare time outdoors. Walking. Windsurfing. Or simply attending concerts in parks. Simple pleasures, not the sophisticated pursuits his mistresses would enjoy.

She pursed her lips. How could she admit how much money had vanished, and that she had no idea where it had gone? The large cash withdrawals her credit-card statements reflected told her nothing.

"You had no debt three years ago. And some nice pieces of jewellery." He gave a pointed stare at the ring she wore. The ring Mandy had given her just before she had died and Angelo had claimed to have bought for Mandy in Monaco.

"I don't know what happened to all that," she said honestly.

He gave her a searching look. "You don't remember?"

She nodded.

"I was more than generous," he said. "I indulged your desire to party, to shop until your cupboards were overflowing. If you'd behaved better, you might not be in this predicament."

Surely Angelo wasn't suggesting they might still be together? Not when she knew the kind of man he was. A playboy. A man who traded one beautiful woman for another, as soon as their temporary sell-by date was over.

Her lip curled. "You mean, if I was still your mistress? Putting up with your demands, your—"

"I thought you'd forgotten everything. So how do you remember how demanding I was?" His tone held a sensual rasp, belied by his shrewd gaze.

"I read gossip cuttings. How do you think I learned about our affair?"

He reached out and put finger a finger under her chin. He put enough pressure to tilt her head up, so that he could stare down into her eyes. "So you came here not only to earn money and regain your memory, but to learn more about us?"

The sudden flare of heat that followed in the wake of the touch of that one finger shocked her. *No.* She was not going to respond to his very obvious attraction. He was the last man on earth to whom she could afford to be attracted.

A spoilt playboy who'd had a fortune handed to him on a plate. A dilettante who destroyed people without compunction. Keeping her voice level she said, "I know exactly what kind of man you are."

"Do you really?" He raised a dark eyebrow, looming over her.

Too close. Too male. Too…everything.

She backpedaled. "I don't remember anything, but I know how you make me feel."

"And how is that?" The pressure of the pad of his index finger lessened. The tip trailed down her throat and settled just below the tender hollow at the base of her neck. The touch felt like a brand.

Oh, no. She spotted the trap too late. She swallowed. "Repelled."

He bared his teeth in triumph at the tiny give away as her throat moved. "Ah, you tempt me to prove you a liar."

Gemma gave an uneasy laugh. "Perhaps I haven't been completely honest with you."

His pupils expanded. "Go on."

"I came here to ask for your help." She sucked in a breath. "I woke alone in a hospital in London with no memory of how I got there, who I'd been with at the time of the accident or where I'd been."

His hand dropped away.

Gemma could breathe again.

Until he spoke. "You weren't able to track down information from the people with you at the time of the accident?"

She had to be careful. She couldn't afford to trip herself up. "The only clue about where I'd been was a bunch of old pay slips from Palace of Poseidon." She'd found them in her sister's things. "Later I found out that I'd worked here...that we'd had an affair."

More lies. It hadn't been later. Mandy had e-mailed her from Strathmos, crowing about the fabulously wealthy man she'd landed.

Gemma stared at him defiantly. "That's why I'm here. I thought if I came...back...met you, I might re-member something about—" she paused "—my past."

His expression altered subtly. He came closer. "Is it working?"

"No." Her voice turned husky. She picked up a towel and draped it over her bare, exposed tummy. "I had hoped by staying on Strathmos some things might come back to me. But they haven't." She paused for a beat, peered up at him over the top of her sunglasses. "But perhaps if you helped, if you let me ask you some questions, maybe something you say might act as a trigger. And the past might come back to me."

She waited, holding her breath, her blood hammering in her head, causing it to ache with tension. What had Angelo done to reduce Mandy from a confident, somewhat reckless party girl to a pale, shaking ghost of her former self?

She *had* to find out.

At last he gave a curt nod. "But if it doesn't work, that's it. Okay? You leave as soon as your contract is complete." He rose to his feet. "We'll start tonight, after your show."

"I'd rather meet in the mornings."

"I'm a busy man. If you want my help then you'll have to meet me tonight. In my suite."

"No." Gemma shook her head emphatically, her hair swirling around her face. The last thing she wanted was to be alone with him. The attraction he held terrified her. While she desperately wanted to know what he'd done to her twin, she was not about to let him destroy her in the process. "I'll meet you after the show in the Dionysus bar."

For a moment Gemma thought she'd lost him. Then he said, "You're on."

Five

When Gemma hurried into the Dionysus bar later that night it was buzzing. She hesitated, scanning the press of people, until Angelo rose from a table near the window. Outside, the resort's landscaped gardens were lit by floodlights. Beyond them she could see the lights of vessels winking out on the dark sea.

"Sorry I'm late," she gasped. "I had to shower and change." She indicated to the shimmery wraparound dress that she'd slipped on.

"No problem." He pulled out a chair for her. "How did the performance go?"

"Good. It never fails to put me on a high."

Angelo beckoned to a waiter. "What can I order for you to drink?"

"A white-wine cooler would be good—with lots of sparkling water, ice and a little lime, please."

He gave her a long look. "Are you sure that's what you want? Your performance is over. You can have something more…robust if you want."

The euphoria left her. She sagged into the chair. "I don't drink much of the hard stuff. But thanks."

Gemma watched him as he spoke to the waiter. What had his relationship with her sister been like? Mandy had always loved to party…and the kind of men she'd picked tended to have no problem with that. But Angelo seemed almost disapproving. Not what she'd expected from his playboy personna at all.

When he turned back, Gemma—unable to let his comment pass—said, "Strange for an hotelier to be watching his guests' liquor consumption." With a sweep of her arm, she encompassed the full-to-capacity bar. "Can't be good for business."

"You're not a guest, you're an employee," he said quellingly. "And you don't have a great track record."

"What do you mean?"

He shook his head. "Be grateful that you don't remember."

"But I *want* to know."

"You're better served moving on from those events. It's enough for you to know that you had a…problem."

A problem that he had exacerbated?

Gemma studied his expression. To be fair, it didn't look like he'd approved of Mandy's antics…whatever they had been. Was it possible that he'd had nothing to do with Mandy's slide from grace?

He forced me. I loved him. I wanted to please him. I was ready to do whatever he wanted. And it made me feel good. I'm so sorry for failing you all.

The memory of Mandy's words caused Gemma to steel herself. No. Angelo was *not* uninvolved. He'd destroyed her twin.

But before she could tell him what a low-life skunk she considered him, their drinks arrived.

Angelo passed a long glass to her. "So what do you want to ask me?"

She stared at him blankly.

"That's why we're here, remember?" His smiled was sardonic. "So that you can ask me questions, to try and jolt your memory."

Oh, yes. She gave herself a gentle shake. Nothing would be served by telling him what she thought of him. Better to focus on what she'd come here for—to learn what had happened to Mandy…to find a way to make Angelo pay.

Gemma took a sip of her drink. It was cool and refreshing. "You wanted to know why I need money. In addition to the medical expenses—" she broke off, reluctant to perpetuate that lie, then blurted out, "I want to know why there was thirty thousand owing on my credit card. Do you know where it went?"

"I have no idea."

"I drew cash out with my credit card and ran through it in your casinos, didn't I?" She was pushing him now, but she wanted answers. She wanted him to confess what he'd gotten Mandy into. "*Your* casinos. *Your* fault I'm thirty-thousand in the red."

"You liked to gamble…I didn't force you. But I wouldn't call you an addict."

Gemma flinched. "But it would've been more than I could afford."

"Your chips went on my account. It didn't cost you a euro. You must have accumulated your debts—" he picked the word with fastidious care "—after you left me."

"So where I did I go from Strathmos?"

He lifted a negligent shoulder. "I have no idea."

"Nor did you care—certainly not enough to buy me a ticket to make sure I reached home safely."

A frown creased his brow, he picked up his drink and leaned back. "I'm a generous man. I gave you a more than a plentiful allowance while you lived with me. Gold cards, a supply of cash that you ran through like water." There was distaste in his tone now. "You could have saved that for a rainy day."

Gemma opened her mouth to argue, then shut it again. His words held the unmistakeable ring of truth.

"I regret the hit-and-run left you floundering for your memory." The sympathy in his eyes faded as he continued, "But you're an adult. You've worked in nightclubs in London, Paris. You considered New Zealand a backwater. I assumed you'd simply find another big city, another big-spending benefactor to fund your love of the high life."

She blinked. While he'd clearly enjoyed having Mandy in his bed, it didn't sound like he'd held her twin in high regard. Poor Mandy.

He set his glass down. "After I found you with Moreau I didn't give a damn where you were going. Right then I hoped you'd drown in the sea. You'd betrayed me, in the worst way that a woman can betray a man. I couldn't wait to see the back of you."

Gemma flinched at his bitter words. Yet under the white-hot anger she suspected that Angelo was telling the truth. He *didn't* know where Mandy had gone after leaving him. Could that mean that she'd misjudged him? Had he had nothing to do with Mandy's problems? Had they only started after her sister left Strathmos?

Her shoulders sagged. She'd had such high hopes that Angelo would provide the key to the puzzle. Then she thought about what he'd said, and lifted her head. "Did I leave the island with Jean-Paul?"

He shrugged. "It's possible. I wanted him out my sight, too."

Perhaps the Frenchman could provide a clue to what had happened. Angelo's face had tightened at the mention of the other man. She changed the subject. "You said that you inherited a string of family hotels from your grandfather. How did they transform into this?" Gemma gestured to the bar and, beyond it, the resort.

"On my twenty-first birthday, I inherited three islands and a chain of three-star holiday hotels geared to foreign budget tourists. My grandfather had been ill for a while. The hotels were shabby, showing their age. While they were well booked over the summer months, they were deserted in winter. I knew I could do more. I wanted resorts where occupancy was guaranteed all year round."

"That's why you went for casinos?"

He nodded. "But I wanted more than glamorous casinos. I wanted places where everyone in the family would have a good time. That meant themed resorts, cinemas, a variety of shows that would draw people back again."

"You achieved everything you set out to do."

He nodded. "It took a while. I first worked at upgrading the hotels I had. I knew the first spectacular resort had to be built here at Strathmos. It was my dream. I hadn't been back to the island since I left as an eighteen-year-old. Once I got it up, Poseidon was born."

"And now Poseidon's resorts are associated with worlds of fantasy." She tried to hide her admiration by giving the words a bite. "The Golden Cavern. The Never-Ending River." She named some famous drawcards.

His gaze narrowed. "You remember? You remember visiting them with me?"

The damned amnesia. She'd nearly given herself away. Slowly she shook her head. "I told you, I tried to put together the missing parts of my memory so I read up about our relationship in the tabloids. There were bits about Poseidon's Resorts, too. Like their fantasy themes and what they're worth today. About how innovative you were." And on the Internet there had been endless details about the wealthy, powerful and good-looking Angelo Apollonides, Mr. Eligible Bachelor Billionaire of the Year. But she wasn't telling him any of that. The last thing she wanted was for him to think he interested her. Gemma shifted, uncomfortable with where this conversation was heading.

She could barely hide her relief when the duty manager arrived and whispered into Angelo's ear.

"I'm sorry," he apologised. "I am needed. And we've barely gotten started."

"Don't worry. We can talk again some other time."

"Shall I order you another drink?"

"No, I'm done." She pushed the empty glass aside. "I might wander over to one of the coffee bars. And then I'll make my way back to my room. I can use an early night. Don't worry about me."

He rose and gave her a slow smile. "I find that I can't help worrying about you." And her heart twisted.

And then he was gone.

Still thinking about that delicious smile—and her reaction to it—Gemma picked up her purse and threaded her way through the packed bar to the exit—where she almost ran into Jean-Paul.

"Steady, *cherie.*" He caught her by the elbows. "Can I buy you a drink?" His dark eyes lingered on her appreciatively.

Sensitive to Angelo's accusation that Mandy had cheated on him with the Frenchman, and Angelo had warned her in no uncertain terms to stay away from him, Gemma's first response was to refuse. But what if Mandy had left Strathmos with Jean-Paul? Gemma hesitated, then thrust her scruples aside.

She needed to talk to this man.

"I'd love a drink." She gave him a bright smile to make up for her hesitation. He was back in minutes with two glasses.

"What is it?" she asked, eyeing the clear liquid uneasily.

"Surely you didn't think I could forget, *cherie?* You're the only woman I ever knew who drank triple vodka and tonic like water." He gave her a very knowing smile. "The secret of your success, you called it. And what made you so exciting."

Angelo strode out of the Apollo Club. It hadn't taken long to calm two furious patrons after an accusation of cheating in the discreet back room where a poker game with extremely high stakes was being played.

In the elevator he greeted an American IT billionaire and his wife who came to the Palace every few months.

Hurrying out the elevator, he glanced at his watch. Gemma should be back in her unit by now. Downstairs, he stopped beside a porter kiosk and called reception requesting to be put through to her room. It rang unanswered.

Perhaps she was still in one of the coffee shops.

He made his way to the entertainment complex. He didn't find her in the first coffee shop. Nor in large alcove with soft armchairs where a pianist played Chopin. But as he passed the Dionysus Bar he caught a glimpse of copper flame.

Gemma.

Frowning, he ground to a halt and looked again.

It *was* Gemma. And she was not alone. Jean-Paul Moreau was standing beside her barstool, his arm resting on the bar beside his drink, looking utterly enthralled by her.

What the hell was she doing with Moreau?

He'd warned her to keep away from the man. The silver dress she wore showed off her curves and her hair was a vivid flag of colour against the pale fabric. Seated on the barstool, her sleek legs were shown off to maximum advantage.

Three years ago he'd felt nothing except anger and disgust for Gemma and he'd hardly thought of her in the intervening years. So what the hell had changed? Why could he not stop noticing every detail about her? Especially given that it was clear that nothing had changed—she still hankered after Moreau.

He gave a grim smile when she jumped as he stopped beside her.

"Angelo! I thought you were—"

"Busy?" he finished, and gave Moreau a cool nod.

"Well…yes."

"I sorted the problem out and came back to finish our conversation."

"Oh." Her eyes went round. She glanced in Moreau's direction.

Trying to work out how to dump the Frenchman, Angelo suspected.

"Another vodka?" Moreau offered.

Vodka? Angelo narrowed his gaze. A flush rose in her cheeks. *Guilt.* "I thought you didn't drink much of the hard stuff any more? In fact, I seem to remember mention of a hot drink in a coffee shop after I left you earlier."

"Gemma is of age," Moreau interjected. "She can drink whatever she desires."

"I told her to stay away from you." Angelo shot the Frenchman a killing look. Then he said to Gemma, "What the hell does it matter? Have another goddamned vodka with him."

Deeply disappointed he turned and walked away. He told himself he didn't care what she did. Gemma Allen was bad news. A liar. A faithless little cheat. The anger she'd ultimately caused him three years ago had not been worth the pleasure she'd given him in bed.

And she hadn't changed. The sooner he put her out of mind the better.

"Angelo…"

His long, angry strides had already carried him out

the bar, across the entertainment complex and he was headed for the lobby to the elevators that would take him to his penthouse.

"What?" He swung around, glaring down at her as a bolt of sensation shook him as she caught his sleeve. He didn't want this attraction. Not to this woman.

She released him. "Forget it."

"No, you're here now. So talk."

"I wanted to explain why I had a drink with Jean-Paul."

Her eyes were wide and dark. Gentle and pleading. He looked past her, clenching his jaw. All she wanted was his help to regain her memory. Nothing more. Better he remember that. "Drink with whom you please."

"I wanted to find out if he knew anything about the thirty thousand—"

"Forget about trying to find out what happened to the damned money. It's gone. Put your stupidity behind you. So you have some debt, so what? You're young, you can work it off." A pause, then he added softly, "On your back if need be."

Gemma's expression changed. He saw the fury, the darkness in her eyes as she registered the taunt. Her hand came up. She swung wildly. Angelo ducked, she missed. A glass vase from the glass table beside the elevator crashed to the ground. A party of guests took one horrified look at them and hurried past. Gemma barely noticed. Angelo knew he should rush after them, offer them a free night, gambling chips. Damage control.

But he didn't.

Right now Gemma had his full attention.

"How dare you?" She hissed. "How dare you say that, you…you…"

"Gorilla? Neanderthal?" Behind him the elevator opened. He took a deft step backward. "Who knows, I might even be convinced to consider taking you back to my bed and if you're very, very good—maybe I'll help clear that debt." And he hit the button for the roof garden.

She rushed forward, balling her fists and swung again. "I wouldn't sleep with you if you were the last—"

"Neanderthal in the world?" he finished with a hard laugh, and caught her flailing hands. "You might not be so lucky then. You've done it before, why the scruples now?"

He felt her stiffen with outrage. He secured her arms behind her back and pulled her up against him and his mouth slanted across hers.

She tensed.

The elevator shot upward. As his tongue delved into her mouth, Angelo felt her give and lean into him and the familiar arousal shafted through his lower body.

How could he have forgotten how soft her skin was? How full of life her red hair was? Or the little moaning noises she made into his mouth as she pressed against him? He couldn't remember her feeling…tasting…this good.

Hell, so maybe he had amnesia, too.

Distantly he heard the ping of the elevator door opening and the sound of talking and laughter. The rooftop garden was occupied.

Releasing her hands he pressed the ground-floor button and then they were sinking. Her tongue stroked against his, hot and deliberate. The fire inside went wild. He released her hands and cupped her buttocks, pulling her towards him. She came eagerly, rising on tiptoe, her body soft, melting against him like warm golden honey, and he ached with want.

He was tempted to yank open the bow on that wrap-around dress, unfurl her, rub his hand between her legs to check if she was damp enough to take him and slide into her slippery warmth. Only the knowledge of where they were stopped him.

An elevator. *Hell.* Given how annoyed she'd been minutes ago, she'd slap him for sure. Hard. Even if only after he'd driven them both to completion, tasted her satisfied sighs. No, better to take it slow.

Instead he slid his hands up…over the feminine curves of her bottom to her waist and back down again tracing the tiny string of an excuse for underwear she wore. Heard her breath catch…and hold. Taking advantage of her expectancy, he fingered the thong through her dress.

She wriggled against him, and he drove his tongue deep into her mouth, giving her a taste of what he wanted, what he really craved. She arched against him and he felt his erection leap.

The car shuddered to a stop. He lifted his head. "Carry on like that and I'll forget my good intentions. I'll hit the button for my suite. Three steps and we'll be in the dining room. Three minutes and we can both be naked. Is that what you want?"

"No." She shook her head wildly, her face shocked and pale. "I don't want this…you." She stumbled backwards out of the confined space, her hands covering her eyes. "God, what am I *doing?*"

He followed more slowly. Putting an arm around

her shoulder he guided her away from the public lobby. Out of sight. "What we've done many times before?" he said helpfully. Her hands dropped away from her face and she bit her lip, her teeth white against the bee-stung bottom lip as she glared at him. But something in her eyes, a deep agonised confusion made him stretch his hand out. "Hey, it's okay, I know you don't remember. But it doesn't matter."

"It matters." It was a wail. Then her head was back in her hands, her fingers knotting through the long dark red curls. "It matters more than I can tell you."

"It doesn't." He stroked her shoulder and noticed absently that his hand was trembling. "I'll tell you something, it's even better now than it ever was in the past. It's more…I can't explain. But I can't seem to get enough of you. The taste of you, the feel of your body up against mine. I want you, Gemma. Badly."

"Believe me, that's not good." The smile she gave him was wan.

"It will be very good," he promised, "you'll see."

"I can't." Her expression grew resolute. "Angelo, I can't make love to you—"

Irritation twisted inside Angelo. He wanted her. He wasn't accustomed to women saying no. "Why? You want to."

"That's arrogant." *But true.* She was terrified she was going to cave in to his demand. She drew a ragged breath. There was one thing he would understand. "I can't make love with you until my memory returns."

He cursed.

"Who knows," she added, "there might be someone else—"

"Someone so important that you don't remember him?" he sneered. "Someone like Jean-Paul Moreau?"

That only made her expression harden. "That's it. Good night. I'm finished with trying to talk to you. I'm going to bed. Alone."

Six

The ringing of the phone woke Gemma. Any plans she'd harboured to sleep late on Thursday—her day off—fell apart when Mark Lyme, the manager of the entertainment complex, told her that Lucie had come down with a flu-like virus. Immediately Gemma offered to take over some of Lucie's performances and arranged a time to meet with Mark to discuss a suitable program.

The Dionysus was a very different set-up to the Electra Theatre, and it had been years since she'd worked in a bar environment. Most of the day was spent putting together the program with Mark and Denny, another performer, for the first fill-in performance early that evening.

The substitute show was rough and ready but it was enough to satisfy the crowd. They sang a couple of duets, Denny told some jokes and they invited some of tourists to sing along karaoke-style.

Gemma caught a brief glimpse of Angelo in the back of the bar halfway through the evening. He was waiting for her and she found herself accepting his invitation to dinner. At first she fretted that he might try to kiss her…seduce her…but her worries proved to be unfounded. Angelo behaved like the perfect gentleman.

Lying in bed that night, Gemma covered her eyes and moaned out loud. *She was so confused.* Who was the real Angelo Apollonides?

By Friday Lucie's temperature was raging and Dr. Natos, the resort doctor, had prescribed bed and rest.

Gemma and Denny met for another rehearsal. During a brief break, she found Angelo at her elbow, holding two paper cups. "Coffee? I'm sure you could use it."

"What's that saying about not trusting Greeks who come bearing gifts?" She slanted him a provocative glance.

"Hardly a gift. Consider it an apology."

After a moment's pause she took the paper cup. "An apology?"

He looked abashed. "For my behaviour the other night. I should have apologised over dinner yesterday. But I didn't."

"Oh." She took a sip. It was strong and sweet and pungent.

He frowned. "I'm confused."

That made two of them! She slanted him a wary glance. "Why?"

"I had no intention of having anything to do with you. But I keep thinking you've changed. Then something happens—like seeing you with Jean-Paul—and I think I'm wrong. You're still the same." He raked his fingers through his golden hair. "Have you changed?"

She shut her eyes. *God.* How on earth was she supposed to respond to that? Not honestly. It was too late for that. She had to soldier on. And then there was the fact that she wasn't ready to face the rage and scorn in his eyes when he discovered her treachery. Not yet.

She'd tell him when she was about to leave. When her contract had ended. And she had uncovered the truth about Mandy. Whatever that might be.

He waved a hand. "Forget it. That's a stupid question. Sit down, you could probably use the break."

Gemma followed him dragging her feet as he led her to the cluster of seating in a small lobby.

His cell phone rang. Fishing it out his pocket, he studied the caller ID. "My mother," he said. "Excuse me."

Angelo could feel Gemma's eyes resting on him as he responded to his mother's well wishes. He listened with half an ear to a story about the car her latest husband had bought, laughed when expected. Conscious of keeping Gemma waiting, he cut the conversation short.

"For a playboy, you have a good relationship with your mother," Gemma said, her eyes curious.

He didn't rise to the bait. "Even playboys have mothers. And, despite all the wealth in the world, her life has not been easy," he answered guardedly. "She fell pregnant with me when she was very young. The man abandoned her. I never met him."

Not *my father,* but *the man,* Gemma noticed.

"Oh."

It must have been hell for a young boy.

"So is today your birthday?"

"Yes—I'm blessed with two celebrations in one month. Last week it was my name day."

"Name day? What's that?"

"A day all people bearing the name of a particular saint celebrate. So on the eighth of November anyone called Angelo celebrates. My mother thought I was an angel when I was born." He gave her a sardonic smile.

She laughed. "Did you get gifts?"

"Most people simply called to send greetings—that's what my cousins, Tariq, Zac and Katy did. My mother sent a gift. Some of the villagers who've known me all my life baked for me."

"O-kay." She suppressed a smile. From what she'd seen of him so far, he'd struck her as a jet-set prince. "I didn't have you pegged for the kind of guy who received home baking."

"I love home baking. But you didn't—too fattening, you said. In fact, you hardly used to eat at all. Your appetite is better now. You've stopped all those diet pills." He gave her a frank, appreciative look. "Now that I think about it, you've picked up a couple of pounds. It suits you. Makes you sexier than ever."

The air sizzled between them.

When she saw Mark waving, Gemma wanted to swear. Angelo had been opening up. She drained the cup and threw it in a trash can. "I have to go," she said to Angelo.

"I'll see you later." He gave her a wry smile. "And I

won't try to seduce you. At least not until your memory returns—unless you ask me very nicely."

That night Gemma and Denny delivered a far more polished show. Her own Friday night show in the Electra Theatre followed, and Gemma returned to her unit exhausted but more than satisfied with how the evening had gone. Kicking off her shoes, she switched on the kettle and made for the loveseat in the sitting area.

The knock on the door came as a total surprise. More surprise followed when the handle rattled and Angelo walked in, clad in dark trousers and a white dress shirt with black snaps. "You've forgotten to lock your door."

"Good evening," she said. "Shouldn't you be partying?" Surely there was no shortage of supermodels or starlets who he could've flown in to help him celebrate.

His gaze went past her to the bare table and neat kitchenette. "I take it you haven't had a chance to eat since your show?"

"No." She liked to wind down first. Then realization dawned. "I'm not having dinner with you. I'm tired."

"You need to eat."

"It's too late to go out."

"Who said anything about going out? We can eat right here, have a picnic on the bed, just like old times. I've ordered some of your favourites from room service. Bollinger, caviar, some crackers." He flashed her a triumphant smile, his teeth white and even against his tanned skin. "And you can't refuse—it's my birthday."

Her favourites.

Mandy's favourites. Suddenly she was wide-awake

and very, very edgy. A picnic on a double bed with Angelo sounded lethal. Even more dangerous than going to dinner with him in one of the resort's restaurants. Given her deception, spending time here in this small, intimate space would be stupid. "I'd rather go out."

Her unease was interrupted by another knock, softer this time.

Angelo's gaze locked with hers. "Too late. Dinner has arrived. No need to do anything. Just relax and enjoy. Nothing is going to happen between us. Not until your memory returns. I promised, remember? And I don't break my word."

But she had no intention of keeping hers.

There would be no return of her rogue memory. *Damn.* How had it ever gotten to the stage that Angelo Apollonides was starting to look like he had more honour than she did?

In the end, Angelo's impromptu birthday supper proved to be a lot of fun. They sat thigh to thigh on the loveseat and ate gourmet food off utilitarian white crockery.

Gemma was under no illusion that Angelo had set out to make her relax. And it was working. She found herself laughing at a story he told about capsizing a catamaran—and liking him more and more as the evening wore on.

On some level a hum of awareness vibrated between them. But it never surfaced enough to make Gemma jumpy and set her on edge. She believed Angelo's promise that he would not try make love to her…and she allowed herself to chill out.

At last the meal was finished. Even the rich chocolate cake, with a single candle on it that Angelo had blown out.

And, seeing that she had no gift, Gemma had insisted on singing "Happy Birthday." For the first time she had seen Angelo flush awkwardly.

After she'd finished giggling at his embarrassment, she'd risen to make coffee and Angelo had followed to help. Only to discover that tiny kitchen area was too cramped for two. So he settled for propping himself up against the counter and watching her prepare the blend. When the coffee was ready, she bustled around, tidying up and they chatted drinking the rich dark brew.

The mug clattered on the countertop as he set it down. When he commented, "Your hair suits you like it is now." She turned from packing away the crockery she'd rinsed off to smile at him, only to find him holding the framed photo of Mandy with their parents.

Gemma's heart came to a standstill. And then it started to race. After the rush of adrenaline came relief. Now he would discover the truth. With a shock Gemma realised that she wanted this masquerade to end. She was not cut out for deception.

His glance shifted between the photo and Gemma. "This must have been taken around the time I—" he hesitated "—knew you."

Her eyes narrowed. He hadn't realised the truth. He'd put the small external differences between her and Mandy down to the passing of time and superficial changes. As his gaze lingered on her, Gemma suspected he was considering the changes that lay below the all-covering jeans and shirt. As he'd noticed, she'd never been as thin as Mandy.

His eyes kindled an urge within her. The flame flickered, danced. Slowly. Sensuously. A womanly desire that refused to be banished.

"I like the curls more than the straight style you wore back then." He glanced down at the photo and back to her and his mouth softened into a smile that she suspected was supposed to melt her innards.

A hint of annoyance doused the desire. How could he not tell the difference between her and Mandy? Suddenly, perversely, she wanted to be found out. "My hair has always been wild," she said, a little tersely. "Curls are much less work."

"So why straighten it?"

She shrugged. "That was the fashion then."

"And you always do as fashion dictates, do you, Gemma?" Suddenly there was an edge in his voice. An edge she didn't understand.

"Excuse me?"

But his attention had returned to the frame cupped in his hands. "Are these your parents?"

"Yes." Gemma moved closer until she could also see the three figures in the photo. Dad was staring sideways at Mandy, while Mum smiled into the camera.

"Your mother's pretty. I can see her resemblance to you—and where the red hair comes from."

"Her name is Beth. She's really easygoing, despite the red hair." Yet despite Mum's normal placidity she'd been vocal in her opposition to Gemma coming back to Strathmos to confront Angelo. Mum had been worried, had begged Gemma to leave the past behind. But Gemma couldn't. She *had* to know…

"And your father looks so proud of you. Who's your mother smiling at?"

Gemma closed her eyes as a sharp burst of memory slivered through her of that sunny day in her parents' suburban garden against the foot of Pigeon Mountain in Auckland. She could remember the scent of the damask roses. She could feel the warmth of the sun on her back. She could remember Mandy laughing—

"I don't remember," she said tonelessly.

Something in her eyes must have alerted him to her confusion and pain because he came swiftly towards her. "Hell, of course you don't. And I'm a stupid idiot to ask such questions."

He was so close that Gemma could smell the scent of his skin overlaid with a tangy aftershave. A hint of amber, of musk…and something else.

Arousal.

A chill shot through her. No! She scuttled backward and collided with a chair jutting out from under the bench top and would have tripped if Angelo's hand hadn't shot out and stopped her from falling.

"Hey!" He yanked her upright. "Are you okay?"

His eyes were a rich turquoise, the colour of the sun-lit sea with no hint of black or grey. The thick brows above were pulled into a frown and Gemma read concern.

She could almost believe—

Damn! She broke free with a sharp twist. She recognized the sensation that unexpectedly flooded her. Recognized its warmth, its seductive danger—and it scared her spitless.

She swallowed, her mouth dry.

She'd been convinced that her hatred would fortify her against this attraction, like a talisman against evil.

So how was she supposed to deal with an Angelo she was beginning to like? Underneath the playboy exterior lay a complex man who was so much more than the media portrayed. She was even starting to doubt that he was the selfish manipulative lover Mandy had described.

"Are you okay?" he repeated.

"I'm fine," she said, and gave an elaborate yawn. "Just tired."

He got the hint but after he'd left, she felt more alone than she'd ever felt in her life.

Gemma was surprised when she looked out into the audience on Saturday night to see Angelo seated with a crowd of people at a table in the front of the Electra Theatre. Three women, all beautiful, and two men.

None of them were eating.

They must be here only for the show. She almost stumbled over her next line, recovered and then sang on, trying very hard not to look in their direction again.

She made it through the show without another stumble. By the time she got to the dressing room, Angelo was waiting.

"Come, there are people I want you to meet."

"I'm tired." It was an excuse. A lie. She was too wired to sleep.

In the end she convinced Angelo to let her shower and change and agreed to meet him at his penthouse—a huge space with black leather furniture and modern artwork and an endless expanse of glass that Gemma realised must showcase fabulous seaviews in the daytime.

The crowd turned out to be Angelo's cousins Zac Kyriakos and Tariq bin Rachid al Zayed and three women; Zac's new wife, Pandora, and Zac's sister, Katy, and their cousin, Stacy.

"We thought we'd surprise Angelo," Zac explained. "His birthday needed celebrating."

"You should feel honoured, Angelo," Pandora said darkly, "I braved a helicopter flight for you."

Angelo gave her a hug. "Thank you for coming. All of you."

A late-night meal had been arranged buffet-style on the sideboard. Grilled calamari, prawns on long elegant skewers and oysters on the shell. Spears of asparagus, slivers of capsicum, sticks of cucumber and sliced fruit added colour beside the seafood.

"Help yourself," Angelo told Gemma, setting down a glass of white wine on the low table beside the sofa on which she sat.

"I will." She threw him a smile and he surprised her by leaning over and brushing a kiss across her brow.

"A toast." Zac raised his wineglass. "To Angelo and many more birthdays."

They all echoed it and Angelo reciprocated by lazily raising his glass and proposing a toast to Pandora and Zac. Which led to Pandora suggesting that it was time for another wedding. A horrible silence followed.

"Don't look at me," Tariq grated. "I'm no advertisement for marriage."

Gemma assessed him. He stared back. She detected suspicion in his golden gaze. He was gorgeous in a stern, hawk-eyed kind of way and wore a long, flowing thobe—although his head was bare—that suited his air of command. She couldn't help wondering what had happened with his wife.

After dinner there was a large marzipan-iced cake, with candles for Angelo to blow out. Gemma grinned at him and decided to spare him another rendition of "Happy Birthday."

"Speech, speech," called Pandora. "Zac, *agapi mou,* come and sit." Pandora patted the cushion beside her. She was blonde and beautiful in a wistful kind of way.

Zac landed beside her and, pulling her onto his lap, he growled. "Don't call me *my love* in that fake way."

"Phony was what I said. Not fake." Pandora started to giggle and gave him a look brimming with love and humour, telling Gemma this was a very private joke.

"Ignore them," Katy advised, rolling her eyes to the ceiling. Gemma noticed that Katy had lines of strain around her eyes. "Pandora is the only person I've ever met who can put my overbearing brother in his place." Katy looked around with a frown. "Now, where is Angelo? Ah, getting out of making his speech and catching up with Tariq in the kitchen. Look at them, they must be talking about women."

Gemma noticed how close the men stood, both serious, their heads together. "I take it Tariq's marriage is unhappy," she murmured softly.

"They're separated. I think the experience totally put him off women," Katy confided.

Gemma started to wonder what these forthright women would say about her later.

Katy seemed to read her mind. "Relax, we like you. Almost as much as Angelo does. Otherwise you wouldn't be getting the inside gossip."

"Angelo doesn't like me," Gemma protested.

"Mmm…maybe *like* isn't a strong enough word. We're not going to ask what happened between the two of you in the past—"

Pandora clambered off Zac's lap and came to stand beside Gemma. "Except that we hope you had a damn good reason for two-timing—"

"Hush. We agreed that was none of our business."

"It is none of your business," Stacy said, entering the conversation. She glared at the other two women.

Gemma stared at the three of them, bemused.

And then Angelo was beside her. "Are you okay?"

She turned her head. "Shouldn't I be?"

He perched beside her and slung an arm around her shoulder. "My family can be a little overwhelming at times."

Pandora and Katy started to laugh. "Come," said Stacy, "give them a break."

Later Angelo saw her back to her unit. The night was cool but there was no rain. The fact that the wind had died down meant that they could hear the hiss of the sea. "I think your family may have the wrong impression about us…me," Gemma said.

The lamps that edged the walkway shed enough light for her to see his eyebrows jerk up. "Why?"

"They seem to think that we're an item. And Katy didn't even seem worried that we'd broken off in the past. Although, I did detect some reserve from Tariq."

"He thinks I'd be mad to take up with you again."

"Oh?" The image of their heads close together in the kitchen came back to her. "You talked about me?"

"Tariq talked. He thinks you'll betray me again. Break my heart."

Gemma wanted to object. To deny that she'd ever do such a thing. Just in time she remembered that he thought she was Mandy. And Mandy had always been a flirt, a heartbreaker. So she drew a deep, steadying breath and asked, "So what did you say?"

In the shadows she could feel the force of his regard. "That I never loved you, so you never broke my heart. And it won't happen this time around, either."

Seven

Angelo and his family all left Strathmos on Sunday. Gemma heard the beat of the blades of the helicopter departing just after noon, but didn't realise that Angelo had gone until she found the note in the backstage pigeon hole where her mail was delivered.

Back next Sunday. See you then.

That was all. He hadn't even signed it. But she knew without doubt who had sent it.

Later she heard that he'd gone to Athens, that he'd be flying on to the resort at Kalos for a series of hush-hush meetings about a new opportunity he was investigating. Gemma had expected to feel relief at his absence, a cessation of the tension that twisted within her. But instead there was only an unfamiliar emptiness inside her.

Gemma suspected she was headed for heartbreak. Angelo had made it clear last night that there was no chance that he would ever love her. So she'd better take care to guard her hollow heart.

Gemma took one of the bicycles that the resort made available to the staff and guests and cycled down to Nexos, the small fishing village or *xorio,* not far from the resort.

The tables outside the local *taverna* were all taken. Most by locals playing *tavli,* backgammon. At one end, a fashionably dressed couple, clearly from the resort, shared a platter of *mezze* with olives and pita and a selection of spreads. Another young couple sat holding hands across a table. And a pang shot through Gemma.

There was no chance that she and Angelo would ever resemble these lover-like couples.

She turned away from the tables and chairs and wandered into the bakery beside the taverna, spoiling herself to a couple of *tiropites*—triangles of phyllo pastry filled with cheese—and a bottle of mineral water. She wheeled the bicycle across the cobbles and settled herself on the seawall to watch the fishermen spreading the nets in the sun and eat her impromptu lunch.

All around her, village life carried on. Across the road, two elderly widows dressed from head to toe in black were shuffling into the churchyard of the quaint white-washed church with its domed bright blue roof.

The church reminded her of Pandora's talk about weddings yesterday and Tariq's bitterness. Had he loved his wife? Why had his marriage fallen apart?

Of course, love was not strictly necessary for a marriage—or even for a relationship. Angelo had confessed last night that he'd never loved Mandy. What was it with these men?

Then she thought of the loving tenderness Zac demonstrated to Pandora and an ache settled in the region of Gemma's heart.

Unscrewing the top off the mineral water, she took a swig. She doubted Angelo would ever love anyone like that, without reserve. He was so self-contained, he didn't seem to need anyone.

For a fleeting instant Gemma couldn't help wondering whether he was alone now. His little black book would have no shortage of numbers of beautiful women to call on. If he chose to…

The thought depressed her.

Last night he'd made it clear that he was in no danger of falling for her. So much for her wild idea of making him pay.

She'd fantasised about proving to him that he wasn't irresistible to every woman in the world. That she held him in disdain. And she'd contemplated seducing him, making him fall for her, then rejecting him. But now she'd met him and found that he was so far out of her league that her half-baked plans were absurd.

She didn't dare seduce him. Because she suspected that once she'd made love with him, she would never be able to walk away. That she would be marked as Angelo Apollonides's woman for life.

She brushed the crumbs off her fingers and screwed the cap back onto the empty bottle. Sleeping with Angelo was not going to answer all her answers about why Mandy had died. And she could not betray her sister's memory in that fashion. Or risk her heart for a man who would never feel a thing for her.

In a little over a week it would be time to leave Strathmos…and Angelo. And move on. Strathmos was a foreign world, exotic and removed.

Angelo's world.

The empty place in her chest expanded, chilling her. Gemma took a last look at the fishermen on the beach. They looked so unhurried, so content.

Unlike her.

Biting her lip to stop the tears of loneliness that threatened, she rose to her feet and made her way to her bike. She would return to Auckland and get on with her life as her mother had suggested. Perhaps the familiar warmth of her family and friends would bring comfort. Tonight she would call her agent to line up the next gig.

The time had come to lay Mandy to rest.

With Lucie back at work on Monday, Gemma's frenzied schedule returned to normal. Yet she was restless. And her mood was mirrored by the unpredictable weather. Gusts of wind and bursts of hard rain shook the island. Gemma threw herself into her show and a couple of days passed before she had time to draw breath.

Weather allowing, she'd intended to spend her day off on Thursday windsurfing. The morning dawned clear and sunny with enough wind for a good run across the chop. But Gemma's heart wasn't in it. In less than thirty minutes she was back on shore, refusing to admit to herself that windsurfing alone was no longer what she desired.

She missed Angelo.

Blocking out that traitorous thought, she spent the afternoon in the entertainment centre. The resort staff had started erecting a giant Christmas tree and, with nothing else to do, Gemma stayed to help.

It was bittersweet hanging the decorations. It had been a while since she'd celebrated Christmas. Her family had avoided it…Christmas Day had become a time of grief.

As she reached up to hang a silver ball on a branch, her cell phone trilled.

It was Angelo.

Immediately her pulse quickened; the tree seemed greener, the lights around her brighter. For the first time since he'd departed she felt truly alive.

"Missing me?" he asked, humour in his voice.

"Of course not," she lied. "I've been too busy to think about you."

There was a little flat silence. Then he asked what she'd been doing. Gemma told him about the awful weather, the winds and the rain. He laughed a little when she commented that this was not what she expected of life on a Greek island.

"Christmas is coming," he said, "expect more rain."

"Oh, no." Then she told him about the Christmas tree that she was decorating. "It's always strange to see decorations out in November. I can see why your grandfather's tourists came only in the summer months. And I can understand why you've created the casinos and laid on all the entertainment you do. The resort is seething with people."

"Good." He sounded distracted. There was a short silence. Then he said, "I will be back early on Sunday morning. I always attend the Sunday service in the village when I am on Strathmos. Will you come with me this Sunday?"

Spend time with Angelo?

"Of course. But I need to be back for a rehearsal afterward." Even though she knew she was setting herself up for heartbreak by continuing to see him, Gemma simply couldn't resist.

The rest of the week dragged past.

Gemma had just taken a call from her agent on Sunday morning with an offer to sing in a popular Sydney club where Gemma had sung before, when a dull, droning noise interrupted their discussion.

Clutching the cell phone, Gemma rushed out of her unit. A moment later a huge shadow passed over her. Glancing up, she squinted into the sun and made out the dark shape a helicopter.

Angelo was back.

A thread of dark, forbidden excitement shivered through her. "I have to go, Macy."

"Wait, I need to know what—"

"I can't give you an answer. Not now. I'll call you tomorrow." She wasn't aware of Macy's mutterings; all she could think about was that soon she would see Angelo again.

By the time he arrived to collect her, she'd managed to get her pleasure at his return under control.

A rapid glance showed that he was dressed in a beautifully cut designer suit. She wore a smart sleeveless black dress and her hair had been confined into a French braid. Gemma knew she looked elegant and restrained...no hint of her wild excitement showed.

He didn't kiss her, not even a light buss on the cheek. Instead he stared at her for a long moment, his expression unreadable, and her pulse raced. Gemma got the feeling he'd been about to say something momentous.

At last he held out his hand, and said, "Come."

She took it. His clasp was warm and firm, his hand strong. And her heartbeat steadied.

Once they reached the church, she looked around with interest. Despite the white exterior, inside the church, colours ran riot. Just inside the tall double wooden doors, almost a hundred slim white candles flickered. Bowls of bright pink and red cyclamens and a huge vase of crocus added more colour. On the walls, saints with gold-leaf halos looked down on the packed pews.

They found seats near the front. A large woman beckoned to them, gave a very brief smile to Gemma and spoke rapidly to Angelo in Greek as she shifted along the wooden pew. Trapped between the older woman and Angelo, Gemma was very aware of the warmth of his thigh pressing against hers. When the priest appeared, she forced herself to concentrate.

The service was long and unlike any service Gemma had ever attended. Villagers wandered in and out in an ever-changing stream. Children played on the floor beside the windows. And the priest chanted in ancient Greek, while rich incense filled the church.

Afterwards people spilled out into the churchyard, congregating in small groups under a vine-covered pergola. Angelo kept her close to his side, his arm around her waist. A cat sat on the low wall not far from them; Gemma gave the animal a wary look.

The strange juxtaposition of the exotic resort, the simple church with its ancient ceremonial customs struck Gemma. Had Mandy seen this side of Angelo's world?

Gemma tilted her head to Angelo. "Have I been here before?"

"I asked you to come with me often enough in the past, but you didn't want to."

So Mandy had never been to the church with him. Given her twin's love of sleeping late and her preference for the good life, the refusal made sense. "Do you come often?" Gemma changed the subject.

He propped a foot up on the low wall beside her. The cat saw it as an invitation and came closer, purring and rubbing against his legs. Angelo bent to stroke the appreciative feline. Gemma backed away.

"Are you frightened of cats?" he asked.

"No, allergic," she replied. "I don't need red eyes or a fit of nonstop sneezing."

"Then let's move along." They found a new spot and watched as two girls came to play with the cat. "I come to this church every Sunday morning when I'm on Strathmos. I was baptised here."

"Oh. I didn't know that."

"It's not the kind of thing we usually talk about, is it?" His mouth kinked up. "In fact, we never spoke much at all in the past. I didn't even know you were allergic to cats.

We've talked more in the last couple of weeks than ever before. Maybe it has something to do with the amnesia."

That brought back her deception. Mandy had never been allergic to cats. Gemma certainly didn't want to talk about how she'd deceived him. Even though she knew that she would have to. Soon. On Tuesday she would be giving her last show. And then she'd be leaving. For good.

To distract herself, she asked, "Who was the woman who made space for us in the church?" Then added hastily, to justify her curiosity, "She looked familiar. Does she work at the resort?"

"That's Penelope." He pronounced it Pen-e-lop-i with the stress on the *O*. "You met her, when you were here before. Perhaps your memory is starting to return. You should let Dr. Natos check you out at the resort."

That was the last thing she wanted. "Maybe my head is getting better." He didn't look convinced. "Who is Penelope?" She asked again. "In case we bump into each other—she'd think me rude if I didn't know."

He shot her a strange look. "That didn't worry you much in the past. You never had much time for her. She was my governess when I was a child."

"*A governess?*" It accentuated the divide between them. She hadn't been deprived, but hers hadn't been an upbringing populated with governesses and servants and limitless privilege.

"Someone had to teach me to read and write. I didn't get sent to school in England until I was ten."

"You went to school in England?" That would account for his flawless English—no hint of an accent, no misuse of idiom.

"Yes, my mother thought it was for the best. My grandfather couldn't sway her."

"Did you enjoy it?"

"Not at first," he admitted. "It was a long way from home. I didn't speak good English. Initially I felt so isolated. I wanted to come home."

"Home? Here? To the resort?"

"No, there was no resort. There used to be a house on the island."

Gemma gave the hill behind the village a sweeping look. "A house?"

"I pulled it down and built the resort on the site of the wreckage."

Something in his voice gave her reason to pause. The tanned skin had stretched tautly across the high, flat cheekbones. He looked remote and ruthless.

Gemma shivered. There was so much she still didn't know about him. And now it was too late. She would be leaving soon.

After they got back to the resort, Gemma hurried to the entertainment centre to help Mark with the Christmas show rehearsal. She wouldn't perform in that. Tomorrow would be her last appearance. In a couple of days, she'd be back in Auckland. And she'd have to put the pieces of her life back together again.

"Gemma." She started when she heard her name called. Mark and Lucie were watching her with quizzical expressions.

"Wakey, wakey," Lucie called. "You look like you're off in dreamworld."

Gemma felt herself flush. Nightmare world, more like. "Okay, where are we?"

"In the Apollodrome," said Lucie with a cheeky smile. "Rehearsing for the Christmas spectacular."

"I remember." Gemma flinched the instant the words left her mouth. Lucie and Mark wouldn't realise the savage irony of that.

"Can you sing the Christmas medley?"

"I don't know the words," Gemma called back. "I'll sing something else to give everyone a chance to do the movements."

"Gemma's not booked to sing in the Christmas Eve spectacular." Angelo's voice broke in as she strode forward. "Stella Argyris will be performing."

Gemma stiffened.

"I asked Gemma if she would stand in for Stella," Mark moved forward and gestured to Gemma to get into position. "Stella's not due to arrive for another ten days but many of the other performers are here. I want to get the show on the road, so to speak."

"I've worked with the divine Stella before," Lucie murmured to Gemma. "She's a cat. A man's kind of woman. She'll be itching to get her claws into our gorgeous Greek boss."

Gemma's heart splintered. "Lucie, hush. He might hear you."

Lucie shrugged. "So what?"

Gemma wished she had a fraction of the other girl's insouciance. "Tomorrow is my last day. I want to leave on a good note."

"Judging by the way he's looking at you, I'd say you've hit the highest note already. Stella's gonna hate you."

Gemma whipped around to see what Lucie was on about and encountered Angelo's intimate gaze. "Hurry up—I've got plans for the afternoon."

Gemma turned scarlet. She launched into "O Holy Night." The instant she started to sing "the stars are brightly shining," she knew she'd made a mistake. She'd always loved this carol on a deep, emotional level, but now as she sang the image that came to mind were the silver-white stars in the sky over Strathmos. Why couldn't she've chosen to sing "Away in a Manger," she wondered frantically, at least that would've had no deep, soul-rending connotations.

Angelo seemed to have turned to stone. He was staring at her like he'd never seen her before.

Gemma's lashes feathered down, blocking him out her line of sight. The next line poured from her, her voice swelling, her throat thickened with emotion and her smoky voice became even more husky than normal. The climax came too soon and by the time the last words left her, Gemma was spent.

There was a moment of silence.

"Wow," Lucie broke it, sounding awed. Gemma opened her eyes and blinked. Behind Lucie, Mark had started to clap and one by one the dancers joined in. Only Angelo stood unmoving. Gemma started to feel a little ridiculous; she clambered down the stairs, off the stage.

Finally, Angelo shook himself. He headed off her escape route. "You sing like an angel."

With shock Gemma realised that his voice was hoarse. As if he'd been as moved as she'd been.

"I love that carol," she said, and thought how trite it sounded.

"You sang 'Happy Birthday' to me the other night, but this…this…is something else." He sounded awed. "To think I never even knew you could sing when you were with me. What the hell else did I not know about you?"

At his words Gemma came crashing back to earth. The magic vanished. She was Gemma Allen. Not the Gemma Allen Angelo believed her to be—that was Mandy—but another creature all together. The tangle of deceit she'd created had spun out of control.

After the rehearsal Angelo and Gemma had a light lunch and after she'd changed, he took her sailing. The afternoon passed in rush of wind and laughter.

That evening the applause after her show was even more fervent than usual. And Gemma knew that the audience had sensed the energy and emotion that the day spent with Angelo had unleashed inside her.

She was aware that this could not go on, would soon be over. She still hadn't phoned back Macy about the offer of work in Sydney. By now the job would be taken. Gemma knew she was living for the moment, until it all came crashing down on her head. As it must.

So when Angelo took her back to his penthouse for a late dinner after the show, she didn't protest. This was it. Her last chance to spend time with Angelo in the bubble that she'd created.

During dinner, they spoke of mundane matters, the candles on the table creating a golden haze around them. But beneath the everyday words, something buzzed, vibrating between them, an inexorable force. By the stillness of his body, the light in his eyes, Gemma knew he was aware of it, too.

Setting his knife and fork down, Angelo said, "I haven't helped you regain your memory at all, have I?" His eyes were dark with emotion. "Your return to Strathmos has been in vain."

She should confess now. But she didn't. She didn't want to extinguish that glow on his face that existed for her alone. She wanted to bask in it—for just a little longer. Once the bubble world was gone, it would be burst forever. There'd be no going back.

"Not in vain," she said finally. "The job has been great. And…I met you." Then she hastily tacked on. "Again."

An unmistakable passion flared in his eyes. He pushed back his chair and stood. "Come here."

Gemma knew what he was asking. If she went, everything would change. A moment of fear flickered in her chest. If she went to him…she would have to accept that she no longer believed he had destroyed Mandy and caused her to self-destruct.

That he was not the utter bastard Mandy had painted. That, for her own reasons, Mandy had lied.

"Come," he said again.

Slowly she rose to her feet and started to move around the dinner table. He met her halfway. Took her hand and dropped down onto the long leather couch and pulled her onto his lap.

Need uncoiled within Angelo. A need to see her smile again, to banish the shadows from her eyes, a need for her to be happy, a need to touch her…a need that grew and grew.

What the hell was happening to him? How could he care so little about Gemma's past betrayal? All he knew was that the whole week he'd been away from her had dragged like a prison sentence.

Experience had taught him that Gemma was treacherous, faithless. One side of him craved her, wanted to believe her promise that Jean-Paul meant nothing to her, wanted to believe it could be different this time… and fought to convince that other, more cynical side of Angelo that she had changed.

Her head was turned away from him. From this angle he could see the rise of her cheekbone, the straight line of her nose. He raised his hand, smoothed the wild tangles back to reveal the soft creamy skin at her neck.

"Ask me to make love to you," he breathed. "So that I don't break my promise to you."

He watched her throat move as she swallowed. When she turned her head, he met her gaze and he read the same desire that consumed him, as strong as a relentless tide.

"Please make love to me, Angelo."

A slow sensation rumbled like liquid thunder in his chest and, leaning forward, he brushed his lips across her silken skin. Her mouth opened. She tasted soft and sweet.

A long time later, she gave a breathy gasp and shifted, so that she knelt across his lap, her body tight and expectant.

His hands came up to her shoulders, dislodged the thin shoestring straps and eased the top of the dress down. She wore no bra. One glance revealed that her breasts were high and firm, the nipples dark and his heart began to pound.

He pulled her up…towards him…took the waiting nipple and surrounding flesh into his mouth. The nipple peaked under the stroke of his tongue.

Angelo pursed his lips, sucked, felt her body jerk and wrapped his arms tightly around her.

Her still-clothed belly moved in slow, insistent motions against him. In one swift movement he peeled the Lycra dress off and revelled in the sensation of her naked skin beneath his hands. He stroked her back, the sleek, rounded globes of her tight buttocks; the piece of stretchy lace that qualified for underwear was no barrier to his touch. His fingers slid beneath the thong.

She was warm and wet and his fingers moved effortlessly in the sleek furrow. He could tell by her ragged breathing that she was hot, that she wanted this as much as he did.

As his fingers moved back and forth, his mouth echoed the rhythm against her breast, until she gasped out loud and he felt the suppressed shudder that shook her.

Then she pushed away.

"I can't take more."

Before he could object, she'd slid off his lap, knelt between his thighs. He felt her fingers at the zipper of his trousers. A rush of want surged through him. He grabbed her head between his hands.

"No."

She tipped her head up, her eyes glazed with emotion.

"Yes."

"No." His control was slipping. He had a turbulent sense that if he let this happen his world would never be the same. That he was poised at a doorway to an undiscovered universe.

He heard the zipper give. Her hands brought him out, hard and potent.

"Gemma."

She ignored his desperate croak, her fingertips soft against his sensitive skin.

Giving in, he flung his head back against the sofa and groaned as she stroked him.

When the warmth of her mouth closed over him, he squeezed his eyes shut at the unbearably sweet heat. *"Gemma!"*

The slow sucking started, driving him to the edge of a dark, unfamiliar abyss where he could hold on no more. Shadows started to dance against his eyelids. His thighs began to tremble and then he was convulsing again and again, trapped in pleasure beyond what he'd ever experienced.

Eight

He carried Gemma through to the bedroom, laid her down on his bed. "My turn," he growled.

He stripped the thong off and started to stroke her with fingers that possessed a magic touch. A fine tension tightened in Gemma's belly. She shifted, the raw silk of the bedcover creating a delicious friction against her back, her thighs.

He touched the little button, her knees came off the cover. She moaned. He moved his fingers and her breath left her. Closing her eyes, she shut out everything. Nothing existed, except this room, this man...and his touch.

And then the heat of his mouth was against her. Slick. Teasing. His tongue probed. She gasped. He licked again. Gemma locked her fingers in his golden hair and pulled him away.

"I can't…"

He lifted his head. His eyes gleamed. "You can."

"I want…more."

He must've understood her incoherent mumbles. There was the sound of foil tearing and a moment later he'd crawled over her, his chest hard and sleek against her taut, aching breasts. Then his mouth was over hers, his tongue hungry and plundering as he took her mouth in a kiss so hot, so wild, that her hips bucked under him. Impatient. Desperate.

His hand closed on her breast. Heat seared through her, stabbing between her legs. She bent her knees up, tilted her hips, hinting, clamouring for more.

Angelo moved against her. She could feel his erection, the blunt tip sliding against her. She was ready for him.

He pushed forward and slid all the way in. Gemma moaned, a hoarse primal sound, as pleasure shafted her. Her arms went round his neck, tightening. And her legs wrapped round him, locking him to her.

There was a moment when he lay utterly still, filling her, and then he pulled back a little, and sank forward again. The friction was intense. The pace ratcheted up.

Gemma's breathing quickened, shallow gasps that sounded overloud in the quiet room.

She squeezed her eyes even more tightly shut, focusing on the friction, the sensation that arced through her, from between her legs, through her belly, to her nipples, to her tongue that slid wildly against his.

There was an instant of darkness, the world went black and then she was shivering into a void of light.

Angelo groaned, and she felt him pulsing deep in-

side her. "Hell, it's never been like that," he muttered
hoarsely. *"Never."*

As his words registered, the brightness faded, and a
shiver of apprehension shook her.

Her final show had arrived. Tonight Gemma wore a
black dress with spaghetti straps that made her dark red
hair appear redder than ever. The low scooped back revealed her carefully cultivated tan and Gemma took her
time applying makeup to emphasize her eyes and lips.
By the time she was finished, she knew she looked good.

Her time on stage passed in a blur. She squinted past
the lights but couldn't locate Angelo at any of the tables.
At last she gave up and tried to concentrate on the words
she was singing, on communicating the meaning of the
song to the audience, but some of the lustre had gone.

She left the stage with a sinking heart. Her time on
Strathmos was over.

On the way to her dressing room, Denny waved and
Gemma gave him a half-hearted smile.

Pushing the door open, her eyes widened at the unexpected sight of Angelo reclining in her dressing room.
Gemma hesitated on the threshold.

He should've looked out of place surrounded by the
heap of glittery clothes that Lucie had abandoned on the
floor. But he didn't. Instead he looked unfairly at ease
as he dwarfed the couch, his long legs stretched out in
front of him.

She averted her eyes from his gold hair and bright,
piercing eyes and the taut body encased in the beautifully fitting dark suit. Warily, she entered the dressing
room and closed the door. "What are you doing here?"

"Waiting for you. Since this morning, you've been impossible to find. I don't intend to let you run out on me tonight."

Last night had been so special…earth shattering… she hadn't been able to face him this morning. She'd needed time alone to come to terms with it.

"I wouldn't have run out on you." They needed to talk. He was going to be furious with her. Her heart clenched at the thought of the coming confrontation.

"Join me for dinner?"

Dark and deep, that voice did stuff to her that should be declared illegal. "Anywhere except your penthouse." She didn't want to make love, it would distract her from what she had to say.

The smile he gave her was irresistible. "*Endaxi.* Okay."

He took her to the Golden Fleece. The decor was rich and warm with exquisitely painted murals on the walls of Jason and the Argonauts performing daring deeds. The high-backed chairs, white table linen and dim lighting, together with the hushed service gave it an outrageously exclusive ambience. As the meal progressed, and the conversation topics remained general, the tension that grasped Gemma started to unwind.

Gemma declined desert in favour of coffee and while they were waiting for it to arrive, she examined a mural depicting Jason with a woman who must be Medea. Angelo followed her gaze. "She was hard work, a sorceress and a witch."

"Yes, but he didn't do right by her. She helped him gain the fleece, he took her back to Corinth and married her. But then decided it was too tough to be married to a woman who was a witch—and a foreigner to boot. So he planned to dump her and marry another woman."

"Except Medea spiked that plan rather dramatically." Angelo's lips curved in a wry smile.

"Poor Glauce," Gemma agreed. "She certainly didn't deserve what she got. Medea's sending a robe steeped in poison as a wedding gift was downright evil."

"You know your Greek mythology pretty well."

"I should do. My father lectured classics. I grew up on the ancient myths. Greek and Roman."

Angelo shot her a surprised stare. "You never told me that."

Uh-oh. Gemma wished she'd kept her mouth shut. Mandy had never been much of a reader, she'd hated what she called "Dad's boring tales."

"So how did you end up a singer?"

"My mother could play the piano reasonably well, so I learned to play, too. I loved to sing, so it wasn't long before I started going for specialist lessons."

"And dancing…what did your mother say about your dance career?"

She drew a deep breath. Should she tell him now? He was smiling at her, his eyes warm. No. In a little while. She wanted just a little longer. "Actually Mum was responsible for that. She was a professional ballet dancer. After w— I…" she broke off at the near give away "…I was born, she opened a dance school and taught lots of little girls instead of performing live—she wanted to spend time with—" *us* "—me. What about you?" She shifted the focus of the conversation to him. "When did you know what you were going to do?"

"On my thirteenth birthday my grandfather took me

out for lunch and told me that one day I would inherit the chain of hotels he owned, and to prepare myself to look after them. My cousin Zac bore the family name, so he would inherit the Kyriakos Shipping Corporation. Tariq was to inherit the oil refineries.

"My grandfather also promised me I'd inherit the three islands he owned—Strathmos, Kalos and Delinos. I'd spent the first years of my life on Strathmos, so I knew it well. After that day I absorbed everything I could about the hospitality industry, about business, that I could lay my hands on."

There was a pause when the coffee arrived. Gemma reflected on the single-mindedness of the man sitting opposite. He'd known what he wanted and gone after it. He been responsible for a large part of his success. There was a lot more to him than the playboy image he projected to the media.

After they'd finished their coffees Angelo walked back to her unit. At the door he took the key from her and unlocked the door before following her in.

Gemma's heart started to knock against her ribs.

"Another coffee?" she asked, desperate for something to do while he stood in her space. Her voice was several notches higher than usual.

"Why not?" Mercifully, he moved away, and Gemma was able to breathe again. He picked up the photo on the bench top and instantly the tension was back, turning her rigid with anxiety. Her breath ragged, she said, "No sugar, right?"

"Black. No sugar."

It figured he wouldn't share her lethally sweet tooth. She emptied sweetener into her coffee and hoped she'd be able to sleep tonight given all the caffeine she was consuming.

"You're holding a cat."

"What?" She stared at him trying to make sense of the comment, to reconcile it with the rising tension that incapacitated her, numbed her ability to think straight.

"In the photo, you're holding a cat." His voice was endlessly patient.

Her brow wrinkled. "Yes, Snuggles."

"You told me you were allergic to cats."

Uh-huh. Gemma stiffened, wary of a trap. "I am," she said slowly. "Snuggles belongs to my parents."

"So why are you holding him? In the churchyard you told me how cats affect you."

Tell him.

She stared at him, her mind went blank. Her tongue felt thick, she scratched for words. "Because he always comes to me. He likes to see me red-eyed and sneezy."

That, at least, was true. Snuggles, the darn cat, had a wicked sense of the misery he caused her. But of course, the real truth was that *she* wasn't holding Snuggles in the photo. Mandy was. And Mandy had no allergy to felines of any description.

The tightrope of lies she was balancing upon became ever more precarious. And when Angelo put the photo down, she said a prayer of thanks and placed the two mugs on the coffee table in front of the loveseat.

Appearing satisfied with her explanation, he sank onto the plump seat. "When are you thinking of leaving?"

"Tomorrow. I'll catch the midday ferry, spend a couple of days in Athens sightseeing and then I'll fly back to Auckland."

"It's too soon." His eyes turned to flame. "Come here."

Tell him. "Angelo—" Gemma backed up at the intent in his brilliant eyes "—I'm *not* going to sleep with you."

"Who said anything about sleeping?" There was an intimacy in his gaze that did dangerous things to her equilibrium. "I just want a kiss."

A kiss…one final kiss… She went into his arms. It felt like she was coming home. And that created a maelstrom of emotions churning within her. Guilt. Confusion. Regret that she hadn't met him long before Mandy.

But it didn't stop her responding to him.

When he lifted his head they were both breathing fast.

"Some kiss," she said.

He didn't smile. Eyes intent, he said, "I have to leave for Kalos tomorrow. I have a series of meetings there. Come with me."

She started to shake her head.

"Please, come. You can stay as long as you like. I don't want you to leave again."

He still thought she was Mandy. But Mandy was dead. And *she* was alive.

Disturbed by the direction her thoughts were taking, she rose. She needed to tell him the truth. And leave. She couldn't allow herself to be tempted to stay. Even though she wanted to. More than anything.

He grasped her hand and pulled her back. She landed on his lap. With an embarrassed laugh she struggled to extricate herself. He wouldn't let her.

Face close to hers, he said, "I want to spend time with you—more than I want you in my bed." There was a hint of bewilderment in his eyes.

And that was when Gemma knew he felt it, too. This strong, enduring bond between them that was turning her life upside down, forcing her to reevaluate who she was and what she wanted from her life.

"Okay, I'll come."

His eyes lit up. He raised her hand to his lips, turned it over and placed a soft, seductive kiss inside her wrist. "You won't regret it."

Gemma gave him a look of disbelief. Of course she was going to regret it. But she couldn't let the chance to spend a few more days with him pass.

Poseidon's Cavern, the resort on Kalos, was magnificent. At the centre of the main resort complex Angelo had installed a giant tank filled with sea creatures and fish. Walking through the lobby, she was drawn to the tank to stare at the rays flapping past the viewing windows.

"This is fantastic." She turned to Angelo. "I've never seen anything like it."

"I brought you here before. Doesn't it stir any memories?"

Gemma's excitement dimmed and she shook her head, hating the lie that she'd trapped herself in.

"Don't worry. Later I'll show the rest of the complex. There's a bar and a restaurant with a fabulous view of the tank. They were designed to feel like part of an underwater grotto. Aside from the theatre and cinemas, there's a water theme park to keep you busy. On the south side of the island we've used the underwater caves in the theme park and we'll take a ride through them to-morrow. It will be a little cool this time of the year, but it's spectacular down there and it's something that we hadn't completed last time you were here."

"That's sounds lovely." But the best part was that it was an experience where she wasn't following in Mandy's footsteps. She wouldn't have to worry about how her twin had reacted.

Not that she was worried about Angelo working the truth out any more. If he hadn't twigged by now that she wasn't Mandy, but her twin sister, it was unlikely that he was going to discover the truth. But she couldn't al-low this to go on.

A week, she decided. She'd give herself a week. And then she'd tell him. That night she made love to him with the fervour of the damned. Afterwards he looked at her with a question in his eyes.

When Angelo disappeared the following morning to his all-day meeting, Gemma took one look at the overcast sky, then spent a couple of hours examining the enormous tank inside the resort and reading the plaques about the occupants. Later in the morning she made her way to the heated conservatory pool where she was stunned by the sight of Jean-Paul tanning himself beside a svelte blonde.

"Cherie." He leapt up when he saw her. Gemma turned her head, and the kiss intended for her mouth landed on her cheek.

"Has Apollonides allowed you out your cage, pet?"

His words riled her. "Looks like you've acquired a pet of your own." Gemma gave the blonde a meaningful look.

"She is nothing. I'd drop her like a hot potato if you showed any interest."

His faked heartbroken expression made Gemma glare at him. "You're a wicked man."

"Who loves to do wicked things, remember?" His voice dropped to husky intimacy.

She didn't want to go there. "I don't want to remember."

"Ah, the big fish pays better. How can I blame you?" Jean-Paul sounded philosophical. A waiter materialised at his elbow. "Ah, pull up a lounger for the lady. Gemma, let me order you something to drink and we can catch up on old times."

Gemma wasn't that keen to catch up on old times but she badly wanted to quiz him about Mandy. So she opted for a coffee—and so did Jean-Paul's companion whom he introduced as Birgitte. She turned out to be Swedish and, besides having a wonderful figure, appeared to be thoroughly nice. Gemma couldn't help regretting her *pet* crack. After they'd finished their coffees Birgitte took off to the nearby spa.

"Are you ready for a swim?" Jean-Paul asked.

"In a while."

"I'm sure it won't be long before Apollonides arrives—and he won't like finding you in my company." Jean-Paul looked pleased at the prospect.

Men! Gemma gave a mental headshake. "Angelo doesn't own me. He said I could drink with whom I liked." But apprehension shivered through her.

"If he pays your bills, he owns you. That's how a man thinks."

"How awful." Gemma took the gap he unwittingly provided. "Speaking of bills, after my last encounter with you three years ago my credit card suffered more damage than I expected. I must have gambled more than I'd intended."

"You're calling it *gambling* now?" Moreau shot her guarded look and Gemma's interest picked up. *He knew.*

She gave him an enticing smile. "What would you prefer me to call my little secret, hmm?"

"*Cherie,* better to keep quiet about that. Apollonides might not be happy about your little habit."

So Angelo hadn't known. Or at least that was what Jean-Paul believed. Gemma frowned. That was not the impression Mandy had given Gemma before her death. *I loved him, he ruined me.*

"Did you share my little secret?" It was a shot in the dark. The memory of her sister's wan, sunken face, her listless eyes, her shaking hands still haunted Gemma.

Jean-Paul's gaze sharpened. "Why are you asking me these questions?" His eyes dropped to the shirt over her swimsuit. He pushed the buttons aside.

"Hey, what are you doing? Take your hands off me!"

"Sorry…I thought…it doesn't matter."

But Gemma put it together. "It was you. You introduced her to the drugs that killed her."

"What do you mean *her?* And what are you talking about, saying I introduced *her* to drugs?" Jean-Paul's gaze darted around, examining everyone in the immediate surround.

Gemma realised her indiscretion. She'd nearly given away the fact that she was not the woman he thought she was. She couldn't afford another slip like that. "You were the source, the supplier."

"But, *cherie.*" He stroked his hand along her thigh. "You know all—"

"I don't remember. I had an accident, I lost my memory. So don't *cherie* me." She smacked his hand away. The way he'd touched her chest made sense. "You thought I was wearing a wire. You're scared of being arrested."

A flash of fear flitted through his eyes. "I'll deny it. Everything. You'd be stupid to start this. You've got Apollonides eating out of your hand." He gave an acid laugh. "I never thought I'd see the day that he took you back into his bed. Not after what he saw. He must want you badly. Funny, I didn't think you were that special myself."

Gemma's stomach turned. She felt ill.

Oh, Mandy…how could you?

As Gemma had gotten to know Angelo, she'd come to wonder how Mandy could have cheated on him. Jean-Paul's words made it clear that her sister *had* climbed out of Angelo's arms into the Frenchman's. Angelo was convinced there'd been other men, too. Maybe he was right. And he believed she was Mandy.

Pain twisted deep inside her. Well, she could hardly object. She'd led him to believe she was her twin. She couldn't blame him for that. But she hadn't given a damn about Angelo at the start of her deception, when she'd arrived on Strathmos. She'd believed him to be the bastard who'd gotten Mandy hooked on hard drugs.

But she'd been mistaken.

It wasn't Angelo who started Mandy down her path to destruction…it was Jean-Paul.

Revulsion swept her as Jean-Paul smiled at her, over-familiar and over-expectant. She had to get away from him. He'd ruined her sister's life, caused her death. Mumbling an excuse, Gemma hoisted her tote over her shoulder and scooted off the lounger, desperate to find a place where she could be alone to think about what she had discovered.

One thought kept festering: how could she ever set her relationship with Angelo right?

Nine

Standing outside one of the boardrooms in the high-tech conference centre, Angelo shook hands with Basil Makrides. "I am pleased you are satisfied with our agreement."

The older man nodded. "I want to spend time with Daphne, with our sons. Too much of my life has been lost on building an empire." There was sadness in his eyes.

Angelo was privy to the tragic situation of Basil's younger son. "I am sorry about Chris. I hope he will recover."

Basil sighed. "We will give him all the support we can. At present he's getting the best care in the world. And Daphne and I will be there at his side when he comes out."

Angelo's step was light as he went to find Gemma. The negotiations with Makrides had ended sooner than he'd expected. He now owned a group of small but exclusive resorts in Australia that he was keen to bring in line with the rest of the Poseidon ventures. He was looking forward to taking a couple of days off and relaxing with Gemma.

She delighted him, enthralled him.

Each day, he grew more intrigued by her, discovered yet another facet of her character. Gemma had changed, more than he could ever believe possible. They meshed in a way that they had never done in the past, in a way that he had never fit with any other woman. He was prepared to let the past go...to start over with her.

He didn't want to think too much about what was happening to him. He simply wanted to enjoy Gemma...her company...and her sexy body.

When he saw her ahead of him, clad in one of the pool's cover-ups, a tote slung over her shoulder, he lengthened his stride.

"Gemma." He snagged her elbow, and she jumped. "Sorry, I didn't mean to startle you."

She turned, her tawny eyes widening when she saw him. Something shifted in the depths, then vanished. "I thought you were busy with a meeting."

"I finished early. And seeing that the squall that threatened this morning has blown away, I wanted to show you the underwater caverns."

Fifteen minutes later, clad in wet suits to minimize the coolness of the subterranean winter water, they each hopped into a giant yellow inner tube that would float them through the honeycomb of tunnels. Because of the cold, there weren't many others in the dimly lit caves, so Gemma pushed off from the wall and scooted across the black water before rebounding off the opposite wall of the tunnel. She gave a squeal of laughter. "This is fun."

"The current will move us along." Angelo's tube bumped into hers, and she laughed again. His gaze lingered on her white smile and pleasure surged within him. "Not scared?"

"Not at all."

"It gets dark a little farther on," he warned.

"Ooh, spooky." She bumped her tube into his, and he rebounded into the wall. Trapped between the cavern wall and her tube, Angelo watched her approach with a wicked smile. Before he could move, she leaned over and scooped some of the dark water into her hand and flung it at him.

Angelo spluttered as the cold spray hit the side of his head. "Is that the way you want to play it?" He growled, using his hands to paddle closer.

"No." Gemma started to giggle helplessly. "Don't wet me more. The water is freezing."

His arm snaked out and hooked around her waist. She shrieked as she slipped off her tube. "Don't dump me in this water, I'm sorry. I won't do it again."

Angelo swept her over the divide between the two tubes. She landed, sprawled across him, her front plastered against his. Instantly he was aware of the softness of her body outlined by the Neoprene suit. The tangle of her wet hair brushed his cheek.

She shifted, twisting away. "My tube!" Her bright

yellow tube bobbed along in the distance, moving fast without a passenger.

"Hold still. You're going to capsize us," he warned, dragging her closer.

She froze. "That's the last thing I want."

"Don't worry, it's only about a metre deep."

"I don't care about the depth. It's the freezing, dark water I want to avoid."

"Be adventurous." Angelo settled her against him. "Live dangerously."

"This is more dangerous than it looks." She sounded breathless.

His arm shifted, he could feel her heart beating wildly. From the exertion? The thrill of the ride? Or something else?

He pulled her closer with one arm, the other holding onto the ring moulded to the tube. "Feel safer now?"

"No," she moaned.

Angelo was smiling when he kissed her. Her lips were cold and wet, but they parted the instant the tip of his tongue stroked hers. The kiss grew wild…deep. He'd never felt this kind of insatiable hunger for a woman before.

Then everything went dark.

He raised his head. "It's the Midnight Bend. We'll round the corner and then there'll be light."

"You think I'm scared?" There was amusement in her voice.

He kissed her again. But she'd moved so he missed the lips he was aiming for in the pitch black, and had to make do with kissing her neck, the softness behind her ears.

"That's so good," she groaned.

He tongued her skin, unbearably aroused.

The tube swung around a curve and they were back in the dim, ghostly light. He pulled away. "Want more?"

"Mmm," she murmured.

This time he made sure he got her lips. The kiss was deep and very, very hungry. Her hand crept up, caressing his nape, then spearing into his hair and pulling him closer still.

Finally he pulled away, breathing hard. "Hold tight," he gasped.

Her hands tightened against his head.

"I mean, hold the tube, hold me. There's a bit of a rapid ahead." He saw her eyes widen, then she was shrieking as the tube started to speed up and go downhill. The tube jerked and shook as the current swept it forward. Angelo braced himself, holding her close against him.

Faster and faster they went.

The last part of the descent was the steepest. Gemma was shaking under the weight of his arm.

"It's okay."

"It's great!"

She gave a whoop of excitement. And that's when he realized she was laughing, that she was high on enjoyment, not shaking with fear. They came careening down the final slide and surfed onto the wide pool at the bottom.

Gemma shifted in his grip, twisted her head around and beamed incandescently up at him. "That was fantastic! Can we do it again?"

And right then Angelo knew why she was different

from every woman he'd ever known. She was so transparent, so intensely warm and joyous.

Gemma was one of a kind.

The next day passed in surges of adrenaline, moments of apprehension and utter pleasure in Angelo's company.

In the morning they spent time feeding the fish in the huge tank and then they went for a walk marked along the island. After lunch, Gemma insisted on trying out ride after ride in the theme park. Protected by the wet suit and high on excitement, Gemma didn't feel cold until several hours later, when Angelo said, "Time to call it a day. We've got guests coming for dinner. You'll like them—the Makrideses are nice people."

Wet and suddenly weary, Gemma allowed Angelo to drape an oversized towel around her and usher her back to the resort.

Back in his penthouse, she stepped gratefully into the shower and let the heat beat against her skin. She lathered her hair, combing the tangles out with her fingers, and afterwards she took her time blow-drying the curls before pinning them up into a sophisticated twist. An easy-to-wear stretchy Lyrca dress followed. A careful application of light makeup and a pair of gold hoop earings, and she was ready to face Angelo and his guests.

She waltzed into the open-plan seating area, only to find the laughing man of earlier gone. Angelo stood with his back to the view over the island, impeccably dressed in black trousers and a black T-shirt, but his jaw was set. "You didn't mention that you had an intimate little tete-a-tete with your former lover at the pool yesterday."

Gemma's heart sank at the coldness in his eyes. She stared at him through her lashes, not knowing quite what to say. She'd wanted to forget about Jean-Paul. Escape. And, to be truthful, she hadn't wanted any mention of the Frenchman to wreck the burgeoning relationship between herself and Angelo.

"Nothing to say? Did you know that Jean-Paul would be here? Is that why you agreed to come?"

"No! Jean-Paul means nothing to me." Angelo's suspicion threw her. She should've expected it. After what Mandy had done, it wasn't surprising. And with that came a further revelation. His opinion mattered because she was starting to have real feelings for him. He was the worst man in the world for her to fall for— Hell, he didn't even know who she was.

The time had come to tell him the truth.

Scanning the piercing eyes, the mouth pulled into a tight line, she knew there would be no forgiveness.

It was way too late.

The elevator pinged, breaking Angelo's fixed, angry stare and Gemma felt weak with relief. Coward, she admonished herself, as he moved fluidly towards the elevator and greeted the man and woman stepping out.

Gemma followed more slowly, wishing the evening was already over. She needed to talk to Angelo alone. For her own peace of mind, she had to come clean. She could delay no longer, however much she wanted to spend time with him.

She forced a smile to her lips as Angelo performed the introductions. She couldn't tell Angelo now, not with his guests here. Later, after they'd gone.

Daphne and Basil Makrides were a reserved couple, both with worry lines around their eyes, though they grew less reserved as the evening wore on. But Angelo remained cool, and Gemma found it increasingly distressing.

Two members of his staff poured them cocktails and served a selection of mezze-style starters. Gemma chatted to Daphne about the resort, about the excitement of the wild ride through the underground caverns, and Daphne smiled.

The conversation moved on to food. Basil and Daphne were well-travelled, and Angelo contributed to the conversation, although Gemma couldn't help being aware of the dark glances he shot her from time to time. She tried to ignore it, chattering gaily and soon all four of them were talking of favourite spots they'd visited.

But the unbearable tension between herself and Angelo caused Gemma's stomach to knot up. When he moved to change the music, she followed him. "I honestly didn't know Jean-Paul would be on the island," Gemma murmured in a low voice that would not reach his guests. "I was surprised when I met him at the pool."

"Maybe not such an accident on Jean-Paul's part."

"For goodness' sake." Gemma rolled her eyes. "He was with a stunning Swede by the name of Birgitte."

Angelo looked surprised.

"Obviously your informant failed to mention that," she said, a touch acerbically. "Although, to be fair, Birgitte did leave to go to the spa for a while. But I also left not long after that. I had no desire to share Jean-Paul's company." She'd stayed only as long as had been necessary to learn what she needed.

Her distaste must have been clear, because his hand covered hers. "I'm sorry."

She jerked under his touch. "Why?"

"For misjudging you. I thought—" There was confusion in his eyes. Pain, and a hint of vulnerability.

He thought she'd been ready to betray him with Jean-Paul. For a second time. *She had to tell him the truth.* A glance in the Makrideses' direction showed her that they were hovering near the dining table. No time now. So she said, "I won't see him again. I promise."

Angelo inclined his head. "Thank you." The liquid voice of Andrea Bocelli swelled through the room. Angelo started to speak, but then he shook his head. "Later."

Later. Apprehension knotted in her stomach. There would be lots to talk about later.

Gemma followed Angelo slowly towards the table where two waiters in waistcoats and bowties were setting out plates with polished-silver covers to keep the food hot.

"Do you have any children?" Gemma asked Daphne after the meal and they'd returned to the comfortable sofas to drink rich coffee from tiny Greek coffee cups. The staff had left, and the four of them were alone.

Daphne stilled. There was an uncomfortable silence and Gemma had the horrible premonition that she'd put her foot squarely in it. Then Daphne replied, "Yes, two sons, Chris and Marco."

Gemma changed the subject and started to talk frantically of the cooling weather and how different it was from Auckland where the weather would now be humid with less than four weeks to go until Christmas.

Gemma chattering on with increasing desperation about Christmas decorations and shopping habits until Daphne said suddenly, "Whenever I try to talk about Chris everyone smiles and talks about something else. It's like he has an unspeakable disease."

"He's ill?" Gemma asked carefully.

"No, not ill, not in the way you mean. He has a… problem."

"Oh." Gemma wasn't sure what more to say. So she said nothing and waited.

"He's in rehabilitation." Daphne named a famous French drug-and-alcohol rehabilitation centre. "It's his third attempt, we're hoping that this time it will work."

Gemma placed her suddenly cold hands over the other woman's. "I'm so sorry."

Daphne's eyes glinted with moisture. "No one lets me talk about it. It's like Chris no longer exists."

"I understand."

"How can you possibly understand?" There was a tinge of anger in the woman's question.

Gemma drew a deep breath. "My sister died of a drug overdose."

Daphne gasped. "I am so sorry. I didn't realise."

"The worst was not realizing she'd been an addict—for some time." Gemma blinked back the familiar tears. "The last couple of months of her life were awful. She self-destructed before my eyes. I was so furious with her." And with her sister's billionaire boyfriend who had gotten her hooked on drugs. *That* anger had been misplaced. "I miss her desperately."

"There are times when I'm so cross with Chris I want to shake him, ask him why he's doing this…and

most of all I wonder where Basil and I went wrong."
The words burst from Daphne. "We gave him everything we thought he wanted."

"It's not your fault."

Daphne looked at her, her eyes sunken in their
sockets, haunted by unhappiness.

"You can't blame yourself. We always try to blame
someone in these situations. It's human nature to try
find an excuse for terrible things that happen."

She had blamed Angelo. Wrongly. Unfairly. It
wasn't his fault Mandy had died. He wasn't the ogre
she'd imagined.

Gemma shot him a glance. He was talking to Basil,
as if aware of her every move, he glanced up, their eyes
tangled…and held. Her heart shifted.

At that moment, Gemma realised she loved him.

She stilled in shock. Then he was in front of her.
"Can I get either of you ladies a nightcap?" Gemma and
Daphne shook their heads.

"The coffee is good," Daphne said.

Angelo slid into the space beside Gemma on the
sofa and his thigh pressed against hers, sending sharp
slivers of desire splintering through her. Wrapping his
arm around her shoulder, he placed a kiss on her brow.
The bold claim took her by surprise, she saw the astonishment in Daphne's eyes as Basil came to stand beside
her.

Twenty minutes later the evening was over and, as
they walked to the door, Daphne swung around and unexpectedly hugged Gemma.

"Thank you for sharing how you feel about your
sister's death, it helped me more than you'll ever know.

At least Chris is still alive, still has a chance to recover. And I've made a decision. I am going to fund a foundation to help warn young people about the dangers of drugs. Basil has spoken about doing something like that in the past. But I was simply too listless to do anything."

Basil threw Gemma a surprised look. It was clear that the topic of Chris and his addiction was not something he was accustomed to his wife discussing. Gemma didn't dare look at Angelo.

Then she told herself he couldn't possibly guess her secret. She forced herself to smile calmly as they said goodbye to the Makrideses.

Angelo locked the elevator with a click. "I didn't know you had a sister."

Gemma's throat closed in apprehension. "Yes."

A frown furrowed his brow. "You told me you were an only child, I never realized you'd lost a sister."

Mandy had denied her existence? Was that what her twin had secretly always wanted? To be the only child, the centre of attention? Did she feel cheated by having to share the limelight with a sister—or worse than that, did she resent the interest that came from being a twin? Something inside Gemma withered at her sister's rejection.

Angelo was speaking again. "What was her name?"

"Mandy." Her answer was terse.

"Is it still painful to talk about her?"

"Very."

"I'm sorry."

His sympathy and tenderness worsened the ache in her heart. His grip on her hand tightened and Gemma's throat tightened. *She loved him.* Her deception pressed in on her. How could she ever tell him? She turned into his arms and lifted her face. His arms tightened around her and his breathing grew heavy.

She wanted to be close to him. Naked. For the last time. Then she'd tell him. And it would all be over.

Ten

In the bedroom they undressed quickly and collapsed onto the bed in a tangle of limbs. A lamp in the corner of the room, between the wide bed and the wall of drawn drapes, cast a pale glow over them.

Angelo moved a little closer. "How did I ever let you go?"

A moment of darkness disturbed the passion that had overtaken her. *He thought she was her sister.* And she had to set him right.

"Angelo—"

His hand trailed across her breast, across the curve, brushing the delicate tip. Gemma sighed as frissons of delight followed beneath his fingertips. She lost track of what she had to say.

Then his tongue came out, probing, tasting the dark

nipple and heat splintered in her belly. Gemma fought a groan as that maddening mouth feasted on her.

He paid homage to the other breast, and when he'd finished Gemma stared at her taut quivering nipples with a sense of shock.

What was it about Angelo that stripped her of all her inhibitions? She wanted him...but there was more. There was a sense of belonging together, a deep-rooted understanding between them that she'd never experienced with anyone else.

It overwhelmed her. It scared her. Because it couldn't possibly survive what she had to confess.

"What are you thinking?" Angelo pulled her against him.

"Nothing." Her voice cracked on the lie. "Nothing," she said again, trying to make it sound convincing to her own ears.

"Then I'll have to give you something to think about." He stretched out a hand to stroke her naked flesh. "You're trembling."

"Yes."

Her breathy reply made Angelo grow harder in anticipation. His every nerve seemed to be on edge, suspended on the razor-edge of pleasure. By contrast, her body was soft, her skin silky under his hand and a wave of tremors shook her.

"Are you all right?"

She nodded, her eyes wide. He paused, determined to take it slow. Then her lips parted, her tongue tip slicked across that luscious lower lip and his control shredded.

A rush of heat seared him. He moved over her, chest

to her breast, his legs sliding along the length of hers, and bent to take that tantalising mouth.

Lower down he was aware of his body pressing into her. Her thighs parted and he tilted his hips forward until no space remained between them.

This close, her eyes were velvety with desire and he was supremely conscious of his strength, the power of his arms braced on each side of her upper arms, the weight of his torso brushing her breasts and the muscles shifting in his thighs. In contrast, she was so feminine, her long legs flexing subtly against him.

Breathing harshly, Angelo lifted his mouth and shifted his weight. Supporting himself on one elbow, he rapidly readied himself with the other hand, hoping he wouldn't erupt before he'd even entered her. The sheath of rubber rolled onto him. She shifted underneath him, tempting, impatient.

As he penetrated her, stretching her, she lay motionless. Finally sheathed deep within her, he lay against her—head bowed, eyes clenched shut—inhaling the sweet fragrance of her skin.

She moved and her inner muscles tightened on him, demanding a response. Pleasure streaked through him and his relentless control frayed. He began the slow sweeps that would take them towards a place he'd never known.

As the pace quickened so did the intensity. His hands cupped her hips, pulling her closer as he drove harder and harder into her. She echoed his ferocity.

When he thought he could take no more, when the pleasure was so great he felt that he would explode if it didn't end, he felt her contract against him, once, twice, and it was enough to tip him over the edge, into the fire that threatened to consume him. And then he pulled her into the curve of his arm, his body warm and relaxed against hers. "Look at me."

Gemma avoided his gaze, simply dropping her head against his chest, nuzzling his skin, breathing in his hot male scent.

She was here now. In his bed. In his life. Did it matter who he thought she was?

She stroked his stomach, let a finger trace the indent between the muscle definition. A wicked temptation called to her. *Kiss him.* He need never know she wasn't Mandy.

After all, if she never told him would he ever learn the truth? Probably not. He'd had many mistresses and none lasted. Their relationship would run its course, too. This sweet madness between them would not last.

But what if it did? What then? Could she keep this secret forever?

No. She didn't want to live with a past that Mandy had already stained with betrayal. She had to tell him. *Now.* While they were immersed in this special, loving glow. Acid ate the back of her throat. She swallowed. He would understand why she'd done what she had. *He had to.*

She pulled away a little, to give herself some breathing space, to gather her courage—and so that she could look into his face, the face she'd come to love so much.

"Hey, come back here, I want to hold you."

Gemma propped a cushion behind her back. "Angelo—" It came out a croak. She tried again. "I need to tell you something." She stroked his cheek with trembling fingers.

"Yes? What's wrong?"

She bit her lip. How…where…to start? She drew a deep breath. "I told you my sister died…"

He nodded.

"She was my twin."

"I'm so sorry. I've heard that twins are very close. It must have been hard. You said her name was Mandy?"

It was Gemma's turn to nod. "She died on Christmas Eve nearly three years ago."

"Three years ago?" Then he snapped his mouth shut.

Gemma could see his resolve not to interrupt, to support her, let her explain. Her love for him swelled.

For the first time she started to hope that he might be able to accept what she was about to tell him.

"Mandy was…well, Mandy. She made me laugh, she loved practical jokes when we were kids. She knew no fear and would try anything." Except Mandy had been terrified of being unpopular. She'd always wanted to be the ahead of the peer group, the first to swear, the first to smoke.

Gemma moved away from him and crossed her legs. "When we were kids we both loved to create shows. I'd sing and she'd dance." She recognized that she was rambling, trying to delay that moment of terrible truth.

"A talented duo. What did Mandy grow up into?"

Gemma hauled in a deep breath, met his gaze squarely. "She became a dancer, an exotic dancer."

Angelo stilled. "So both of you worked as exotic dancers? Did you ever work together? Identical twins… that would've been a card to play." He paused. "Or were you very different from each other?"

"We were nothing alike—even though we looked very similar."

"How similar?"

"Practically identical." The confession was dragged from Gemma. "At school our teachers struggled to tell us apart." Mandy had traded classes with Gemma to avoid those she hated. "And I'm not an exotic dancer, I've only ever sung."

There. She held her breath.

"What do you mean you—" He broke off. A horrible, tense silence followed. He shook his head, his eyes dazed like a fighter reeling from a blow. "What are you saying?"

"You knew Mandy, Angelo," Gemma confirmed. "Three years ago—"

"I knew Gemma." His voice was hard, definite. "Who the hell are you?"

"*I* am Gemma."

"Gemma worked for me, I have a copy of her work permit, her passport, to prove it."

Gemma uncrossed her legs and slung them over the edge of the bed, her back to Angelo. "Mandy didn't have a work permit. She was convicted for shoplifting with a group of friends a teenager. So her application for a work permit was declined."

"Look at me." She heard him move, then he was standing, looming over her. "I want to see your face. We would not give anyone a job without their paperwork being in order."

Gemma took a deep breath. "She had a work permit. She applied for it in my name, without my knowledge. She took my passport and my credit card when she left." And Gemma had never told a soul. When her father surmised that Mandy had been lucky to get a work permit, Gemma had remained silent. She'd been stranded in New Zealand, her career options curtailed—with no chance of working in Australian or Pacific island resorts, furious with her twin, waiting for Mandy to return. She bowed her head, covering her face.

"Didn't you tell the authorities?"

"You have to understand, all our lives we covered for each other. It was a hard habit to break. But I never thought that Mandy would come to any harm, not on a Greek island." Although she had experienced some qualms when Mandy had e-mailed to tell her about the fabulous man she'd hooked up with. Handsome. A billionaire. She'd been even more worried when Mandy had sent her press cuttings and photos of Angelo, whom Gemma had dismissed as a dashing sophisticated playboy. She'd begged Mandy to come home. But Mandy had been in heaven living out her fantasy lifestyle.

Gemma let her hands drop and glanced up at him. "I was more worried that you'd break her heart. You had a reputation as a playboy who went through beautiful woman like a hot knife through butter."

"A lot of that is PR. For show, to attract the jet set." His face darkened. "I'm very generous to my girlfriends. All the women I've been involved with know the score."

Except for her. She'd fallen in love with him. And, at the start, she'd believed Mandy had been in love with him, too. It had never crossed her mind that there'd been someone else in her sister's life.

"So why did you come here?" He flung his arms out wide. "Why the whole elaborate charade of pretending to be your sister?"

"I wanted to get close to you."

He stared at her in disbelief. "You certainly managed that. Did you plan to sleep with me?" There was a cynicism in the lines around his mouth and his bright eyes were dull.

She blinked.

"You did plan this!" He looked at her like she was something nasty.

Gemma swallowed. "In the beginning, I had some stupid half-baked idea that I might seduce you. But I abandoned it." She had to make him believe her. "I thought that you were responsible for Mandy's death."

"What about the amnesia? You told me about a hit-and-run in London. Was that true? Or another lie?"

Gemma looked away and shook her head. "There was no accident. I don't know where Mandy went after leaving here, but by the time she returned to New Zealand she was a pitiful, broken creature. She suffered from moodswings and had muttered wildly about the glamorous man she'd loved...and lost to another woman. I thought that was you."

"Nice to know that you hold me in such high regard," he bit out sardonically. He stalked away, pressed a switch and the wall of curtains started to open. He looked out into the darkness. "When your sister stayed with me, I caught her once using cocaine at a party and I made it clear that I wouldn't tolerate it," he said in a flat monotone. "That if it ever happened again, our relationship was over. She said it was a mistake...that she'd never done it before and wouldn't do it again. I believed her.

"I suspected she had a drinking...problem. I'd tried to convince her that she needed help after she'd had a little too much to drink at a party, stripped her clothes off and started to can-can. She argued that she was fine, it was just a bit of fun…that I was too staid. I broke it off that night, but she was so apologetic, said she wanted another chance. I gave it to her." He turned around, his eyes angry. Unforgiving. "And you thought I was responsible for her addictions? Did she tell you that? Mention my name?"

"No." Gemma felt awful. "I assumed. But I knew she'd had a relationship with you—she was so proud of it."

"So you never read about our affair in the scandal-sheets?" he said sardonically.

Gemma shook her head. "Mandy was in a bad way. We didn't have much time with her once she returned home. She took an overdose and then she was dead."

"Was it deliberate?" His voice softened.

For a wild moment Gemma thought he was about to reach for her, but then his eyes iced over.

Her throat thickened. "I thought so. I thought that you'd driven her away after getting her hooked on drugs, that she coped by turning to the drugs for solace. I thought she didn't want to live without you."

He paced along the length of the window, a dark shape against the night. "No wonder you hated me. No wonder you wanted revenge. But do you have any conception of the kind of danger that you put yourself in? What if I'd been the kind of man you thought?"

"I *had* to do it. She was my twin sister. My other half." And then she realized that was wrong. *He* was her other half. The bond, the empathy, that had been growing between them was stronger than anything she'd ever shared with her sister. She rose to her feet, took a step towards him. "Angelo—"

"Even though she lied to you, stole from you, de-frauded you?" He was angry, she saw. "Mandy used the credit card that you told me you'd mysteriously maxed out and couldn't remember how, didn't she?"

"Yes. But from what you told me, the dates correlate with after she left Kalos, while she must've been with Jean-Paul. And he supplied drugs to her...he admitted that much to me."

Angelo's gaze narrowed. "I'm not having a dealer on my island. I will take care of him. It makes sense. If Mandy no longer had the allowance I gave her at her disposal, then she must have pawned the jewellery I bought her for a fraction of its value." He glared at her. "Why didn't you stop the card when you discovered it missing?"

She shrugged. "I couldn't leave her stranded over-seas with no money if she needed it. I simply never expected her to run up that kind of debt. She knew I'd have to repay it. It must have been for drugs."

"Well, I won't leave *you* stranded." There was a note of finality in his voice. "I will book you a ticket to take you back to New Zealand safely."

It was over. He was dumping her. Gemma lifted her chin. "That is not necessary. I can make my own way home."

"I can't believe what you did." Anger and a mist of complex emotions clouded his gaze.

"I'm sorry," she whispered.

He turned away, stared out into the night. "I told myself you had changed. I thought I had found a woman who was special...one of a kind. But you are even more treacher-ous than your sister. Your betrayal was calculated to—"

"No, I didn't mean—"

"Be silent." He cut her off. Moving to the door, he added, "I will find somewhere to spend the night. By morning I want you gone. And don't return. Because I never want to see you again."

In the slanting morning light Gemma packed her bags, her heart aching, but she had a frightening suspicion that her heartbreak served her right. She'd called reception and been told that a ferry would be leaving in twenty minutes. If she hurried she could catch the boat to the mainland.

Angelo had not come back to the room since their awful confrontation. She'd waited, huddled on his bed, for him to return.

But he hadn't.

The message was clear. She had to accept that it was over. He did not want to see her. That to him her betrayal was worse than Mandy's had been.

Downstairs, the reception lobby was bustling. Gemma waited in an alcove for the shuttle to the ferry to arrive. The mural of a golden-haired sun god driving his fiery horses across the sky brought a bittersweet lump to her throat. She'd ventured too close to the heat and been badly burned.

But she would survive.

"Gemma?"

She turned at the sound of her name and her heart sank when she saw Jean-Paul. He examined her, his eyes searching for she knew not what, while a frown creased his brow.

"What?"

"You are Gemma?" It was the question that only yesterday she would've dreaded.

"Yes, I am Gemma."

"But you are not the woman I—" he paused "—once knew intimately."

Jean-Paul had worked it out. Probably as a result of her slip the other day. She released the breath she hadn't even known she was holding. "No."

"You're a dead ringer for her. She has to be your twin."

Rage surged through the pain. "Dead is what she is. And it's all your fault."

An ugly expression came over his face. "You breathe one word to Apollonides and I'll tell him the truth. That you've been deceiving him, laughing behind his back. You said that you've forgotten the past. That's how you've explained away not knowing things you should."

Behind him Gemma glimpsed the doorman who had offered to call her when the shuttle came, coming towards them. It was time. She rose. "Do your worst, Jean-Paul. Angelo already knows."

And she walked away leaving Jean-Paul staring after her, his jaw slack.

From the hilltop above the resort Angelo watched the ferry pull away, white water churning in its wake. He shoved his hands deeper into the pockets of his windbreaker.

Gemma was gone.

His mouth twisted. He'd told her to leave, and she'd obeyed. So why did he feel no better?

The wind caught at the windbreaker and ruffled at

his hair. He didn't notice. He narrowed his eyes against the sun and followed the course of the ferry until, a long time later, it disappeared from sight.

Then he started down the hill. A police helicopter approached from the mainland, making for the heliport.

Good. The police had organised a search warrant after his tip-off. Angelo couldn't wait for them to search the man's room and arrest Moreau. He suspected it would be a long, long time before the man frequented any resorts.

Just as it would be a long time before *he* forgot about Gemma.

Eleven

It was humid in Auckland in December. Gemma returned to her parents' home after a morning's Christmas shopping with her mother and made for the bathroom clutching the box she'd bought at the pharmacy. In less than five minutes she had the answer she'd dreaded.

"Mum," she staggered out the bathroom. "This is going to be a shock."

"What's wrong, darling?"

"I'm pregnant."

"Are you sure?"

Gemma nodded and held up the indicator stick.

"Oh." Her mother looked like she wanted to say something. Finally she asked, "Do you know who the father is?"

"Of course I do."

"But you're not telling?"

Gemma gave a laugh. To her own ears it sounded hysterical. "I will when I'm ready." She wrapped her arms around her mother. "You shouldn't be so understanding."

Her mother hugged her back. "How can I not be? Do you know how far along you are?"

"Not far at all. I missed a period, that's what clued me in. I've always been so regular."

"Go see your doctor. You may not be pregnant at all. Perhaps your body is just playing tricks on you after the long flight."

"I've been back almost two weeks—it's unlikely to be the flight."

Beth Allen shook her head. "But the pill makes the chance of it happening so remote."

"Except I haven't been on the pill for a while. There was no one in my life, so there seemed little point. He used protection. Something must have gone wrong. I'll go see the doctor, but I doubt it will change things." Deep in her heart Gemma was already sure. "Mum, I should tell you. The father is—" She broke off.

"Yes, darling?"

Gemma swallowed. "It's Angelo Apollonides."

Her mother's hand came up to cover her mouth, but no sound escaped. But her eyes were wide and dismayed as she stared at Gemma. Then she stepped forward and hugged Gemma. "You can tell how it came to pass when you're ready."

They stood like that for a long while, holding one another, and Gemma drew support from her mother's warmth. At last she said, "Thanks, Mum, for your support."

"Your father and I will always be there for you and the baby."

"I know. But I need to you to understand one thing, Mum. Angelo wasn't responsible for what happened to Mandy. It was another guy, Jean-Paul Moreau. I think Mandy loved him, and he rewarded her by making her into an addict. I hope he burns in hell."

"Oh, sweetheart, I have to tell you that is a relief to hear it wasn't your Angelo."

Later Gemma went home to the apartment she'd rented out while she went to Greece. It seemed strange to be living in the middle of the city after the time she'd spent on Strathmos.

Gemma made a pot of weak herbal tea and poured herself a mug. She intended to cut down on caffeine for the next nine months, that meant less tea and coffee.

Taking the mug she made her way to the dining-room table. She lay her hand on her flat stomach and thought about the baby. About the future. And about Angelo.

The phone interrupted her thoughts. It was her agent, thrilled with an offer for Gemma to perform at a brand-new Australian resort.

"It's the chance of a lifetime," Macy was gabbling. "The money is great and it's for six months. You get star billing. You'd be mad to let this pass."

Gemma considered it. The sum would wipe out the debt on her credit card; help her start the baby's life on much more stable footing. She could sublet the apartment while she was gone, that would give her a nest egg. But she couldn't take the job for the full six months. She'd be showing by then and she'd want to slow down.

"Macy, see if they'll do a deal for three months. I'll take that. I'll be ready to start in the new year. But get me the best money that you can."

She set the phone down, feeling a lot better now that she had a plan to get the burden of the debt Mandy had run up under control.

Now she'd have to call Angelo and let him know about the baby. He deserved that much.

Macy called back two days later, ecstatic with the deal she'd managed to secure Gemma. The contract was for four months and would start in the new year, and she'd managed to better the money, as well.

As for telling Angelo about her pregnancy, in the end Gemma's parents convinced her that it would be better to tell Angelo face to face. Her father was quite forceful about it, and was ready to come along, too, until Gemma talked him out of it. But she was pleased to see that he was looking a lot happier. Her pregnancy had given him a new interest in life.

Gemma had argued at first that flying to Strathmos was an expense she couldn't afford, particularly with the costs that the baby would incur, but in the end they'd convinced her.

So a week later Gemma found herself across the world again on Strathmos. She called ahead to make sure Angelo was in residence. The first person Gemma saw when she reached the resort was Lucie.

"Gemma—" the slight blonde threw her arms around her "—you're back."

"Not to stay, I'm looking for Angelo."

Lucie stepped back, her eyes curious. "He's around

somewhere. But it's the Christmas show tomorrow night, you must come watch. Even though Stella Argyris is the star of the show—and she never lets anyone forget it. She's even more of a pain in the butt than I remembered." Lucie rolled her eyes.

"I will." If she was here that long. If Angelo didn't kick her off the island the moment she delivered her news. And that reminded her, she'd need to book accommodation in the village later so that she'd have somewhere to stay for the night. Although, if the worse came to the worse, she had no doubt that Lucie would let her use the sofa in her unit.

"Any idea where I can find Angelo?"

Lucie shook her head. "He was talking to Mark earlier outside Dionysus's—but that was a while ago. Have him paged," she suggested.

"Thanks." Gemma had no intention of forewarning Angelo about her presence.

She wandered around, Angelo wasn't on the overcast beach where the westerly wind blew the sand up in gusts. Nor was he in the entertainment complex, although Mark greeted her eagerly. She didn't catch a glimpse of him in the lobby so she made her way to the casino. The gaming rooms were already occupied by some of the more hardened gamblers and she smiled at the bouncers as she made her way into the Apollo Club, but there was no sign of Angelo there, either.

She'd just about given up, deciding he must be in his penthouse and that she'd have to have herself announced, when she saw him seated in one of the many coffee bars, with a woman who was making every effort to keep his attention, flicking her long dark hair from her face, thrusting her chest forward to show off a superb stretch of cleavage.

Gemma turned away, her heart constricting. What had she expected? He'd told her he intended to forget her, and what better way than with a beautiful woman?

Angelo was gorgeous, wealthy…of course women would throw themselves at him. She'd never expected him to hanker after her. Yet seeing him with someone else hurt. Horribly. She made blindly for the exit. Outside the air was cool, the wintery edge of the wind cutting through her cardigan.

Gemma headed for the entertainment centre. As she rounded a bend, she saw Mark approaching from the opposite direction. She had no desire to talk to anyone so she slipped through a door into the massive Apollo-drome super bowl where the Christmas extravaganza would be held.

She slipped into a seat and fought to blink back the tears that threatened. People came in and out, a couple of guys shifted props across the stage, but in the huge space she remained unnoticed.

It was a while before she gained sufficient control over her emotions to feel up to venturing out. The people had started to buzz in and out and she didn't particularly want to bump into anyone she knew. So she stayed where she was and realised the final dress rehearsal must be about to start. Squinting, she recognised several of the dancers in their workout gear, a couple of the backing singers. Just as she was about to stand to leave, all the lights came up and she saw Angelo walk up the centre aisle.

But he was not alone.

The beautiful brunette clung on to his arm, talking

vivaciously, her fingers tapping against his arm, demanding his attention. Angelo bent his head.

Gemma shrank back and felt a searing stab of jealousy.

When Mark came across the stage, the brunette rose onto her tiptoes, kissed Angelo's cheek and made for the stage stairs. It was then that Gemma realised that this must be Stella Argyris.

Clearly, Angelo already had a new mistress.

She rose clumsily to her feet, intent on getting out of here. She saw Angelo turn as if drawn by some sixth sense and freeze.

Then she was plunging out of the row of red seats, her heart tearing with pain, desperate to get to the exit, to get away from the sight of them…of him.

Why had she come back to Strathmos?

She should have called him, told him about the baby over the phone. She should never have let her parents talk her into doing the right thing.

But her reluctance to lie to herself made her face the truth.

It wasn't because of the baby that she was here. She'd come because she'd hoped that there was a chance to salvage something between them. That Angelo would take one look at her and know that he wanted her forever.

No chance of that. She'd deluded herself. Angelo had already found a new bed partner. Moved on. He wasn't the kind of guy to fall in love with someone like her. So what had she been thinking?

A hand closed around her arm. "I heard you were here, asking for me. What do you want?"

Affronted and upset, she yanked out of Angelo's

grasp. "I made a mistake. I should never have come back." And then she tried to move past him.

He blocked her path, his body broad and intimidating. "So why are you here?"

She shook her head. "It doesn't matter."

His fabulous eyes glinted. "I will decide if it matters. Something brought you a long way back. What?" There was an intensity in his tone that she didn't understand.

She shrugged, ducked around him and started to walk quickly, her head down, intent on getting away from him.

He kept up with her. "We need to talk."

"No, we don't." She rushed down a flight of stairs, her sights fixed on the exit to the Apollodrome. A vision of Stella Argyris kissing him filled her mind. "There's nothing to say."

She reached the exit and broke into a run, desperate to get out of the entertainment complex, to get away from him, before she started to cry.

She could hear his footsteps behind her. She ran faster, dimly aware that people—performers and tourists—were staring at her as she bolted past.

They'd reached the exit doors. Gemma plunged through them, into the salty windy air. She veered away, heading for the pathway to the village.

He caught her arm. "Slow down."

"Let me go."

He ignored her. Pulling her around to face him, he said, "You wanted to see me, now you've nothing to say?"

"Exactly."

"We need to talk."

She stuck her jaw out. "We don't."

"Okay, I'll talk, you can listen. But I suggest we do

this in the privacy of my suite—unless of course you like the idea of public scrutiny."

Gemma looked around. A group of gardeners was staring at them, talking. One laughed and Gemma flushed.

"No, not a good look for the boss to be arguing with his former mistress in public."

Her chest constricted.

"I don't care what people say about me, but I thought it might worry you."

She glanced up. His eyes were hard, his jaw set. Her breath caught. He was so utterly gorgeous. And she loved him desperately…was carrying his baby. She gave in. "Okay, we'll talk."

Except for the addition of a Christmas tree decorated with gold and red balls, his suite was unchanged from the night weeks ago when she'd carried out a vigil waiting for him to return to her. Gemma wasn't sure why she'd expected it to look different. Probably because, for her, everything had changed that night.

And now she carried Angelo's baby.

"Have a seat."

She took her cardigan off, dropped it on the floor beside the sofa and sat. Then gulped when he moved to stand in front of her. "So, tell me why did you come back? What was so important to come all the way across the world?" His eyes were guarded, but she got a sense that his body was wound tight.

She bit her lip. How was he going to react? Would he be angry? See it as an obstruction to his relationship with Stella?

"I'm waiting."

"I'm pregnant."

Whatever he'd expected, clearly, that wasn't it. His head went back, his eyes flaring with shock…and something else.

"Run that by me again?" he said very, very softly.

"I'm pregnant." Tremors of tension shimmered through Gemma as she waited for his reaction.

His eyes narrowed. "You're pregnant. Did you do it deliberately?"

Twelve

"What?" Gemma didn't try to hide her shock.

Angelo's handsome features could have been carved out of marble. "Is this your idea of revenge? Your way of punishing me for your belief that I'd caused your sister's death? Did you plan all along to fall into my bed, to get pregnant?"

"No."

His tension uncoiled infinitesimally. "So why *did* you let me make love to you, knowing I thought you were *Mandy?*"

Oh, dear God, this was the one question she could not answer. Not without giving herself away. Irretrievably.

So she said with a touch of mockery, "Because you turn me on. More than any man I've ever met."

His voice held an edge. "Oh, that's the only reason?"

She shrugged. "Well, yes. What more could there be?"

"What more could there be?" he repeated savagely. Then he landed on the arm of the sofa and slid in behind her. "What more could there be?" A feather light kiss landed on her cheek. "This…" He pulled her across his lap, angled his head and his tongue stroked across her bottom lip, igniting a well of longing within her. "Someone who turned you on. That's all I was?" There was affront beneath the annoyance.

"Well, that's pretty much why you slept with me, wasn't it?"

"Maybe I thought I'd found my dream woman." His voice was ironic. Before Gemma could respond, his hand slid under her T-shirt, found the bud of her breast. "I was wrong. But we still have this, don't we?"

Gemma shoved his hand away. She felt a tearing ache of loss. He *didn't* love her. He could never love her. "I just wanted to tell you that the baby existed. You have a right to know. I won't even put your name on the birth certificate."

"Why not?"

"You want to be listed as the father?" She'd never expected that.

"Of course. No child of mine will grow up with the slur of *father unknown*."

She took a deep breath. "What will you tell people? What about Stella?"

"Stella?" He frowned, bewilderment clouding his features. "Why are you asking about Stella?"

"I saw you. I saw you kissing her."

The frown deepened and his eyes grew cool. "You saw Stella kissing *me*."

She folded her arms across her breasts. "And I saw

you having an intimate little conversation in the coffee shop," she plunged on.

He shrugged. "Stella wanted something."

Stella wanted something. That was for sure. Stella wanted Angelo Apollonides. "Are you trying to tell me that there is nothing between you and her?"

"That's exactly what I'm telling you."

"That you haven't slept with her since I left?"

"I shouldn't need to answer that. Especially since your only reason for sleeping with me was because I was a warm body." The savagery was back, and his lip curled into a snarl.

Doubts swirled through Gemma. What did Angelo want of her? Did he mean that he hadn't had another woman since she left? And given his reputation, could she believe that?

He was moving away. "And you won't need to worry about other women—because we're getting married."

Gemma froze. "Why should I marry you?"

His eyes grew wary. "I would never knowingly allow a child of mine to be raised with the slur of illegitimacy."

She didn't want Angelo marrying her only for the sake of the baby. "But lots of couples have children without the blessing of marriage."

"Not me." Angelo was unequivocal. "I grew up in a time when the world was more harshly critical. I lived with the sharp edge of the slurs. Even if the world has changed, I don't want that for my child."

Any romantic hopes Gemma may have harboured about his proposal died. He didn't love her, this was all about making sure his child had parents who were married.

* * *

Gemma was still trying to fathom how to react to Angelo's bombshell when they made their way to the Apollodrome for the Christmas Eve show the following evening.

Angelo had insisted Gemma stay in the penthouse, in the spare bedroom. And, with nothing suitable in her luggage, she'd been grateful to Angelo when a box emblazoned with the fancy logo of one of the exclusive boutiques in the lobby arrived at the door.

Opening the box, she glimpsed a fabric that glowed like crystal between layers of tissue paper. The dress was soft and clingy and fitted as though it had been made for her. The fabric changed colour from snowy white through to sparkling silver. A pair of silver heels and a tiny silver bag completed the outfit.

Now, as she glided backstage beside Angelo, Gemma felt anything but pregnant and ungainly.

Until she looked into a pair of enraged jet-black eyes and read the malevolence there.

"Angelo," Stella croaked, "my throat is in agony."

Mark rushed up and paled with dismay. "My God, Stella, you should've told us earlier. The show is sold out, ready to go."

"I didn't want to be a bother." Stella lowered her eyelashes. "I thought it would pass."

Gemma gave the woman a hard stare. She looked stunning, her black sheath made the most of her curves and her makeup hid any pallor that might reveal that she was unwell. But with a throat infection, she would not be able to sing.

"Angelo, maybe if I sit down a little while, it might

ease." Stella's hands fluttered at Angelo's sleeve, but he was already turning away.

"Mark, where's the program?"

It materialized with a flourish. Angelo pulled out a pen. "We'll cancel the solo that Stella was going to do, replace it with an item by Lucie LaVie—I'm sure she'll have a hilarious Santa story to share."

"But—" Stella's eyes widened with horror.

"And Aletha—" Mark named one of the other singers "—has been working as understudy. She can sing 'Oh, Christmas Tree' and 'Kalanda, Kalanda'—" he named the Greek version of "Jingle Bells" "—but that still leaves a hole where Stella was going to sing an encore all by herself, we'll just have to scrap that."

"But I can—" Stella interrupted frantically.

"Gemma," Angelo touched her arm. "Would you very much mind singing 'O Holy Night' as the encore? Please? I know you're not booked for this, that you were expecting to enjoy the performance as a guest. But would you do it? For me?"

She'd do just about anything for him. Singing her favourite carol was a cinch.

"Of course." She didn't dare look in Stella's direction.

"Brilliant idea," Mark said. "Gemma stood in for Stella in several of the early rehearsals."

"Gemma doesn't need to—"

"Stella, don't worry yourself about it. You're ill. I know that you would not have jeopardized such a show unless you were very sick."

Gemma whipped around to stare at Angelo in astonishment. *He knew.* He knew that Stella had been after the limelight and he'd dealt with her ruthlessly.

She shivered, suddenly feeling sorry for the other woman.

"Now, go." It was an order. "You need to be in bed, taking care of that throat so that you're well enough to perform for your next obligation." Even Stella caught the not-very-subtle warning and she slunk away without a word.

"Gemma, you'll need stage makeup." Mark was shepherding her to the dressing room. "Sorry to spoil your evening, you're a sport to help out when you must have been looking forward to watching the show from the front row."

"But what's everyone going to say when they find out they're not seeing Stella? She's a well-known singer. She'll have fans that came to see her."

Mark shrugged. "Too late to worry about that. At least they get to see a spectacular show, better than a cancellation."

In the wings Gemma waited. She'd also be singing a duet with Denny. She watched as a fire-eater gave a spectacular performance juggling torches and a whole lot of stunts that had the crowd gasping, then she and Denny were on.

The next ten minutes passed in a rush, she could barely remember what had happened. On the way off the stage, she passed a group of Christmas elves going on, a Russian troupe of acrobats that had the audience "oohing" and "aahing."

The carols sounded wonderful. Gemma started to relax. The finale came, everyone was on stage and the chorus voices were rising. Gemma felt the performers' excitement mirrored back by the audience.

Her hand brushed her stomach. *Hear that, baby? Next year you'll see the show, too.* So hard to believe.

The choir sashayed off, the dancers did a last sequence and with a wave they were gone. The curtains fell and applause followed.

Then Gemma was on the stage all alone. The audience lay like a vast sea of darkness ahead of her as a single spotlight lit her.

She searched the front row. And found Angelo through the bright beam of the spotlight.

She launched into "O Holy Night." She sang it for him...as he'd requested. No one else existed.

Only Angelo.

Afterwards she felt drained, but curiously exhilarated as clapping swept the showroom. She waved her hands in thanks, smiled and bowed. When she looked for Angelo again, he was gone and her heart sank.

An expectant hush fell over the crowd. Gemma started to walk to the wings, still facing the audience, waving, smiling until her cheeks hurt. The crowd started to buzz.

She turned to see what had caught their attention.

Angelo was on stage, coming towards her, his arms filled with a huge bouquet of red roses.

Joy twisted through her.

And then she remembered. This tribute was meant for Stella. Not her.

Stella's red roses.

Meaningless. Nothing to do with love. Nothing more than a goodwill gesture of appreciation.

Angelo reached her. He held a microphone in one hand. "That was a marvellous performance." The audience erupted into a burst of clapping. "Yesterday, I asked Gemma Allen to be my wife. Now, I'd like you all to celebrate her answer with me."

He held the microphone towards her.

The silence was absolute. The audience waited. Angelo, waited, his body taut.

Gemma gave him a despairing glance. What was she to say? How could she marry a man who took mistresses rather than a wife? A man who didn't—would never—love her?

Then a woman in the front row jumped up. "Say yes, Gemma."

Startled Gemma squinted into the lights. The woman was unfamiliar, blonde. She smiled, gave her a little wave.

"Ignore my mother," Angelo murmured.

"Your mother?"

Her voice boomed out over the microphone. Gemma blushed as the audience tittered. Out of the darkness came an indecipherable bit of advice.

Gemma ignored it.

She knew what she was going to do.

She was going to marry Angelo. For the sake of her baby. And for her sake…because she loved him.

"Yes." Her voice was strong and clear and the crowd whooped.

Then the roses fell from her grasp as Angelo swept her up into his arms, his mouth meeting hers in a kiss that held hunger and a touch of desperation.

Gemma wasn't acting as she grasped his shoulders and gave the best—and most public—performance of her life.

* * *

There was a Christmas party after the show. Lucie came rushing over with a tray of glasses filled with champagne as soon as she and Angelo arrived. Gemma laughed. "You're making me feel quite the celebrity."

"You are! You are! How could you keep—" Lucie flashed a sideways glance at Angelo "—such a secret from me?"

Angelo grinned. "I only asked her to marry me yesterday. I wasn't going to give her a chance to say no."

"Really? You railroaded her in front of all those people. Oh, naughty man."

Even Gemma laughed at Lucie's antics. And Angelo held her close to his side, his grip possessive, his hand heavy on her hip. For a while Gemma started to think that this could work, that even though he didn't love her, her love…and the baby…would be enough to meld them together.

Angelo went to fetch her a drink and Mark materialized at her side. "Your worry that the crowd would be disappointed by Stella's absence was all for nothing. Angelo's proposal gave them a once-in-a-lifetime show."

Gemma smiled at him. "At least the fans weren't disappointed." But it set her thinking. Had Angelo thought of it as a publicity stunt? She didn't think so. Her experience of him revealed an intensely private man, who as much as he liked a gorgeous woman by his side, treated that woman like a goddess. He was far kinder, far more complex than she'd expected.

The Angelo she'd read about in the gossip columns

was not the kind of man who would've married his pregnant mistress, and she struggled a little with the vast dichotomy between the playboy public profile and the complex man she'd come to love.

It wasn't long before he returned. But he wasn't alone. "My mother, Connie."

Gemma's eyes widened as she took in the slim, tanned woman. Connie looked liked she'd just stepped out of a beauty salon. Immaculate. Tanned. Not a hair out of place. And she certainly didn't look old enough to be Angelo's mother.

"Hello." Gemma smiled uncertainly.

"I am thrilled to meet you. Angelo told me all about you."

Gemma shot Angelo a questioning look. How much had he told his mother? Not everything, she hoped.

"I met your sister, once, briefly. The resemblance is remarkable."

So Angelo must have told his mother about her deception. "We were very close—even though we had little in common."

"Except my son."

"Mamma." Angelo's tone was furious. Gemma was too embarrassed to even look at him.

"I'm sorry. I'm sorry." Connie's hand covered her mouth, her nails perfectly manicured. "I can't ever seem to keep my thoughts to myself."

Angelo's eyes were clouded as he said, "But you can try. At least until Gemma gets to know you a little better."

"I'm sorry, Gemma. Forgive me?" Connie's long manicured nails rested against her arm. "Come, let's sit down somewhere, the three of us. You can tell me about the names you are thinking of for the baby."

So Angelo had told his mother about the pregnancy, as well. His mother seemed to have taken it well. No drama about a grandchild ageing her. Gemma let out a sigh of relief. On the plus side it looked like her future mother-in-law was totally without guile.

"Angelo, a glass of champagne for me please, and—" she turned "—what would you like, Gemma?"

"Water would be fine."

"Make it Perrier, my son." When Angelo wound his way into the throng she said, "Tell me about New Zealand. I have never been there. Are the men good-looking?"

Gemma laughed. They chatted for a while, Angelo brought their drinks and joined them for a while before he was dragged away by a staff member to welcome a big spender who had flown in to try out the Apollo Club and heard about the Christmas party.

"I'm thrilled Angelo is getting married. He always said he never would."

"It's the baby—I don't think he would've married me otherwise." What was the point of hiding why Angelo had proposed?

"So you are aware that Angelo is illegitimate?"

"Yes." Gemma reached out to touch Connie's hand. "But you don't have to—"

"I do. You need to understand the man you're marrying." Connie sighed. "His father was a handsome man, an entertainer, a singer of love songs. I fell in love with him. He was charming…a show man. I was eighteen. An heiress. Too sheltered. I became his mistress. Within the first month I was pregnant. The relationship did not last. I came home to Athens, to my disappointed parents.

"My father arranged a marriage for me to Mario Apollonides. To give the baby a name. My father built the house on Strathmos for me and my son and my new husband. The truth was hushed up. But, of course, there were rumours and lots of speculation. Too many people knew about my passion for Angelo's real father. Needless to say, the marriage lasted less than five years. So you see, my dear, why my son would never marry a woman just to give a baby a name."

Gemma stared at Connie. What was Connie telling her? Was there another reason why Angelo had proposed? He'd insisted that no child of his would grow up a bastard. Was Connie mistaken? Why would Angelo lie?

"Nor did my staying secluded on the island work," Connie continued. "Before long, I'd met another man— a business associate of my father, a millionaire. I became his mistress."

"And what of Angelo?"

"He stayed on the island…with his governess. When he was old enough I sent him to an English boarding school to get him out of the fishbowl that Greek society is. My father wanted Angelo to live with him, in Athens. But he already had another boy in his care, Zac. I was afraid that Angelo would grow up in his shadow."

Gemma remembered Angelo speaking of school, of the isolation. "He was a long way from home."

"Yes. It was hard for him, of course, coming from such a prominent family. I was linked through his school years with quite a few high-profile men."

Angelo would've hated that. But it explained his

attraction to glamourous, sophisticated women who wouldn't demand more than he was prepared to give. Emotionally or by way of permanent commitment.

And his love-them-leave-them image was born.

"And being illegitimate made it worse. Once, when he was about six he asked me why I hadn't married his real father. I told him I'd made a mistake, met the wrong man. But that I needed to get married, because society demanded it. He told me that he wouldn't make a mistake like that, he would never marry the wrong person."

Gemma stared at his mother.

So why had Angelo told her he wanted to marry her for the sake of the baby? Angelo was so self-contained, how was she going to find out?

Gemma was no closer to an answer when Christmas Day finally dawned.

By the time she'd dressed, the rain had set in, echoing her pensive mood, bringing back memories of Mandy's tragic death. She made her way through to the kitchen and stopped in astonishment at the sight of Angelo preparing breakfast.

"Merry Christmas." He grinned at her and leaned over to kiss her cheek. He looked so happy and relaxed that her own mood started to lift. "My mother called, she will join us for lunch—that gives us some time alone. The coffee is already on the go and the table has been laid."

They ate a breakfast of thick Greek yogurt and honey and fruit topped off with fried eggs and bacon. Afterwards they took their coffee mugs through to the lounge and settled beside the Christmas lights. Christmas…Gemma closed her eyes and thought briefly of Mandy.

Be happy for me, sister.

When she opened them, the lights on the tree winked at her, as if to say Mandy had heard her plea. *Thank you.*

When she looked up Angelo stood in front of her holding a gaily wrapped parcel. Gemma was relieved that she'd had the foresight to purchase a book on Greek legends for Angelo for Christmas.

She unwrapped his gift and took out the beautiful silk sarong. "It's beautiful," she mouthed.

He tore the wrappings off his gift and a smile lit his face. "I haven't read this. I'll look forward to it."

Then he took a little parcel out his pocket and tossed it to her.

"What's this?"

He shrugged. But his bright eyes were darker than usual and he looked almost hesitant. "Open it."

The removal of the gold paper revealed a black velvet box. Her heart stopped.

"Do you like it?" he asked softly.

Speechless Gemma stared at the elegant ring, a row of baguette diamonds vertically positioned in a channel setting.

"If you don't like it, we can change it."

His voice sounded far away.

Time seemed to hang suspended. Gemma couldn't stop staring at the ring. What if he never grew to love her? How would she survive being married for the sake of his child? Finally she looked up. "I don't think I can do it."

He stiffened and his gaze grew guarded. "What? Marry me?"

"You're only marrying me because of the baby."

"I want to be part of my child's life."

Gemma stared at him. "You're a high-powered busi-nessman, you flit from resort to resort. You don't really want a family to drag you down." She tried to sound reasonable.

Angelo walked to the window. For a long moment he stood staring out. Then he swung around to face her. "I've been thinking about what Basil said. I'm going to delegate a lot of what I do. Family is important. I want to be part of my son's life. I want us to be married, to bring him up together."

"It won't work." She bit her lip. He sounded so con-vincing.

His gaze sharpened. "What are you frightened of?"

That you'll never love me. God, he was intuitive. "I'm not frightened. I just don't think—"

"—you can do it." He came towards her and took her hands in his. "You've said that already. But I think you're scared. What are you afraid of?"

Gemma swallowed. "Nothing."

"Then why is your pulse erratic." His fingertips stroked the delicate blue-veined skin inside her wrists. "Why is your breathing so shallow?"

"You know why." She watched him from under her eyelashes. "It's this overwhelming attraction between us."

He shook his head. "If that was all it was you wouldn't be trying to back out, you'd be bright-eyed and eager. No, this is something else." He scanned her face.

She could see that razor-sharp mind thinking. Would he guess the truth?

That she loved him?

"Are you worried that I still have you confused with your sister?"

"No." Strangely that didn't worry her at all.

Some of the tension went out of Angelo. "Good. I'm glad we've got that out the way because the two of you are really not alike at all. I knew you had changed. It simply never crossed my mind there were two of you. I thought you were one of a kind. Now, what are you afraid of?"

Gemma swallowed again. "I don't want to be married to someone who—" She broke off.

"Who what?"

Who didn't love her.

That was the simple truth of it. She'd been contemplating marrying one of the most desirable men on the planet. A man who didn't love her. For the sake of her child.

She must be mad.

"Who what?" he prompted again.

"A man who a zillion other woman are going to find as a hot as I do," she replied after a pause made it clear that he would remain silent until she answered.

"Ah—" he stroked her hand "—now it gets interesting. You'd only need to be concerned if those gazillion women interested me," he said quietly.

She thought about what he'd said. Her stomach rolled over. Could he possibly mean… "So why wouldn't you be interested in any of those zillions of woman?"

"Why did you really agree to marry me?"

There was a burning intensity in his question. Their eyes duelled, held. Indecisively, Gemma gazed into his turquoise depths.

"I'm scared," she confessed.

"Of what?"

"That if I tell you, you'll—" She broke off and shook her head. She couldn't bear it if he laughed…or worse, looked at her with pity in his eyes.

"Would it help if I told you why I asked you to marry me?"

"Because of the baby?"

He drew a deep shuddering breath. "Not because of the baby. For me." His grip tightened on her hands. He leaned closer. "After you left, it wasn't the same. My life was empty. I need you to complete me. I love you."

Her breath caught.

His eyes were bright, unguarded. The love shone from them. "The baby was an excuse, a way of getting what I really wanted. You."

Gemma's breath left her in an audible whoosh. Warmth filled her, her body softened, leaning into him. He felt warm and solid against her. Permanent. "I love you, too."

"At last!" He yanked her into his arms. The kiss that landed on her mouth held a touch of desperation.

And she realised that Angelo had been nervous. He hadn't been sure of her at all. "I was getting cold feet at the idea of being married to someone who didn't love me."

"And I have to admit I wasn't thrilled at marrying someone who wanted me only for my body. Wench." He sat up and grabbed her hand and slid the ring onto her finger. It fit perfectly.

Gemma giggled. "It could've been worse. I could've told you that I was marrying you for your money. To settle my credit-card debt."

"I knew that wasn't a factor."

"How?"

"The offer of the contract to sing in Australia would have taken care of your debt." He slanted her a look. "That's a resort I've recently acquired. I wasn't intending to let you get too far away. Once I got over the shock of your revelation that you weren't Mandy…and the even bigger shock that I wanted you back. I had to make a plan to get you back."

"I should've known!" Gemma laughed with joy. "I almost turned it down. Because I'd discovered I was pregnant. I wanted to work in New Zealand so I could be close to my parents. But the chance to get rid of that debt was too good."

A kiss landed on the top of her head. "Now we'll spend our honeymoon there and I'll spend the four months I have you under contract overseeing the developments I have planned for those resorts."

She cuddled closer. "And speaking of work. I still want to sing. But something Daphne said struck a chord with me. She's talked about starting a foundation to educate young people about the dangers of drugs. I'd like to get involved with that."

"Do anything you want. I will support your decision."

No longer his way. But their way. Gemma smiled to herself. "I'd like to feel that someone like Mandy could be saved. Or someone like Daphne's son, Chris."

He hugged tightly to him. "You have my support, on one condition: we get married before the new year."

She lifted her face to his, hooked her arm around the back of his head and pulled his mouth down to hers. "Deal!"

*   *   *

Angelo had one final surprise for Gemma. He flew her parents out to Strathmos for the wedding and watched her stunned delight as they walked into the penthouse to surprise her.

He put himself out to charm her parents. Two nights before the wedding the four of them had dinner in the Golden Fleece and afterwards they strolled down to the Apollo Club.

Later they shared a nightcap in the penthouse. By the time her parents were ready to call it a night, it was ten o'clock. After kissing her mother good-night and giving her father a hug and seeing them to the door, Gemma turned to Angelo with a gleam in her eyes that made his throat tighten and said, "I fancy a long, hot soak."

They wallowed in the huge spa tub in his bathroom. Angelo lounged across from her, his damp hair had darkened to bronze but his eyes were as startling, as vivid, as ever.

"Tired?" Angelo's tone was gentle.

She opened her eyes. His gaze held a tenderness she'd never seen before. "More like lazy. I feel like I never want to get out the water."

He smiled. "Oh, I guarantee you'll want to."

Her heartbeat bumped up. Her skin prickled, every inch of her instantly awake and energized.

"Angelo—"

Under the water his hand slid over her belly. "Our baby."

She smiled at him. "Our baby."

His gaze very intent, he said, "I love you, Gemma. Only ever you."

"I know," she murmured. "And for me there will only ever be you."

His eyes started to smoulder. "I believe you. I know you will never betray me.

"Come." He pulled her over him and water washed around them both at the sudden movement.

Gemma became intensely aware of the supple strength of his chest against her back, the hard length of his erection against her buttocks, ready and waiting.

Her head fell back into the crook of his shoulder where it joined his jaw, uncaring that her hair would be soaked.

When his other hand came up to play with her nipple, locking her in the circle of his arms, Gemma made a frantic, keening noise in the back of her throat and bucked her hips.

Angelo laughed softly in her ear. "More?"

The sound she made was barely coherent. One of his hands left her breast, snaked downward and slipped between her thighs.

There was something so intimate about being spread over Angelo's body, unable to see him, but aware of every arch and muscle of his flesh. She felt surrounded by him. He was under her, his arms around her, and all the while the wild flames licked between her legs.

She started to pant. She closed her eyes, focusing on the desire that burned through her.

When Angelo moved, her eyes snapped open. The next instant he hoisted her up onto the lip of the bath, parted her knees and knelt in front of her. She cried out as he entered her.

Heat ripped through her, wild and ferocious.

He moved again, Gemma's hands closed around his head, her fingers digging into the dark gold hair, and then she felt herself give.

"Angelo!' It was a cry of desperation, of satiation.

Angelo stood at the door of the church he'd been baptised in, waiting for his bride.

Connie, along with her latest husband and Gemma's parents, sat in the front row. From where he stood he could see Penelope dabbing the tears of happiness from her eyes. Tariq sat beside Connie, looking very grave, his white robes flowing behind him.

At the altar stood Zac and Pandora who'd agreed to be *koumbaro* and *koumbara* and crown him and Gemma in the wedding ceremony.

At last Angelo heard the drone of a motor and moved towards the entrance. A white limousine emblazoned with the resort's crest came down the winding road and slowed as it reached the church. He narrowed his eyes against the light, trying to catch a glimpse of Gemma.

The village priest materialized beside him. "It looks like your bride has arrived, my son."

Angelo started to move.

The priest's hand caught his arm. "Wait, let her alight."

The driver came around and opened the door.

One taut, elegant leg appeared. Then the other. Finally his bride emerged in a dress so white it dazzled him. He stepped forward, and barely noticed the priest's hand falling away, all his attention focused on the woman ahead.

She smiled at him and offered him her hand. He took it in both of his and raised it to his lips.

"I love you. I honestly do."

She rewarded him with that radiant smile that he knew would brighten the rest of his life.

* * * * *

STOP PRESS

The wedding of playboy hotelier Angelo Apollonides to songbird Gemma Allen was celebrated on the Greek island of Strathmos. When asked for comment, Apollonides stated that he and his wife would be honeymooning in Australia where he has recently acquired a string of brand-new resorts. "I will be taking it easier in the future, and I intend to learn to delegate and spend time with my wife and family."

Rumour has it that, having shaken off the title of the Most Eligible Bachelor in the Universe, Apollonides intends to waste no time in starting a family.

* * * * *

Don't miss the next Tessa Radley story.
Be sure to pick up
The Desert Bride of Al Zayed,
available from Mills & Boon® Desire™
this November.

RICH MAN'S
VENGEFUL SEDUCTION

by
Laura Wright

Dear Reader,

I don't want it to end.

Seriously, I loved writing this series. Three strong women with secrets who run a wife-for-hire agency out of my home town of Minneapolis…then slide three incredibly hot, alpha males in there to torment them.

LOVE IT!

Rich Man's Vengeful Seduction was the first book I thought of for this series. I wanted a hero who was as close to a devil as I could get. A millionaire bad boy who was just as wounded as the heroine and would believe he had to make her suffer as much as she'd unknowingly made him suffer. And I came up with Damien Sauer. I think the concept of two people who have known each other before, have loved, have been intimate, then one leaves, is an incredibly powerful plotline and my absolute favourite to write.

I hope you enjoy! Shoot me an e-mail and let me know what you think.

laura@laurawright.com

Best,

Laura

LAURA WRIGHT

has spent most of her life immersed in the world of acting, singing and competitive ballroom dancing. But when she started writing romance, she knew she'd found her true calling! Born and raised in Minneapolis, Laura has also lived in New York City, Milwaukee and Columbus, Ohio. Currently, she is happy to have set down her bags and made Los Angeles her home. And a blissful home it is – one that she shares with her theatrical production manager husband, Daniel, and three spoiled dogs. During those few hours of downtime from her beloved writing, Laura enjoys going to art galleries and movies, cooking for her hubby, walking in the woods, lazing around lakes, pottering in the kitchen and frolicking with her animals. Laura would love to hear from you. You can write to her at PO Box 5811 Sherman Oaks, CA 91413, USA or e-mail her at laura@laurawright.com.

To Isa, the strongest, smartest
and most amazing four-year-old I know!

One

There was nothing more unsettling than a devil in church.

Swathed in a black chiffon Vera Wang bridesmaid dress, her red hair piled on top of her head, Tess York stared at the man in the fourth pew, her palms going damp around the base of her bouquet of red peonies. His name was Damien Sauer and he was tall, dark and fierce looking—just as she remembered him. Once upon a time they had been together, boyfriend and girlfriend, lovers and friends, but then another man had come along. A man who was mild and shy and had seemed the safe choice at the time. Back then, she'd been a sucker for safe, and had walked away from Damien and the look of seething animosity that had followed her out the door.

The scent of pine from the decorative holiday garland strewn around the church ceased being romantic and festive and instead gave way to a horrible bout of nausea. *What is he doing back here?* she wondered nervously. He didn't belong here anymore. As far as she knew, he'd gotten out of Minnesota years ago and had moved to California. Rumor had it that he'd taken on the real estate market, flipping houses at the rate of two per month. Supposedly, he was unstoppable, went into every deal without a conscience and was now worth millions.

Tess was hardly surprised by his success. Six years ago he'd worked as lead carpenter for a construction company in town. His ideas were so clever, so innovative, his handiwork so skillful and beautiful, he was wanted by every contractor in the city.

But local jobs and local pay hadn't been enough for Damien. He'd wanted more and had been willing to risk everything to get where he wanted to go.

Tess watched him sit immobile in his seat with that arrogant lift to his chin as he witnessed Mary and Ethan exchange wedding vows. Tension moved through her neck and shoulders like a snake in search of a fat mouse. She had done everything to bury her wretched, mistake-filled past, erase the so-called life she'd lived, married to the most worthless of husbands. Along with her partners, Olivia Winston and Mary Kelley, she'd helped build a winning wife-for-hire business and had created a smooth, comfortable life for herself. All she wanted to do these days was act as though the past had never existed and continue to live happily and cautiously in the present.

But the devil had shown up in church.

Behind her, someone took to the keys of the piano, playing the introduction to *Phantom's* "All I Ask of You." Everyone in the wedding party turned—as rehearsed—to watch the two performers walk to the piano, then sing.

Everyone except Tess.

She couldn't take her eyes off Damien. Maybe if she stared hard enough at him he'd get up and leave. She almost laughed out loud at the stupid thought. He wasn't a man to be chased out, scared off. He had the strongest will of anyone she had ever known.

Her gaze moved over him. He had grown leaner in the body and broader in the shoulders since she'd last seen him, but his mouth was as hard as his expression now, as though he didn't make a habit of smiling.

What is he here for? Does he know Ethan? Or God forbid, Mary?

Tess shifted, her black heels feeling suffocatingly tight. There was no way she was ready to spill her guts about the past to her partners…

Beside her, No Ring Required's culinary expert, Olivia Winston leaned in. "Hey, I know the singing's not Broadway caliber, but no spacing out, okay?"

"Yeah. Right. Sure," Tess muttered, utterly distracted.

The pretty brunette frowned at her. "What's wrong with you?"

"Nothing," Tess said quickly.

"Doesn't look like nothing," Olivia muttered.

Refusing to make a scene at her partner's wedding, Tess forced herself to face the singers. She had to get a grip here. Maybe Damien didn't even know she was there—maybe he'd forgotten all about her. Maybe he was married…with two kids and a dog named Buster. After all it had been six years. Look at all that had happened to her….

But as she half listened to the singers belt it out for the bride and groom, the music swelling and filling the church, she had an odd feeling, as though she were being watched, as though little bugs were crawling into the red curls at her hairline and nipping at her skin. It was a feeling she'd had only one time before.

The day she'd turned her back on the devilish Damien Sauer and walked out.

"Sir, would you like me to take you home?"

As his driver navigated through the congested downtown Minneapolis traffic, Damien sat in the back of his limousine, the collar of his black coat kissing the hard line of his jaw. "No. I'm going to the Georgian."

"I'm sorry sir. I don't think I heard you—"

"Take me to the Georgian Hotel," Damien said evenly. "I'm going to the reception."

"But, sir, you never go…" The driver's voice trailed off.

"Is there a problem, Robert?" Damien asked impatiently, as outside the long, black car, snowflakes pelted the windows.

"Sir?" Robert glanced up into the rearview mirror, his pale brown eyes not exactly meeting that of his employer's. "If I can speak frankly—"

Damien raised a brow. "You may…if you keep your eyes on the road while doing it. This isn't the dry and mild Los Angeles weather. The roads in Minneapolis can be pretty slick."

"Yes, sir." Robert turned his attention back to the road, two hands locked to the wheel.

Damien released a breath. "So, what do you want to know?"

"In the four years I have been working for you, this is the first wedding reception of a business associate you have ever attended."

"Is it?" Damien said tonelessly.

"Yes, sir."

"Hmm."

"Very important business then, sir?"

The car slowed, made a turn then stopped. Damien looked up, frowned. "Are we here?"

"Yes, sir, but there's a line of cars ahead of us."

They were more than a few yards from the entrance to the hotel, but Damien wasn't a man to wait. He reached for the door handle and pulled. "I'll get out here, Robert."

"But, sir?" The driver glanced over his shoulder, uncertain. "Shall I—"

"No, no. Stay in the car."

Robert nodded. "All right, sir."

Damien was half out the door when he turned back. "And, Robert?"

"Yes, sir."

"To answer your question, this reception is about something far more important than business." He stepped out of the car. "Be out front in one hour."

The ballroom in the Georgian Hotel was *the* most spectacular sight in Minneapolis for a wedding reception, beautifully appointed with gilded ceilings, crystal chandeliers and a black-and-white-marble dance floor. In any season the room could knock you off your feet, but in December, there was an extra shot of fabulous as the ballroom was decked out in white Christmas lights, spruce trees, mistletoe, and atop every black glass place setting, handmade chocolate candy canes nestled sweetly inside mini Christmas stockings.

Tess York was a self-described chocoholic, and five minutes after her arrival to the hotel her mini stocking was empty. Beside her seat was Olivia's, and the only reason a candy cane still lay safely on her plate was that Tom Radley, No Ring Required's very first client five years ago, and a family friend of Mary's, had taken Tess by the hand and forced her onto the dance floor before she could snatch it up.

On a rectangular stage beside the dance floor, a woman who sounded shockingly similar to Natalie Cole belted out love songs.

Next to Tess, Olivia and her fiancé, Mac Valentine, moved to the music. The pair were so handsome, so sharp looking they could have easily been mistaken for a Hollywood couple. Stunning in a black bridesmaid dress similar to Tess's, her dark hair long and loose about her bare shoulders, Olivia turned her brown doe eyes on Tess and cracked a smile. "You are one amazingly bad dancer, you know that?"

"Gee, thanks," Tess said dryly.

"Not true," insisted Tom Radley, sidestepping to avoid contact with the heel of Tess's shoe as she executed an awkward spin. "Don't listen to her, Tess." He glared at Olivia. "She's as graceful as a swan, light as a feather."

Olivia snorted. "As long as she doesn't step on your feet, right?"

"Easy now, my love," Mac said, pulling his girl closer.

Tess made a gesture with her hand as though she was flicking away an annoying bug. "Move along, Winston. I'm sure there are other people on this dance floor whose self-esteem you can destroy tonight."

Olivia laughed. "Right. As if you could ever be bested, Tess. You have more confidence in your little pinky than a grizzly bear at feeding time."

"Hmm," Tess said, her brow creased. "Not sure how I should take that."

Ever the gentleman, Mac jumped in. "As a compliment. And I think you dance beautifully." He attempted to look innocent, but the guy's smile had way too much rascal in it to be believable.

"Flattery won't get you anywhere with me, Mr. Valentine," Tess said, ducking her head to walk underneath Tom's arm as he led her into a spin.

Mac shrugged, then turned to his fiancé and leaned in to kiss her neck. "How about you? Will flattery get me anywhere with you?"

Olivia snuggled closer in his arms. "Yup."

Tess rolled her eyes. Leaning into her partner, she whispered, "Let's move away from the lovebirds before the cherubs flying over their heads accidentally shoot us with their arrows."

Laughing, Tom said, "You got it," and steered her away.

But when they reached the other side of the dance floor, there was a man standing there. He was clearly waiting for them, his cool blue eyes regarding them with an interested, though unfriendly stare. He was tall, wide in the shoulders and dressed in a very expensive tux. His black hair was cropped short and his full mouth looked hard and capable of cruel words.

Tess's heart leaped into her throat and remained there, pounding away unsympathetically. It was one thing to have him sitting ten feet away, his gaze trained on Mary and Ethan as they gave themselves to each other—it was another to have him in front of her, reaching for her hand.

Damien Sauer glanced at Tom, lifted an eyebrow. "If you don't mind."

Slightly nervous, Tom's answer came out sounding winded. "Of course I mind. But…well, I'm good at sharing."

"That's admirable," Damien said darkly, easing Tess from Tom's arms into his own. "I'm not."

Tess was not the kind of woman who would allow a man to call the shots—not anymore, at any rate. If anyone else at any other time had jumped in and pulled her away from her partner the way Damien had, she'd have been tempted to deck him. But this man was different, and so was her reaction to him. It was as though time had never separated them, and once in his arms, she felt so good, so warm, she didn't even attempt to pull away from him.

As the music played all around them, Damien settled into a slow rhythm, his gaze burning into hers. "Hello, Tess."

She hadn't said his name out loud in six years. Guess now was as good a time as any. "Damien Sauer. Wow. It's been a long time."

"Not that long," he said. His voice was deep, deeper than she remembered, but the tone was the same and it washed over her, bringing back a hundred different emotions. "I saw you at the engagement party, and I thought you saw me. Maybe not."

"No, I did. I mean, yes. But I didn't think…" She shrugged at her own inability to speak coherently. "I guess I wasn't sure…"

"You're stuttering, Tess," he said, arching a brow. "That's not like you."

No, it wasn't. But strange, complicated things had always happened when this man touched her. And right now his hand, wrapped lightly around hers, and his body just inches away were making her breathe a little funny. "What I was trying to say, completely inarticulately, was that I didn't know you and Ethan were friends."

"We're not," he said plainly. "He's looking to buy one of my properties and I was looking for an invitation to his wedding."

Her heart dropped. "Really?"

"Yes."

"Why?"

He gave her a sardonic grin. "I've heard that your business is quite a success," he said, ignoring her question. "You've done well for yourself."

His words sounded more like an observation than a compliment. "I think so. But not as well as you, it seems."

He nodded. "After you left town, I became very focused."

Of course he was going to go there. Make her damn uncomfortable, maybe break out in a sweat. "Well, focused can be good."

"Yes, it can. In fact, I might go so far as to say that I owe a great deal of my fortune to you."

The scent of the spruce tree to their left was overpowering. "I'm sure that's not—"

"Don't be so modest, Tess. You were an inspiration…"

It was too much. The whole thing—his sardonic compliments, her nervousness. She was not going to put herself in the position of being freaked out around a man anymore. She stopped dancing. Music played and people swayed, but she stared expectantly at Damien Sauer. "What's going on here? Why did you come?"

"I wanted to see you." There was zero warmth behind his eyes, and the look he gave her chilled the blood in her veins.

"Well, you saw me," she said, turning away. "Thank you for the dance."

He took her hand and placed it through his arm. "I'll take you back to your table."

She thought about wrenching her arm free, but she wasn't going to cause a scene, so she let him lead her. As they walked, Tess couldn't help but notice the way women stared at Damien: hungry, needy. Just the way she'd stared at him once upon a time.

When they got to the table reserved for the wedding party, Tess sat and hoped that Damien would just take off, that the dance and the verbal sparring would be the end of it. But he didn't leave. Instead he sat beside her.

"So, how's Henry?" His voice was low and cold.

She stared at him, looked into those deep blue eyes and found clarity. He wasn't here on business or to just "see" her. He'd come to the wedding to confront her or hurt her. But why now, after six years, she wasn't sure. She looked directly into his eyes and said evenly, "My husband passed away. About five years ago."

Damien nodded, but didn't look surprised. "I'm sorry."

"Are you?"

His brows lifted. "I could say no but what would that make me?"

She shrugged. "Cruel."

"How about honest?"

"How about both?"

Out of the corner of her eye, Tess spotted Mary and Olivia on the other side of the dance floor, and her heart jumped. They were staring at her and Damien, curious looks on their faces. Tess knew her partners well enough to know that in about thirty seconds they were going to be headed her way. She wasn't about to have her past and past mistakes laid bare at her partner's wedding.

She turned back to Damien, hoping that her face had not gone pale. "Dinner is going to be served soon. Maybe we can catch up another time."

"Are you trying to get rid of me, Tess?" he asked, studying her face.

"No."

"I can tell when you're lying. Always could."

"Fine." Her jaw tightened. "My partners are on their way over here and they know—"

"Nothing about me?" Damien finished for her, a flash of venomous pleasure lighting his eyes.

"They know nothing about you or Henry or my life before we started the company."

"Why is that?"

"It's none of your business." There was no time for this. Mary and Olivia were just a few feet away. "You can say whatever you need to say. But not here, not now. Another time."

He considered this for a moment, then nodded. "All right."

Relief accosted her, and she said quickly, "Okay. Goodbye, then."

He stood. "I'll see you tomorrow, Tess."

She looked up. "What?"

"I'll be at your office tomorrow at one."

"No!"

Mary and Olivia were almost upon them. Damien leaned in close to Tess's ear, the heat from his breath making her hair stand on end and her heart twist painfully. This she remembered, and long ago this she had loved.

"I'm not here to reminisce about old times," he uttered darkly. "I'm here to collect on a debt that was never paid."

Tess's head started spinning. What debt was he talking about?

"Six years ago," he continued, "you made a promise to me. One that was never fulfilled. I'm here to make sure you fulfill it. Because if you don't, everything you hold dear will crumble."

He stood just in time to greet Mary and Olivia, shaking their hands and complimenting the bride on the ceremony and reception. Dumbstruck, Tess just stared at her plate and the empty stocking. Through the din of her overactive brain, she heard Damien wish them both well, then walk away.

"Nice," Olivia said, taking her seat beside Tess. "Very cute."

"Gorgeous and charming," Mary remarked, righting her tiara before sitting in the chair designated for the bride. "And looking smitten with our girl here."

"Did you get his number, Tess?" Olivia asked.

Tess nodded and said hoarsely, "Yes. I've got his number all right."

Two

In the four and a half years that Tess York had been with No Ring Required, she'd called in sick three times. The first time was in the winter of 2004, when she'd had the flu so badly, she'd passed out on the way to her car. The second time was last summer when she'd had her wisdom teeth out, and the third time was today when she'd woken up with a nasty little hangover.

She wasn't a big drinker. Actually she wasn't even a little drinker, but last night, after seeing Damien and having the past hurled back in her face, she'd enjoyed a few glasses of champagne too many.

Garbed in ratty old sweats and stretched out on the couch with her cat, Hepburn, Tess stared at the TV. Trying to ignore her pounding head, she watched

Montel Williams take a seat beside his favorite psychic guest, who was telling one audience member after another that what they probably had in their house was a ghost who had unfinished business.

"Maybe you can give us some advice on how to get rid of those ghosts," Tess muttered at the screen.

So far, she'd only taken steps to avoid hers. Mary was already on her honeymoon, so Olivia was going to be the only one in to work today. The one appointment Tess did have wasn't on the books, and she was more than willing to skip it.

As the psychic rambled on about heaven and the light, Tess let her eyes close and her mind shut off for a while. She must've drifted off because when she woke up, there was a soap opera on the television and someone knocking on her apartment door. Her head still pounding, she padded over to the door and looked out the peephole.

When she saw who it was, she swore silently, turned around and sagged against the door.

Damien.

"Tess?"

Accompanying her headache, her stomach twisted sickly at the sound of his voice.

"Tess, I know you're there."

"What do you want, Damien?" she yelled into the door.

"You know exactly what I want. I was pretty damn clear last night. Now open the door."

"I'm sick."

"Yes, Olivia was kind enough to tell me that. After I'd driven all the way over there."

Tess sighed. This was not how she did things—hiding behind doors so she wouldn't have to deal with uncomfortable meetings and threats from an old boyfriend. That was the way the married Tess had handled herself, the Tess who'd had a reason to feel nervous and afraid. But that part of her life was over.

She flipped the lock and opened the door wide.

Damien stood there, filling up her doorway. Freshly shaven and showered and dressed in a navy blue suit so fine it probably came straight from the Gucci runway show in Milan.

Knowing she looked like her cat's chew toy after a gnarly play session, she lifted her chin and said in her most superior tone, "I never agreed to see you, Damien."

A slow, cool smile curved his lips as he looked her over. "Well, there she is."

"There who is?"

"The firecracker I used to know. The woman worthy of that mass of red hair." He leaned against the doorjamb. "After last night and hearing all that stuttering and fear of what your partners might find out, I thought she was gone. I wondered what or who had taken that fire out of her."

Well, he could keep on wondering, she thought dryly. There was no way he was ever going to know anything about her life with Henry, about the scars that remained.

He narrowed his eyes, studied her. "You look…"

"Sick?" she offered.

"Did you drink last night?"

"That's really none of your business."

"Champagne gives you intense headaches, remember?"

"No," she lied.

He crossed his arms over his chest. "Are you going to let me in?"

"I think you can say whatever cryptic thing you need to say from here."

"Fine, but I did bring you matzo ball soup…well, actually Robert picked it up." He held up a white deli bag. "And you look like you could use it. But you can't eat it standing in the entryway."

"Who's Robert?"

"My driver?"

She rolled her eyes. "There's a point at which someone has too much money."

"Not really."

He tried to walk past her, but she stopped him. "Soup first."

He handed her the bag, and she let him pass. After a quick look around her living room, he sat on the couch. She picked up the remote and switched off the television, then dropped into the leather armchair a few feet away.

His brow lifted. "Are you afraid of me?"

"Fear is a useless emotion," she began. But then she shrugged. Instead of inspirational quotes, maybe honesty…or some form of hybrid might be a better tack to take with this man. "After what you said last night, or didn't say, I think feeling apprehensive isn't a bizarre response."

His gaze grew serious, his mouth hard. "No."

She placed the deli bag on the coffee table, then looked up at him. "Enough bantering back and forth. You and I both know this isn't a social call, so let's get to it."

He sat back and regarded her. "Do you remember the red house in Tribute?"

A rush of memories flooded into her mind along with a deep burn of sadness. It had been their spot, a starter home, in a tiny town, that Damien had bought for a song as his first investment property. In the high days of their romance, they had walked the main drag of that town, sharing their plans for the future, then later they'd shared a bed.

She met his gaze and nodded. "I remember."

"I want to renovate it."

This surprised her. "You never did?"

"No."

"Okay. So, what does this have to do with me?"

"You made a promise to me in that house, one week before you left."

Tess's heart plummeted into her stomach, and she searched her memory.

"You promised to help me renovate. You wanted to make it a home, if I recall correctly." His voice dropped, soured. "I expect you to keep that promise."

"You can't be serious?"

"I am."

And then it all came back in a rush. It had happened a week before she left, just like he'd said. One week before Henry had asked her to be his wife. One week before she'd forced herself to realize that with a man like Damien she'd never have the kind of life she'd planned for herself. The kind of stable, family-friendly life she'd promised herself when she was seventeen, after her parents' deaths. She stared at him and shook her head. "But why? Why do you care now—"

"It's a chapter I need to finish," he said, his tone cool. He stood, then reached inside his coat and pulled out an envelope. "Here are the keys, the address—in case you've forgotten—and a formidable amount of cash."

"What—"

"I need you to start right away."

He was crazy. She stood. "Damien, I have no intention of—"

"I need the job done in two weeks."

She didn't even try to suppress a bitter laugh. "Impossible."

"I leave in two weeks, back to California. I want to make sure everything is done. And I want a full remodel, not just a coat of paint and new towels for the bathroom."

She put up a hand. "Stop right now. This is not going to happen. Two weeks is Christmas."

He shrugged. "You can do your shopping up in Tribute."

"Not funny, Damien. I have a business to run—"

"Yes, and if it will make you feel better, tell your partners that I hired you." His gaze moved over her hungrily. "My wife for hire for two weeks, fixing up my home."

Awareness moved through her, but she shook it off. She walked to the apartment door and opened it. "I'm not going to play this game with you anymore."

He didn't move. "Good, because I don't play games. You will go to Tribute and you will fix up the house."

"Or what?"

"Or that business of yours will have to find a new location, which will take a lot of time and money that a new business can't really afford."

"Are you actually threatening me?" The words ground out from between her teeth. "Because I don't take kindly to threats."

"I'm telling you to think about your future," he said, his tone dark with warning. "And the future of your partners."

"What the hell does that mean?"

He walked to her, faced her. "I know the owner of your building and I think I could convince him to not renew your lease in January."

Her heart took a nosedive. "How do you know our lease is up in January?" She was shaking now, her breathing uneven. "Do you have this jerk owner in your pocket?"

"I don't have to. I'm the jerk."

Tess held her breath, and silence filled the space. She was trying to process what he had said and, more important, what it meant.

"I own your building, Tess."

She shook her head. "I don't believe you."

"My company owns your building," he said evenly. "Three years now."

"Why are you doing this?"

"I have a business, too."

"What is this business of yours? Revenge? Hurt feelings because I chose another man over you?"

He seemed to grow a foot taller before her eyes, and his gaze became dark and menacing.

She looked directly at him. "You need to grow up, Damien."

His lips formed a sneer. "I'll expect you at the house tomorrow afternoon. Don't disappoint me."

"Who are you?" she called after him as he walked down the hall. "The man I used to know would never do something like—"

"The *boy* you used to know was a fool," he said over his shoulder as he walked into the elevator. "Enjoy the soup."

Tess shut the door with a little too much force. That bastard. *Never. No way.* He could take his threats and shove them where the sun don't shine. She spotted the deli bag on the coffee table and snatched it up, stalked into the kitchen. But as she dumped the soup into the sink, her rational mind started to rear its unwanted head. If he did own her building—a fact she would check immediately—he could follow through on his threat and kick them all out on their backsides.

Did he really hate her that much…?

Tess leaned on the counter and released a breath. Her headache from earlier was gone, but it looked like she was about to get another…one that would last about two weeks.

According to some major athletes and those perfect people who work out a lot, exercise is the best way of reaching a state of true introspection.

Well, Tess was counting on it.

"So, renovating a house? Like new paint and drywall? Or we talking air ducts and toilet flanges?"

It was 7:00 a.m. and Tess had met Olivia at the gym for a workout. Earlier that morning, say around 6:15, she'd sat in her office at NRR and gone over lease agreement after lease agreement, only to discover that Damien's company did indeed own her building. It hadn't taken her long to get it—there was nothing to do but face the fire. Damien was in need of some vengeance, and from the look on his face yesterday he wasn't going to hesitate to kick them all out of the building if Tess didn't comply with his demands.

So, at eleven o'clock, she was leaving for Tribute. She'd get in, do the job and get out.

"I'm not sure what I'll find when I get there," Tess said to Olivia, her breathing uneven as she picked up the pace when the treadmill inclined a notch. "Guess I'll have to wait and see."

Beside Tess, Olivia rode a stationary bike at a snail's pace. "The client didn't give you specifics?"

"He asked for a full remodel."

"Who is the client, by the way? Do I know him?"

Tess hesitated. She wanted to tread lightly here. "He's the man from Mary and Ethan's wedding."

Olivia's brows shot up. "Mr. Tall, Dark and Dreamy? The one who came into NRR looking for you yesterday?"

"That's the one."

"Wow. He moves pretty fast."

Tess bit her lip. She hated to lie to her partner, but there was no way she was going to explain the past and the present circumstances. Or what was at stake if she didn't take this job. "We spoke this morning. He needs the job done ASAP. He needs to get back to California in a couple weeks."

"He's looking to sell the place?"

"I think so."

"That's a big job to take on right before Christmas. You sure you want to tackle it?"

"Yeah. Not a problem. I'll probably do a good portion of the work myself, then hire a few subcontractors."

"You're gonna have to pay double because of the holiday." Sweat-free and smiling, Olivia stepped off the bike and came to stand by the treadmill. "Speaking of which, what are you doing for Christmas?"

Ah…same thing she did every year. Join a few people in her building on Christmas Eve for some food and music, then just relax on Christmas Day. She shrugged. "Not sure."

"I want you to spend the day with Mac and me."

Tess grinned at her partner. It was a nice offer. "That's sweet, Liv. But—"

"No buts."

Tess stepped off the treadmill and grabbed her towel. "We'll see."

"And you know," Olivia continued. "Mac has a friend…"

"That's nice," Tess said quickly. "Everyone needs friends."

Cocking her head to the side, Olivia gave her a soft smile. "I want you find the right man."

"I don't want the right man, Liv."

Olivia laughed. "How about the wrong one, then?"

Been there, done that. She tossed Olivia a tight smile. "I have to go home. Shower and change, take the cat to the vet, then get on the road."

She nodded. "I'll call you."

"Okay."

Tess owned a pretty great SUV. It was sleek and black, had four-wheel drive, leather seats, a killer sound system and an easily accessible cup holder for her coffee. It also had a panel that displayed the outside temperature.

Normally Tess glanced at this panel once during her regular drive time, but on this trip she'd checked the thing every few minutes. Mostly because she couldn't believe how quickly the temperature dropped—five degrees every thirty minutes.

Northern Minnesota in winter was as close to the Arctic as most people ever got. Freezing temperatures arrived in October and stayed around until April, making everyone up there a bit nutty. Tess shook her head. And she was about to spend the next two weeks there. Good thing she'd packed her parka.

Just before two o'clock, she pulled off the freeway and drove the short distance to downtown Tribute, which was comprised of four wide, unclogged streets with a handful of mom-and-pop stores, a gas station and a diner. It hadn't changed much in six years, and for a moment Tess recalled how she and Damien had shared a burger in the diner and a good deal of necking behind the gas station.

Tess slowed to a crawl as she drove down Yarr Lane, then pulled into the third driveway on the left. She killed the engine and stepped out of the car. The yard was three feet deep in snow, but other than that the little red cottage looked very much the same as it had. Which, incidentally wasn't saying much.

To start with it needed a fresh coat of paint, a

clean doorknob, coach lamp, knocker and new address numbers. And that was just on the outside.

As she walked to the door, she recalled thinking that Damien had bought this house for them, for a future together. But he had been quick to point out that he'd purchased the house as an investment property: the first of many—to be fixed up and sold for a profit. Hearing that had crushed her, made her realize that they'd wanted very different things from life.

She unlocked the house and stepped inside. It was completely bare, not one piece of furniture, and there was dust on every visible surface.

She did a quick walk through and found that the two small bedrooms were well maintained, just in need of a cleaning, new fixtures and a few coats of paint. The kitchen and bathroom, however, were, in a word, horrible. Outdated and showing years of wear. Both spaces needed new floors, countertops, some drywall patching, new appliances, fixtures and paint.

She stood in the living room and stared. The place needed a lot, a complete overhaul. First thing she had to do was go into town, get some cleaning supplies and the phone numbers of some skilled labor.

"So you're the city girl Damien hired?"

Startled, Tess whirled around. Walking into the house was a woman in her late sixties, bundled up in a dark-blue down jacket and matching ski cap. She had smooth chocolate-brown skin, high cheekbones and cat-shaped violet eyes. She was short and a little plump, but even at her age she was startlingly beautiful.

Tess stuck out a hand. "Hi, I'm Tess York."

"Wanda Bennett," the woman said, shaking Tess's hand with the firm grip of a lumberjack. "I'm the property manager here in Tribute, and the owner of the food market in town."

"It's nice to meet you."

The woman nodded, then glanced around. "Sweet place, but it needs some work."

"Sure does," Tess agreed.

"Never understood why Damien left it to rot like this. Not his style."

No, it wasn't his style. And he had just left the place to rot until he'd found the time to blackmail his former girlfriend into fixing it up. Tess didn't think that sharing this information with Wanda was appropriate. Of course, the woman had called Damien by his first name, so maybe they were friends, maybe she knew exactly who Tess was and what she was doing here.

"So, you're probably wondering why I barged in like this?" Wanda asked.

"You said you're the property manager…"

"Sure, I turned on the heat and water, but Damien wanted me to give you this." She took a fat envelope out of her jacket pocket and handed it to Tess. "Here."

"What is it?"

"He wired it this morning. He thought you might need more than what he gave you," Wanda explained.

"For fixing up the place. He wants it furnished, as well."

Tess looked inside the envelope. A three-inch stack of hundred-dollar bills. Good Lord. He'd already given her four times that much. But then again you never knew what problems might come up in an older house. She looked up at Wanda again. "Is there a furniture store in town?"

"Nope."

"Lighting, hardware?"

"There is a hardware store in Tribute—it's on Main, next to the diner—and you can get furniture and light fixtures in Jackson, that's about fifty miles away." She paused for a moment, then said, "But I think Damien might want this place fixed up with the local flavor. A few people make their own furnishings around here, I'd talk to them."

"Do they work quickly? I'm under a bit of a time crunch."

Wanda shrugged. "Depends."

Tess sighed. Looked as though she was just going to have to figure everything out on her own. She gave Wanda a quick smile and said, "I'm going to head over to the motel and check in, then."

"Ruby's place?"

"Yes. I saw it in the phone book."

Wanda pressed her lips together and looked at the ceiling.

"Is something wrong?"

"Nope."

Tess's shoulders fell. "What? Is Ruby an ax murder or something?"

"No. Ruby's lovely." She pointed to the envelope in Tess's hand. "It's just that before you go to Ruby's, you might want to go here first."

Tess glanced down at the address written on the envelope. "What is this?"

"Damien asked that you be there at four o'clock."

"Four o'clock when?"

"Today," Wanda said evenly.

Tess looked down at her watch. "It's three-thirty now."

She waved her hand as if it was nothing to worry about. "It's just a short drive. I'll give you directions."

On a sigh, Tess grabbed her purse and searched for a pen. She had really wanted to clean up the place before it got dark. Damn Damien and his demands. "So, what's at this address?" she asked Wanda. "A contractor or a plumber or something."

Wanda shrugged her shoulders again. "Or something."

Tess glared at her. "Did Damien tell you to be this annoyingly evasive?"

At that, a smile tugged at the woman's lips and she pointed to the pen in Tess's hand. "I'll give you those directions now."

Three

The drive took under five minutes, but it was all uphill, and the roads were slick, as daylight had decided to knock off a little early. When Tess pulled into the driveway and saw the house, she thought she'd made a mistake with the directions. She glanced down to check if she had the correct address.

She did.

Who in the world lived here? she wondered. An artist? A famous, reclusive artist who had cut off his ear, then moved to Tribute for the peace and quiet and frigid climate?

Tess got out of the car to a blast of arctic air and looked up at the massive glass fortress. Whoever lived here, she mused, had better have something to do with the renovating process.

She walked to the front door. It wouldn't surprise her if this was some kind of roadblock that Damien had put up to mess with her—picking out artwork for the walls before they were even painted, or something equally wasteful in the time management department. Sure, he wanted the house done in two weeks, but he wanted to make every move she made that much more difficult in the process.

Her teeth chattering, she rang the bell. Thankfully, she didn't have to wait more than ten seconds before it opened. For a moment she thought she'd come face-to-face with Danny Devito. Then she realized the impossibility of such a thought and granted the man a friendly smile. "Hello. I'm Tess York. I have an appointment."

"Of course." He stepped aside. "Please come in."

The first thing Tess noticed when she walked into the entryway was how warm the space was. Not the architecture. That was sleek and sexy and ultramodern. But warm in temperature. Even with the sun going down outside, the light that had been filtering in from the many windows all day heated the house toasty warm.

The man she'd mentally referred to as Danny Devito took her coat, then gestured toward the open living area. The space was perfectly outfitted with expensive, modern furnishings—some that could double as pieces of artwork—that matched the home's architecture. "Come with me, please."

Tess gave the man a grim smile. "I'm sorry, no can do." She had a rule about this kind of situation. If she didn't know where she was and who was in charge, she remained close to the exit. "I'll wait here."

The man looked a tad worried. "He wouldn't like that."

"Who is he?" Tess asked.

"My employer."

Tess rolled her eyes. This was getting nuts. Forget Damien's orders. If he wanted to have this guy's art or whatever the man was selling, then he could get it himself.

Perhaps sensing that she was ready to bolt, "Danny" said in a hopeful voice, "If you could wait one moment, Ms. York?"

Tess released a breath. "Okay. But seriously, this had better get clear real soon."

Like a fretful mouse, the man scurried away, through the double-height living room and its beautiful floor-to-ceiling soapstone fireplace. Tess started counting to sixty. She got to fifty-one before she heard the butler returning.

But it wasn't the butler.

She heard him before she saw him, and her gut went tight. "Giving the help a hard time, are you Tess?"

Tess watched him walk toward her, the master of the manor, dressed in jeans and a black sweater, looking too gorgeous, too dangerous for words.

She shook her head as he approached. "Your house, huh? I should've guessed." She pointed a finger at him. "And, for the record, I wasn't trying to give anyone a hard time. I was being firm. But maybe he's not used to strong women coming here."

"Olin," he said, walking into the living room. "His name is Olin."

Tess followed. "Right. Well, maybe Olin's not used to you having strong women around."

Damien's eyes were cool and brilliant blue as he sat in a black leather armchair. "Only one woman comes here, and she's plenty strong."

"Only one, huh? How progressive of you," she said sarcastically, taking the chair across from him.

"You met her today, in fact."

"Wanda?" Tess said.

He nodded. "She's a good friend."

"How nice."

"I don't bring the women I date here."

The women. Plural. So, there were many. Of course there were many. She pushed away the nip of jealously in her gut and got down to business. "Why am I here, Damien? And with all the mystery?"

"Mystery?" he repeated.

She put her hand up. "No, forget it. I don't need an answer for that. I get it. You wanted me to see your amazing spread, how well you've done—and I have. It's fantastic, you're successful. Okay?" When he said nothing, just looked mildly amused, she pressed on. "Now, I have a job to do—one that was forced on me—and I'd like to get it done as soon as possible."

"I didn't have Wanda tell you that it was my house

you were coming to because I assumed you'd still be pretty pissed off at me and you'd probably stand me up. And I needed you to see this house so you could see my style, what I wanted for the red house."

Oh. Well, that made a small amount of sense. "You want the red house to go modern? It's a cozy little cottage."

"Cozy cottages can and should have modern touches."

"Fine. Okay. Cozy, but modern it is." She stood. "If I could get my coat, I need to go over to the motel and check in before it gets dark—"

"No."

She stared at him, puzzled. "No, what?," she said, laughing. "I don't get my coat back?"

"You're not staying at the motel, Tess."

"Excuse me?"

"No motels or hotels."

This guy was something else. "Where am I supposed to stay, then?"

Damien sat back in his chair.

Tess crossed her arms over her chest. "If you think I'm going to stay here, then the LA smog has really rotted your—"

"No. You're not staying here."

Her hands balled into fists, and she said through gritted teeth, "What do you suggest, then? Building an igloo?"

"You'll stay in the red house." He said it as though it was the simplest, most logical solution in the world.

Her stomach churned with irritation. "The red house is filthy and unfurnished."

"You'll change that."

Nostrils flaring with anger, Tess stood there, her body rigid. She wanted to scream at him, maybe clock him with that mean left hook she'd learned in self-defense class at the Y. But that was just what he wanted—a mad, frustrated, vulnerable Tess York.

Not going to happen.

"So, more punishment, is that it?" she said tightly.

A slow smile pulled at his lips.

Tess nodded. "Have at it, Sauer. Just know that when this is all done and you're back in California making another million, the only thing that'll have changed on this end will be that small amount of regret I felt when I walked out on you."

His gaze flashed with icy contempt. "It's getting dark. I'll have Olin get your coat."

"Don't bother." She left him standing there and walked to the entryway. After pulling her coat from the stainless steel closet, she left.

Every weekend for one year, Damien had come to Tribute to supervise the building of his hilltop house. It was everything he'd ever wanted, a twelve-thousand-square-foot glass house; a modern, minimalist fortress that overlooked the little red house he couldn't let go of. He had designed the house so that he could see the red cottage from nearly every window. It was how he'd wanted it, needed it.

Whenever he looked down at it, he was reminded of her, and the feeling of betrayal had spurred him on, had made him wise and passionless and highly successful in business.

Damien took the elevator to the roof and stepped out on the deck. Snow was falling in sweet, tiny flakes, melting at once as they hit the heated stone floor. He could see for miles from up there, but he didn't even try to look beyond the borders of Tribute. His gaze rested where it always did—on the red house. A tiny speck of a place that mocked him big-time.

Right now it was dark. Obviously, she wasn't back yet.

"Sir?"

"Yes?" Damien didn't turn around to address Olin.

"Dinner is ready, sir."

"Nothing for me tonight."

Olin paused for a moment, then uttered a quick, "Yes, sir," before he disappeared.

Damien wasn't hungry. Not for food, at any rate. What he wanted was her. Her body and her soul. He wanted to make her hate him, then make her love him, then crush her as she'd crushed him.

And, after their meeting earlier, it looked as though he was well on his way....

"Seriously?"

Ruby Deets looked suitably remorseful as she shook her head, her platinum-blond beehive shifting as she moved. "I'm sorry, hon. Wish there was something I could do for you."

Starving and running out of the half cup of patience she had remaining, Tess leaned against Ruby's front desk. "You can. You can give me a room."

"Can't."

"He doesn't own you."

"No, that's true." Ruby leaned in, her double chin just hovering above the tarnished welcome bell. "But he does own the motel."

Tess grit her teeth. Of course he did.

"Is the grocery store still open?" she asked.

Ruby checked the clock on the wall. "You got another thirty minutes."

"Okay, thanks."

"You must've done something to really piss him off," Ruby remarked dryly.

"He's a man," Tess said, then turned to leave, calling over her shoulder, "They're not that hard to piss off."

Three hours later Tess sat on a blanket from her car in the red house's tiny living room. After she'd gotten rid of the cobwebs, scrubbed down the walls and mopped the floor in the one room, she'd built a fire in the brick fireplace and opened her deli sandwich and chips.

Between the rough accommodations and all the thoughts running through her brain, from Damien to the remodel to her past, she was not going to be sleeping much tonight.

For about a half a second, she'd contemplated going home and just explaining to Olivia what she was up against. Her partner was pretty understanding and very cool. No doubt, she'd pat Tess on the back, whip up a five-course meal—three of them heavy on the chocolate—then suggest they find a new office building immediately.

Oh, such a tempting thought.

But Tess was no coward, no quitter. She would take control of this situation and turn the red house into a comfortably modern masterpiece. Then, when the two weeks were up, she'd pack up and go home, put Damien behind her for good.

She took another bite of her egg salad sandwich. To make this work, she would have to stay one step ahead of him, try to anticipate what he would throw at her next. Because if there was one thing she could be sure of, it was that Damien Sauer had plans for her. Possibly destructive plans, and she had to be ready.

Four

"Bed's in the trunk, Tess."

"Thanks, Mr Opp." Tess pulled several hundred-dollar bills from the envelope stash. It was close to four in the afternoon and she was pretty wiped. She'd been cleaning since sunup. Later, on a trip into town for a late lunch, she had found the name and address of a man who sold handmade furnishings and gifts. She'd purchased a beautiful walnut bed, complete with mattress and box spring, as well as a few other pieces for the living room that she was going to pick up later in the week.

Mr. Opp took the money and gave Tess a tired grin. He was a tall, lanky man in his early seventies, who had a pack of little dogs that continually weaved their way in and out of his legs whenever he stopped to talk. "How about a few more sheets of *lefsa?* Butter and sugar on top?"

"No, thanks," Tess said graciously, eyeing the stack of round, flat potato bread. A half hour earlier she had made quite a dent in that stack. "I don't think I could eat another bite."

He grinned and said kindly, "I'll wrap up a few for the road, then."

"I'd appreciate that." With the limited selection of food in Tribute, she wasn't about to decline the offer. Especially when the food in question was ridiculously delicious.

She gave Mr. Opp another round of thank-yous, then got in her car and took off. As she drove back to the little red house, she felt better, as though she might be getting a handle on the situation. After last night and sleeping on the hardwood floor, just the thought of having a bed to sleep on tonight was a massive improvement. Sure, it was going to take every ounce of muscle she had to lug the thing inside and set it up, as Mr. Opp had no delivery service, but hey, it would be worth it.

The sun was settling itself into the horizon when she pulled into the driveway. Before bringing in the bed, she decided to grab some firewood from the side of the house first. She'd kept the heat on all day, but as she'd discovered last night, it wasn't the greatest source of warmth in the world.

After piling four logs into her arms, she pushed the front door open with her hip and went inside.

Immediately she felt something strange. She bent and gently rolled the logs to the floor, trying not to be too noisy. Her heart started pounding against the walls of her chest, but she wasn't sure why.

Was someone in the house? Something?

Animal or human?

She glanced around for something to use as a weapon. No baseball bat, and the chopping ax was outside beside the woodpile. Without thinking, she grabbed one of the logs, swung it back over her right shoulder. Her throat tight with nerves, she moved cautiously through the living room. This was crazy, she thought, stepping into the kitchen and flipping on the lights. There was nothing here, probably just her imagination.

But she let her guard down too quickly. As her arm fell to her side, someone seized her, grabbed her around the waist and spun her, then pinned her back against the countertop. The log dropped to the floor and made a crashing sound. Tess screamed, thrashed around until she saw who was holding her. Then she stopped cold and stared at him. "You!"

His face just inches from hers, Damien Sauer whispered, "Making yourself at home."

"You scared the hell out of me!" she said caustically, trying to break free of his grasp.

But Damien didn't release her. "And you almost knocked my head off my shoulders with that log."

"What a tragedy that would be," she said sarcastically.

Amusement glittered in his eyes. "You seem testy today."

"Do I?"

"Living in the lap of luxury not agreeing with you?"

"Living here is fine. It's the unwelcome guests I have a problem with."

"Then you should keep the door locked."

She ignored the truth in that statement. "What are you doing here? Aren't you supposed to be watching me jump and squirm from under that ten-thousand-square-foot magnifying glass you got up there?"

"Twelve thousand."

"What?"

"Twelve thousand square feet."

She rolled her eyes. He was one of the most arrogant, self-centered…

"I'm checking in," he said, his sapphire gaze moving over her face. "On my wife."

A ripple of laughter escaped her. "That arrangement is going on only in your head."

He leaned in, his mouth just inches from her. "And in your partners' heads, as well, right?"

How was it possible to want to kill someone and kiss them at the same time? They stood there, so close, the scent of snow and leather emanating from Damien as he baited her with his words and his full lips.

Ignoring the prickly warm sensation inside her breasts, she forced her gaze to meet his. "I want you to let me go now."

At her words, something changed in his expression. It was no longer playful, more serious, and he released her, backed up, even walked away into the living room. For a moment Tess just remained there, her back against the butcher-block countertop. She'd said those exact words to another man many years ago and many times before, but with very different results. Damien confused her. He wanted to punish her, yet his punishment was all mental…

With a quick breath, she followed him into the living room. "As you can see, I've cleaned the place. That's about as far as I've gotten in the one day I've been here. Oh, that and I bought a bed."

"A bed?"

"If I'm staying here it's at least going to be tolerably comfortable."

"Where is it?"

"In the car."

He was opening the front door and disappearing outside before Tess got a clue about what he was doing. "I don't need your help, Damien," she called, running after him into the frosty cold air of twilight time. "In fact, I don't need anything from you, except maybe…"

A foot from her car, he paused and turned around. "Except what?"

From three to five in the morning last night, she'd given this idea much thought. Damien wasn't going to be the only beneficiary in this deal. Tess didn't do things that way anymore. "I'd like you to promise me something."

He raised a brow.

"After I do this job, you'll sell the Minneapolis building."

He crossed his arms over his chest. "Which building is that?"

She cocked her head to the side. "Don't be obtuse."

For a moment he just stared at her, looking both emotionally and physically cold, puffs of warm air escaping his mouth. Then he turned around and walked to the back of her car. He had the trunk popped and the headboard out in seconds. "You didn't lock your car door, either?"

"I didn't think this was chop shop alley, Damien."

He carried the headboard up the walk, and Tess followed him. "The building I'm referring to is the one that houses No Ring Required. I want you to sell it."

"Why should I?" He put the headboard inside, then went back for more.

Again, she followed after him like a hungry puppy as he removed parts of the bed frame from her SUV and brought them inside. "Because it's the right thing to do, and underneath that badass exterior you're a good guy."

"No, seriously, why should I?" he said dryly, returning to the car and hauling out the mattress and box spring.

"Because I'm willing to walk away from this if you don't."

He snorted. "You wouldn't. I know you—"

"You know nothing about me, Damien!" She said the words so loudly, so passionately, he stopped in the doorway and stared at her.

She shook her head. "You have no idea who I am now. What I've..." She needed to go easy here. "What I've seen and experienced in the past six years. I'm willing to let you humiliate me, give orders and use me for the next two weeks, to protect my business and my partners. But I won't do it for longer than that."

He didn't move. His chin was set and his eyes narrowed.

She walked to him, her tone low and cool. "You clearly don't need the money. And after we're done here, I'd think you'd want to put me back in the past where I belong."

"That easy?"

"Yes." She held out her hand. "Okay?"

Damien didn't speak for a moment, then he reached out and took her hand in his.

The warmth of his hand instantly seeped into her body, her bones, and for just a second a flash of the past came roaring into her mind. She saw herself in Damien's arms in this very house, saw him kissing her neck, then her mouth.

She pulled her hand away, knowing her cheeks burned. "If you're done here, I have work to do."

He nodded darkly. "I'm done." He walked past her, down the path.

Then she noticed something. "Hey, how did you get here? I didn't see a car."

He glanced over his shoulder. "Walked."

She couldn't stop herself from asking, "You want a ride back? It's kind of far."

He shook his head. "No. It's just far enough."

He disappeared down the street and into the darkness so quickly she didn't get a chance to ask him what he'd meant by that.

Damien arrived home hungry and cold as hell. But all in all, the walk had been a good one. Time to clear his head, make new plans and fill his lungs with clean air. Couldn't do that in Los Angeles.

Olin was hovering at the front door when Damien walked in. "Sir?"

"You look panicked, Olin."

He took Damien's coat and tossed it gently over his arm. "Mrs. Roth is here and she brought along a Mr. Kaplan."

Damien checked his watch. "It's eight o'clock."

"I told them it was too late, but they insisted on waiting." The man leaned in and whispered covertly, "Mrs. Roth called Mr. Kaplan a land developer."

Damien chuckled. "Yes, I know who he is. How long have they been here?"

"Twenty minutes." Olin stood taller. "I'll go back and tell them you don't wish to be—"

"No. I'd told Irene to come by anytime." He should've specified anytime during the day. But this was a special circumstance, part of his plan, and he couldn't afford to be his usual overly demanding self. "Tell them I'll be right there."

"Yes, sir."

"Where are they?"

"The study."

"Fine." He started up the stairs.

"Sir?"

Damien turned. "Yes, Olin?"

"I know it's not my business to ask, but if you're thinking of selling this house, I would be most grateful to know—"

"I'm not selling."

"Oh."

"Not this house, anyway."

There were times when Tess York believed she didn't feel anything—that the ugliness and shame of her past had made her numb. Then, out of the blue, she'd get a few gentle waves of emotion. They were normally accompanied by memories, not good ones, but even so, the waves did remind her that she was still alive and able to feel. And she had to take that as a positive.

Tonight Tess sat on the new bed and rubbed oil onto the snakelike skin of her inner thigh. She was riding a wave right now, where the reality of the massive burn scar that Henry had inflicted that last night before she'd left him was meeting up with the emotions of the memory. It was an odd thing, too, because she always felt the scar, felt her jeans rub against it or the shower water pummeling it.

Tonight, however, it burned.

She couldn't help thinking it was Damien's presence in her life again, the notion that if she had picked him, her life might've been so different—that this scar wouldn't have existed. But who was to know. In his own way, Damien had turned out to be a monster, too.

Outside, snow started to fall. Tomorrow was a big day, the real renovation could begin.

Tess put her salve away, got under the covers and closed her eyes.

Five

The trouble with picking a paint color was twofold: too many choices, then there was the what-if-this-looks-hideous-on-the-wall factor. Normally Tess could get past these minor roadblocks in about fifteen minutes. In her five years with NRR, she'd chosen color for over a hundred walls, but this morning she'd been at Hardy's Hardware for an hour, unable to make a decision.

Tess stood in front of the paint chips and stared at the blur of color, a shiny bald-headed Frank Hardy beside her. She shook her head. "I just don't know."

"You could go white," Frank suggested.

"True…"

"What's the plan for the house?"

"I'm not sure." Maybe that was part of the problem here—no clear goal. Damien still hadn't told her what he was going to do with the house after she fixed it up.

Frank took a chip labeled Basic Eggshell off the board and held it out for her. "Neutral is good."

Sure. Good, but kind of boring. "The thing is, Frank, the man who owns the house is just not a neutral guy, and it's not a neutral house."

"Do I know this guy?"

"Probably."

"Who is it?" Impatience with the nutty woman was starting to register on his face. "Maybe if I knew who you were working for I could be a better help to you."

Maybe, but she wasn't experiencing the greatest luck with the people in town who knew she was working for Damien. Best to keep that information to herself. "I think I'm just going to go for it." She started handing over paint chips. "I'll take the Ryegrass for the kitchen, Toasty and Svelte and Sage for living room and dining room, Buttercream for the bathroom and Ramie for the bedroom."

He looked relieved. "And the exterior will have to wait for warmer weather."

"Yes. But even then, the house will always remain red."

The man's voice came from behind them, and both Tess and Frank turned to see Damien standing there. He looked very tall under the store's low ceiling and very handsome in jeans, black sweater and wool coat.

"For a project that's supposed to be done by me and only me, you're around an awful lot," Tess said, only mildy irritated. "What are you doing here?"

"I'm in dire need of a rake," he said with complete seriousness, walking toward her.

"Yeah, right. You were spying on my paint choices."

Damien smiled lazily. "I'd like to see what I'm getting for my money."

Tess gave him a look of mock disgust. "Where's the trust, dude?"

His brows went up. "Dude?"

Sticking out his hand in Damien direction, Frank grinned. "So, you're the not-so-neutral guy, huh?"

Damien shook it and grinned. "She was talking about me?"

"Didn't know it was you, but now that I do, I get it."

"Get what?" Tess asked Frank.

Frank shrugged, stuffed his hands into the pockets of his stained overalls. "Why it took you so long to decide. Mr. Sauer does that to all the ladies."

Tess snorted. "What? Make them crazy?"

"In a word, yup."

Tess cocked her head to the side and said in a high, breathy, girlie voice, "Well, I just can't decide anything, you make me too crazy."

Frank burst out laughing, pointing at Tess. "I like her."

"Yeah." Damien's sapphire gaze moved over her face in a hungry, possessive way, sending an electrifying jolt of awareness right into Tess's core. It had been so long since she'd felt something stir her up that way. She hardly remembered how good it was to feel turned on. How unfortunate it was that the man who had done the stirring was also the man who wanted to punish her, then put her behind him and forget she ever existed.

Frank cleared his throat. "All right. Give me a half hour for the six gallons."

Tess thanked him, then walked outside with Damien beside her. It was a crisp, winter morning with just enough sun to make being outside moderately tolerable. From lampposts to street signs to shop windows, the town was dressed for Christmas, and, feeling in pretty good spirits that day, Tess suggested they take a walk down the sidewalk to enjoy the sights.

As Damien walked beside her, he said, "I stopped by the house."

She was about to ask him once again about his ongoing involvement in the renovation but decided against it. He was here, in town, and had made himself involved. He was a man who did what he wanted and got what he wanted. Trying to stop him would surely prove fruitless.

"And how's the drywall looking?" she asked.

"Satisfactory. I see you found Jamie and Max."

She nodded. "Best drywallers in the county."

"So they say," he said as they rounded the corner. "Where are you off to now?"

"I have a date."

He came to a dead stop on the sidewalk. "What?"

His eyes were fierce and practically black as he stared down at her.

A shiver of satisfaction moved through her at his reaction. But she mentally flicked it away. "I have a date with a flooring salesperson."

She watched him process this information, then make a satisfied grunt before continuing down the street. "Driving into Jackson?"

"Yep. They have a flooring outlet there. I'm thinking maybe some prefab oak."

He sniffed imperiously. "Prefab? No. Absolutely not."

She looked him over. "You know, you've turned into quite the snob, Sauer."

"Why? Because I like good quality, natural materials?"

"Prefab can be really nice."

"I only want the best materials used on this house."

"Why?" A sudden gust of snowy wind assaulted her, and she pulled the collar of her coat tighter around her neck. "What is the plan for this house, Damien? I mean, correct me if I'm wrong, but if you're going to do your thing and flip it, isn't the rule to put in the best product for the cheapest price?"

Damien was quiet for a moment, then he said neutrally, "I won't be flipping the house."

Okay. So, he wasn't selling. Why did that make her feel so relieved? Why did that make her feel anything at all?

The town was small, and soon they ran out of

sidewalk and shops, and they were headed into the park. Neither one of them suggested turning back, and as they neared an abandoned, snow-covered swing set, Tess turned off the path and made a beeline for the swings. She brushed off the tuft of snow covering the plastic red seat and sat. Damien stood nearby and watched her swing back and forth gently.

"If you could choose anything for the floors," he said evenly. "Never mind the cost, what would you choose?"

"You mean, my fantasy floor?"

He nodded.

She thought for a moment, then sighed. "Oh, let's see. Probably, thick planks, antique wood, maybe barn wood."

He nodded. "Okay."

"Okay, what?"

"Do it."

She laughed, continuing to swing back and forth even though it was starting to make her nauseous. "That kind of floor can run twenty dollars a square foot."

"Just order it, but make sure it's here at the end of the week."

"That's impossible."

"Nothing's impossible. Pay whatever they ask for the shipping and they'll get it here in a week." His cell phone rang and he glanced at the number, seemed to deem it unimportant and slipped it back in his coat pocket. "In fact, I want you to pick everything for the house with no thought to the cost. Make all your choices fantasy choices."

She put her feet down and skidded to a stop. "Come on, Damien."

"What?"

"Make all the choices fantasy ones? To what end?"

"I'm not following."

She shook her head. "I don't get this. What are you doing?"

"Is there something wrong with enjoying your work?"

This went past enjoying her work. "Is this some show of how much money you have?"

His eyes narrowed. "I don't put on shows."

"You have to know that I'm not interested in your money and what it can buy. It doesn't impress me. It means nothing to me. Less than nothing."

He laughed bitterly. "I find that hard to believe."

"What does that mean?" she demanded.

"It's why you went with a man you didn't love."

"What?"

"Henry offered you security," he said, walking over to her. "With him you believed your future would be set, financially and otherwise. Isn't that true?"

"Yes, it's true."

"And what did I offer you?" He stood before her, his face taut, his gaze searching hers. "Not much— just a hope for a future."

"Do we really need to do this?" She pushed herself off of the swing. The paint was probably done.

Without another word, she walked past Damien. But she didn't get very far.

"And now look at us," he called after her. "Your future, your security is in my hands."

She stopped, just feet away. The past wouldn't rest as long as there were others still living in it. And Damien clearly was. He sounded so cruel, so unhappy, so delighted. It was disgusting and foolish, and she couldn't stop herself from turning around and walking right back up to him. When she was there, in his face, her breathing unsteady and her jaw trembling, she blurted it out. "Do you want to know why I went with him? Why I left you?"

"Yes."

"I loved him, Damien."

"I don't believe you."

She said the words slowly. "I was in love with him."

His jaw was clenched so tight she thought it might snap. "You were in love with what you thought he could give you."

"It's all the same."

"No, it's not."

"How would you know?"

She turned around to go, but he grabbed her arm and pulled her back to face him. "If you loved him, what was it you felt for me?"

She lifted her chin. "Lust."

His eyes darkened with rage. "Then you won't mind this."

She didn't have time to react as he leaned in and covered her mouth with his, his free hand cupping her nape.

His kiss was hard, punishing, and she wanted to be repelled by it, by him, but she wasn't. Every muscle, every inch of her skin trembled and ached. Yes, it had been a long time since she was touched this way, but it wasn't that, it was Damien. He was an artist, always had been. The way he held her, his lips taking greedily one moment, then pulling back to nibble and slowly suckle.

Tess sagged against him, her fists wrapped around the collar of his coat, her hips pressing into his thigh.

Her pulse slapped against her rib cage. She wanted more, so much more. If only they were back at the red house, not outside in the park….

Delicious, mind-numbing heat quickly turned to anxiety as she realized where she was and what she was doing and who had started it all. She released him, pushing him away as she stepped back. Her brain felt foggy and she shook her head.

"That will not happen again." She didn't look at him, couldn't, her body was still humming.

This time when she turned and walked away, he didn't reach out to stop her. But his words echoed through the snow-covered park, a dark, delicious warning…

"Don't be so sure."

"Slow down, Damien, for heaven's sake."

"I'm fine."

"You're going to choke." Her hands planted on her formidable hips, Wanda Bennett watched Damien devour the plate of food she'd just set in front of him. Inside her food store, there was a diner counter where she served the basics, from grilled cheese to pancakes. It all depended on her mood. Today her mood had run in the direction of everything egg related. Eggs weren't really high on Damien's list of favorite foods, but he never tried to persuade Wanda to do anything else but exactly what she wanted to do. She was just like him, arrogant and stubborn as hell. If there weren't such a difference in the colors of their skin, he might wonder if they were related.

"Aren't you going to Minneapolis this afternoon?" she asked him.

"Yes." He had a four-o'clock meeting with an investor. "I have to be at the airport in twenty minutes."

"Why aren't you eating on the plane, then?"

He shrugged.

"Steak and champagne is a helluva lot better than my greasy egg sandwich."

"No, it's not," he said sullenly.

She glared at him expectantly. "What's the problem? Is it the girl? The redhead?"

Damn right it was the girl. Always that girl. Why couldn't he be done with her? Why couldn't he have stopped himself from going there, kissing her, tasting her. Now all he wanted was more. "I need a napkin. Or a hose."

Wanda ignored him. "Yeah, I figured she wasn't just an employee. But she's not really your type, either."

"I don't have a type."

"No? I suppose it's just a coincidence that every woman who's ever followed you up here has weighed less than a toothbrush with a figure to match. And," she pointed out dramatically, "I swear a couple of them have shown up on the covers of those rag mags over by the register." Wanda shook her head. "Never understood why a man like you would take company with women who don't know their nose from their elbows…but it's none of my affair."

"No, it's not." He stood and tossed money on the counter. "Truth is, Wanda, those women are wonderfully uncomplicated. No strings, no—"

"No real feelings?" she interrupted.

Damien shot her a defensive look. "I have to go."

She pressed her lips together and shrugged. "Okay, go."

Wanda was the one woman in his life who never pressed him for anything more than what he wanted to give. "She is my past," he said with far too much irritation. "She made me what I am."

A slow smile touched Wanda's full lips. "And what is that?"

"A soulless, uncompromising pain in the ass."

She grinned broadly. "A devil in the bedroom and in the boardroom?"

Damien's brow lifted, and he matched her grin with one of his own. "You'd never marry me, would you?"

"If you were ten years younger…maybe."

He leaned over the counter and gave her a peck on the cheek. "It's supposed to snow tonight. Be careful going home."

* * *

It was nearly midnight, but the last thing Tess felt like doing was sleeping. She was running on Double Stuff Oreos and diet cola, and had just finished the demo of the kitchen and bathroom floors, removing all the old tiles. The installers were coming tomorrow with the antique hand-hewn limestone she'd found through Frank at the hardware store.

She cranked up the stereo she'd bought that afternoon. She had a thing for eighties music, especially Prince, and as she poured the old tiles from the dustpan into the garbage can and hauled them outside, she danced. She was in the middle of the livingroom, on her last load of tile, when it happened. The floorboard beneath her creaked, then cracked, then suddenly gave way.

She had no time to react as her slipper-clad foot dropped through the subflooring. For a moment she just stood there, one foot on the floor, the other in a hole.

"Damn dry rot," she muttered, dropping onto her backside and easing her foot out. But as she did, the pain came on fast. Then she noticed her slipper had fallen off, and her naked foot was sporting a good deal of blood. Confused, she cupped her foot and rotated it so she could see the ball and heel, find the source of the blood. Her stomach clenched when she saw it. There was a nasty-looking gash on the ball of her foot.

"Crap." She took off her other slipper and pressed the soft side against the open cut, then she hobbled to the bedroom where she kept the emergency kit.

After cleaning the wound with hydrogen peroxide, she grabbed a butterfly Band-Aid. She tried to get the cut to close well, but every time she moved, it hurt like hell and blood seeped out everywhere.

She was going to need stitches. How in the world was she going to make that happen?

"Tess?"

Her heart leaped into her throat as fear gripped her. Then she recognized the voice, and relief spread through her. Before this moment, she'd never thought she'd be so happy to hear his voice. "I'm in here, Damien—the master bedroom."

He walked in, looking cold, tired and thoroughly pissed off. "Are you completely insane?"

"Is that a serious question?"

"It's after midnight and the front door is wide open."

"I was working."

"If I hadn't been driving by—" Then he saw the blood on her foot, on the slipper, on the floor. "What the hell happened to you?"

"Rotting floorboard."

"I saw it when I came in, but I thought it was demo." He squatted down and inspected her foot.

"I think I sliced it on the edge of the board next to the one that gave way, or maybe there was something sharp on the subflooring—I don't know."

"Did you clean it with anything?"

"Yes and I tried a butterfly bandage, but nothing's stopping the blood. I think I need to go to the emergency room."

He got up and went to the bathroom, came back with a roll of toilet paper. He used nearly the whole thing, but in seconds he had her entire instep wrapped up like the foot of a mummy.

She gave him a nod and a smile. "Thanks."

"Sure." Then without warning, he lifted her up and gathered her into his arms.

"What are you doing?"

"Taking you to the emergency room," he said, walking out of the bedroom.

"I can call—"

"Get serious." He stepped around the rotting floorboard and walked out the door. "An ambulance takes forever. I'm here and I'm taking you."

"Are you sure this won't mess up your plans to punish me?" she said dryly. "You know, by actually helping me?"

His jaw tightened as they headed for the black sedan in the driveway. "You got hurt on my watch. There's nothing else to say. Now, just shut up and put your arms around my neck, you're starting to slip."

Six

As Tess sat in a plastic chair in the cold half-empty emergency room, Damien paced. Waiting was not his strong suit. Sure, there were a few other people in the E.R., but none of them had anything too serious going on, none of them belonged to him, and none of them made his gut tighten with just a look.

Anger bubbled up in his blood, and he searched the room for someone who looked as though they wanted a good verbal sparring match. But no one would make eye contact with him.

"You look like a caged animal, Damien. Sit down."

He stopped and stared at Tess. He hadn't noticed

before but she was wearing a pair of red flannel Christmas pajamas and her hair was piled on top of her head, a few wavy strands falling about her neck and shoulders. Not surprisingly, she still wore the one remaining black slipper. She was a mess, but a very sexy mess.

He scowled at her. "Are you keeping pressure on your foot?"

"Yes. Now sit down. You look nuts."

"I look nuts?" he said, ire in his tone. "You want to know what's nuts?"

"I'm guessing that's a rhetorical question," she said, her makeup-free face looking very, very beautiful, yet very pale.

His voice dropped to a whisper. "Nuts is wearing slippers during demolition."

"It was late."

He threw his hands in the air. "You were knocking out tiles."

"I wore boots for that part."

"Well, why the hell didn't you keep them on for the cleanup? What did you do when you went outside?"

"I have duck shoes outside the front door. I slipped into those."

He groaned. "Women."

"We're great aren't we?" She gave him an innocent smile. "Complicated, mysterious…"

"That's not where I was going."

Her smile suddenly evaporated, and she closed her eyes and sucked air through her teeth.

Switching from anger to concern, Damien dropped down beside her. "Does it hurt?"

"Not any worse than a tooth extraction," she muttered through gritted teeth. "Without the pain meds, of course."

He cursed. "I'll be right back." He stalked over to the front desk and spoke to the nurse, "That woman with the cut foot needs to see someone right away."

Staring at a patient chart, the nurse didn't even look up at him. "We're busy tonight, sir. She'll have to wait."

"It doesn't look all that busy to me," he said with a thread of irritation running through his tone. "There's a guy in here with a cold, and another guy who's too drunk to even fill out his paperwork. The woman I brought in is bleeding."

The nurse looked up then and shrugged. "I'm sorry. Rules are rules."

Screw rules. Damien took out his cell phone and, right there at the reception desk, punched in a number.

"Sir, please go outside to use your cell phone," said the nurse.

Damien ignored her. The phone rang three times before it was picked up.

"Hello."

"Greg, it's Damien Sauer."

"Damien?" came the tired male voice. "Everything all right?"

"Sorry to call this late, but I'm having an issue at your hospital."

"You're at the hospital? What happened?"

"Not me. A friend. She needs to see a doctor, but we're dealing with first come, first serve, and to be honest there are no emergencies ahead of us—"

The man cut him off. "I'll take care of it right now."

"Thanks."

"I'm sorry about this, Damien. I'm sure they would never have allowed this to happen if they knew who you were."

Damien hung up the phone with the president and CEO of Tribute Memorial Hospital, but he didn't move from the reception desk. Seconds later a call came through on the emergency room phone that sent everyone in a panic. The nurse who earlier had brushed him off now simultaneously blanched and smiled as she told Damien she'd be right with him, then rushed away with several other members of the hospital staff.

Thirty seconds later, two nurses and a doctor burst through the double doors with the cleanest of squeaky-clean wheelchairs, and Tess was whisked away to a private room.

"All right," Tess said to the male nurse who had lifted her from the wheelchair and was gently placing her on a bed. "What did he do?"

She was pointing at Damien, who only shrugged and said, "I'm going to find you some ice chips and the best wound specialist in this hospital."

He was just outside the door when he heard Tess say, "Seriously, did he threaten you guys?

The male nurse laughed. "No, miss."

"Then what's all the fuss?"

"The man who brought you in is Damien Sauer."

"I know."

"Then you also know that he donated the new emergency wing to the hospital?"

Tess sighed. "No, that part I didn't know."

Damien drove his car up the steep hill without hitting a rock, hard chunk of snow or pothole. Pretty damn impressive. Not that the woman next to him had noticed. She'd been asleep for the past ten minutes, the painkillers they'd given her at the hospital working their magic. But as he pulled into the garage and killed the engine, she stirred, her hands closing around her purse, a soft moan escaping her lips.

He looked over at her, lifted a brow. "Hey."

She turned to him, her eyes heavy and tired. "Hi." Her foot was wrapped in a bandage and in his trunk was the pair of crutches the hospital had given them. "Where are we?" she asked.

"You're staying with me."

Tess came awake immediately, even sat up a little in her seat. "No."

"Don't be an ass, Tess. You heard the doctor. You need to stay off your foot for a few days."

"Not here."

"You need the help."

"I don't," she said defiantly. "I can handle this myself."

"How?"

She paused, then let her head fall back against the seat. "Fine, I need help." She rubbed a hand over her face. "But I'll get it from someone else."

"Who?"

"I'll go home, back to Minneapolis. You can get someone to finish the job."

There was no way he was letting her out of his life just yet. He needed so much from her: to make her love him again; to feel her mouth again; to leave her cold like she'd left him. "I don't want anyone else to finish the job." His voice grew dangerously low. "That wasn't our deal."

"Well, how do you think the house is going to get done? I won't be able to do anything major for at least two days. I have a tiling guy coming tomorrow to help me lay the tile, and there's no way—"

"I'll do it."

She stared at him. "What?"

"I'll help the guy lay tile. I've done it a hundred times."

"Not lately, I'm willing to bet."

"You think I can't get dirty?" Damien asked with a touch of heat.

Her mouth twitched with amusement and she returned bluntly, "No, I think you can definitely get dirty."

"Was that an insult or a sexual innuendo?"

She shrugged. "Who knows? Depends if it was me talking or the drugs."

He chuckled. "Perhaps a little of both. Now, to-morrow I'll meet the guy at…what time?"

"Eight," she supplied, looking unconvinced. "You sure you're up for all that manual labor now that you're Mr. Sauer, millionaire real estate mogul who donates hospital wings on a whim."

"That had nothing to do with a whim. That was a kick-ass tax deduction."

She looked at the ceiling. "Oh, that kind heart of yours, Damien."

Laughing again, he got out of the car and came around to her side. But when he got there, Tess was starting to fade a little. The twinkle in her eyes from a moment ago had disappeared, and she was sitting back against the seat, looking miserable. With supreme gentleness, he bent and slipped his hands underneath her. "I'm going to carry you."

"And I'm going to let you," she whispered.

"Pain's back?"

"With a vengeance and a hammer and some kind of hand-crank drill."

He shook his head, grinned. "You're the only one I know who can joke through their pain."

"Who's joking?"

He carried her into the house, through the living room and up the stairs to the second floor. He'd called ahead and had instructed Olin to fix up the room overlooking the garden. He'd never admit it to anyone but himself, but he'd had Tess in mind when he'd designed the room. It had a huge bed with a down comforter, a lavish bathroom and wall-to-wall windows. Even in the sea of pain she was riding, she smiled when she saw it.

"Nice room."

"It has a great view in the morning." He laid her on the bed, her back against the pillows.

She looked up at him. "Is this your room?"

"No."

"Then how do you know about the view in the morning?" She stopped herself, put a hand up. "Forget I asked."

He sat beside her. "What are you rambling on about?"

"Your stay in this room with your many guests. You have had women stay in here before, right?"

"Does it matter?"

Her face contorted with pain and she practically barked out the word, "No."

"All right. Relax now. Can I help you take off something?"

She smirked. "Cute."

A grin tugged at his mouth. She was something else, this one, he thought as he opened the bottle of pain medicine she'd been given at the hospital pharmacy. He took out a pill, then he handed her a bottle of water from the bedside table. "Take this."

"With pleasure." She popped the pill, drank the water, then sank back against the pillows, closing her eyes. After a moment her eyes drifted back open and they locked with his. "Hey."

"Hey."

"Thank you."

"For what?" He felt himself softening with her, and it killed him.

"Helping me out. It should just be the one night, then—"

"Stop, Tess."

But she wouldn't. "I'm a pretty quick healer. Tomorrow I should be a lot better, and I won't need to be watched over or—"

"I get it," he interrupted with an edge to his voice. "You don't want to rely on anyone." He reached over and pulled the covers up to her chin, then he stood. "Go to sleep now."

She nodded and closed her eyes, and Damien turned to leave.

Yes, he wanted to touch her again, make her need him, but he had to be vigilant. If he got too close, cared too much, there was a chance he might end up needing her again—and that he could not allow.

Tess was dreaming. It was one of those situations where she knew she was dreaming and she wanted to stay in it, and see it through to the end. She was dancing the tango in a competition, and her partner couldn't seem to hold her correctly. Every time he tried, she'd slip out of his arms. Around them, other couples dipped and stomped and made grand gestures with their arms, but Tess just stood there in the middle of it all, waiting,

waiting for this guy to get his act together and take her in his arms.

Not far away, at the judges' table, was Damien. He sat on a throne, a crown on his head, watching them, his eyes flared and his jaw set as though he found the whole thing repellent. As the music dissolved and the couples danced off the floor, Damien stood and walked toward her, his hand outstretched…

And then Tess opened her eyes. The music was gone, along with the activity and drama. She was in Damien's guest room and her foot was bandaged and it stung like the devil. She blinked, then glanced around. The curtains had been drawn on only one side of the massive windows, leaving the other side exposed. Outside, the sky was a bleak gray as if it was just too tired to contemplate morning….

Maybe in an hour or two, it seemed to say.

On the other side of the room, Damien was asleep in a chair by the fireplace. Tess's first reaction to seeing him there was to feel comforted by his presence. But that was no good, right? Comforted by the man who wanted her to suffer so he could get her out of his mind and his life? That mentality didn't sound like something she would ever be comfortable being around.

She just stared at him, a heart-stopping Adonis in a blue sweatshirt and jeans. Had he actually slept in that chair all night? she wondered. And why? Seriously, why was he even letting her stay at his house?

Why did he seem to despise her one moment, then treat her so gently the next?

Her gaze caught on something beside him on the floor. Her suitcase. He had gone back to the red house for her things. Her belly clenched. He was expecting her to remain there for more than a day.

She shifted in the bed, tried to get comfortable, but the bandage on her foot was awkward and the sting had morphed into a painful ache and stiffness.

Well, his expectations were going to be met, she thought. She wasn't going anywhere. A wave of panic moved into her already tight belly. She hated feeling stuck, feeling as though she were unable to get up and go, no matter how desperately she wanted to. It reminded her of those endless, or seemingly endless, days and nights in Henry's house, where he watched every move she made and pulled her back if she tried to put even a pinky toe across the line.

"You're awake."

Her head came up with a jerk. Damien was staring at her, so handsome, so devilish with his dark eyes and stubbled jaw. "I'm awake."

"You okay?"

"Can't sleep."

"Does your foot hurt?" He got up, came to sit beside her on the bed.

"Only if I move it."

"Then don't move it."

Her heart stuttered. Why did he look concerned? Was this just a way of helping her to get better faster, getting her back to work? Was he willing to be extra nice just to get her to finish the house?

As she downed two more pain pills, she thought about how her mind worked now. The belief that there was always a motive behind any action. She hated it. But wasn't there was always a motive with men?

She gestured to her bag on the floor. "Thanks for getting my stuff."

"Sure."

She took a deep breath. "You know, Damien. I'm not comfortable here."

"I know."

"With you taking care of me."

"I know."

"In fact, it makes me a little crazy."

A smile tugged at his mouth. "Too bad."

She returned his smile. "You should go back to your room, get some sleep."

He didn't move. His gaze raked over her face, then paused at her mouth. "Yeah, I probably should."

But instead he leaned in and kissed her.

Seven

Damien knew the moment he tasted her that he had just bought his ticket to hell.

Nothing—not even a bandaged, aching foot—was going to stop him from taking more. It was as if time had never passed. She smelled the same—that sweet, cool vanilla scent that had always driven him insane. He touched her face, her soft cheek, felt the skin tighten as she opened her mouth and deepened the kiss. The action tied him in knots, had his head pounding, his heart, too.

He dropped his head back, stared at her, into those large, hungry gray eyes. He'd never wanted anything more than he wanted her at that moment, and when she gave him a small, tentative smile, he crushed his

mouth to hers, devouring the wet heat of her, changing angles with every breath, her long red curls
tickling his face.

On a soft sigh, Tess placed her hands on either side
of his head, her fingers snaking into his hair, forcing
him closer.

Damien went hard as granite. This was going to
be punishment for them both, pleasure for them both.

He ripped his mouth from hers and kissed her
neck, nuzzling at the spot where her pulse pounded.
She moaned and fisted his hair, tugging him closer.
He nipped at her skin the way she used to love as
his fingers madly searched for the buttons on her
pajama top.

"Kiss me," she whispered. "Kiss me so I can't say
no."

Her words excited him, yet were a warning, too—
but he was too far gone to care. He wanted her mouth
again, wanted to taste her tongue, suckle and bite and
make her shiver, make her wet.

His mouth covered hers as his fingers flicked open
the buttons on her top. He could hardly wait to feel
her, that soft, milky skin beneath his palm. He cursed
against her mouth as his hand slid beneath the flannel
and over the full curve of her breast. She moaned and
arched against him, and the sound filled him with
longing. He liberated the buttons of her pajama top,
then lowered his head and gently lapped at the soft
peak, then again and again, circling the pink flesh
until the nipple turned dark and hard.

Tess let her head fall back against the pillow as he continued in easy, lazy circles. Then, when his body and mind were about to explode, Damien took the hard bud into his mouth and suckled deeply. Again and again he suckled until Tess's mewling sounds turned to deep moans. He continued as he let one hand drift down her belly to the top of her pajama bottoms. Her reaction was quick. She stiffened and her hand came down over his.

His head came up and he looked at her.

She swallowed, shook her head. "It's…it's my foot. Hurts."

He turned away. "Dammit. I'm sorry." He felt like a giant ass. What kind of man hit on a woman in pain? Maybe the kind who was only looking for a little payback. He stood. "I'm gonna go."

"Back to bed?"

Not a chance. "I'm going to the red house. Get things set up for the tile job."

"It's so early."

"By the time I get there the sun will be up."

"Okay."

He raised a brow at her. "You're not to move."

"Damien…"

"If you need anything," he said, his body feeling as tight as a jackhammer. "Olin is here, and you just have to call down."

"I'll be going to the ladies' room alone," she said with a half smile.

"Of course." He walked over to the fireplace and

grabbed her crutches. "Use these only if absolutely necessary."

"Yes, sir." She gave him a mock salute.

"Now, if you get bored, there's some books on the nightstand here, and—" he gestured to the large trunk at the end of the bed "—there's a television in there. You just have to use the remote."

"Seriously?" she asked, surprised.

He nodded.

"It's inside the trunk?"

"Yes."

"Fancy."

She sat there, in bed, her cheeks flushed, her hair tousled and sexy and Damien felt as if he was going to explode.

Too damn much already. He couldn't stare at her for one more second. He turned around and walked out of the room, calling over his shoulder, "I'll be back around noon."

Once upon a time, a rabbit was caught in a trap. It sat there for hours until it felt as though it was going quite mad, then it proceeded to gnaw its foot off. Yes, it was bleeding and in pain as it limped through the forest, but it was free.

With her crutches tucked under her arms, Tess explored the second floor. It was all she could do. No up and no down. She had ruled out the stairs, as she had easily envisioned herself falling down them and being bedridden in Damien's ultramodern house long after he'd returned to California.

Slow and steady, she walked down the hallway, past a few more bedrooms, then a workout room and a billiard room. None of these rooms did anything to pique her curiosity. But then, at the very end of the house, in a large, square-shaped room, she saw a library. Heavy on charm, the space was lined in books and artwork. The furniture was a mixture of leather and chenille, and in the middle of one wall, a river-rock fireplace.

Perfect. A lively blaze danced in the fireplace, and after Tess grabbed a few random novels from the shelf, she sat in front of the fireplace on the brown leather couch.

As she was relaxing, her foot propped up on the coffee table, she saw something move out of the corner of one eye. She turned to see the man she had dubbed "Danny Devito" enter the room.

He inclined his head. "Good morning, Miss York."

"Hi, there. Olin, right?"

"Yes, miss."

"Good, because I wanted to apologize for the other day. I was pretty rude."

Olin shook his head. "No, miss."

"Oh, c'mon, Olin, it's okay. You can say it."

The man smiled, but it was a very thin-lipped one, as though he were fighting the urge to laugh. "You seemed…frustrated."

"I was. But I'm sure that's not the first time you've

seen a frustrated woman—you know, with who your boss is and everything."

Olin's smile faded. "Can I get you something, miss? Breakfast? Coffee?"

"No, thank you."

"I could help you back to the room, if you wish."

Boy, she knew where this was headed. "Thanks, Olin. But I'm good here."

Olin's brown eyes were filled with nervous energy. "It's just that Mr. Sauer said you shouldn't be out of bed, miss."

"I'm sure he did."

"I'm sensing a *but* miss?"

She smiled. "But I don't take orders from Mr. Sauer."

The man grimaced.

Tess shrugged. "I'm good here, really. No worries, Olin, okay?"

Olin didn't look convinced, but he nodded anyway. "Yes, miss." Then inclined his head and left the room.

Tess returned to her book, but after thirty minutes or so she started to get a little antsy. Propped up on crutches once again, she circled the room, not really looking for anything in particular. But when she came to an ancient-looking desk in an alcove off the main part of the library, she was intrigued. She went to the desk and sat. There were only two things on the desktop: writing paper with a modern DS embossed on the top of it, and a very nice pen. This had to be Damien's desk, Damien's chair.

She'd never been much of a snoop, but something about being at Damien's desk without him knowing made her ultracurious. She reached down and opened the long, thin drawer just under the desktop. Her pulse quickened as she searched through a few papers, a map of China and a small bag of sour candy. She didn't know what she was looking for until she found it. Two photographs. The first was of her and Damien in her college apartment, the one right off of campus. What was he doing with this, she wondered, staring at the picture.

She and Damien looked so young, and so totally happy. Why couldn't she remember that feeling?

She looked at the second photograph. How the hell had he gotten this? The photo was of her wedding day. She and Henry were standing close, holding her bouquet between them. Tess narrowed her eyes. Unlike the other picture, she didn't look exactly happy, but she did look hopeful. Things hadn't started to change yet; Henry hadn't shown his controlling side yet. Henry smiled back at her in the picture, and a shiver moved over her, settling on the scar covering her inner thigh—that hateful scar that would never go away, and would have to be explained if she ever let a man touch her below the waist.

Flashes of her early-morning makeout session with Damien went through her mind. She'd almost gotten that close with him, and he was the last person she wanted to know about her scar.

She took a deep breath and stuffed the pictures back in the drawer. Just as she closed it, she heard, "You never used to be a snoop, Tess York."

Startled, she pushed away from the desk and stood. She fumbled for her crutches.

"Need some help?" he asked.

"Nope."

He walked to her, his blue eyes glistening with mischief. "Find anything interesting?"

"Huh?"

"In my desk. When I came in you seemed fixated on something."

"Spider."

His brow lifted. "You saw a spider?"

"A big, black, hairy one," she explained, knowing full well that he not only didn't believe her, but thought her a total idiot as well. She let her head fall forward and blurted out the truth. "Okay, I was snooping and I saw the two pictures in there. I'm sorry, it was rude…"

He said nothing, and his expression was unreadable. Was he mad? Annoyed? Embarrassed? Who knew. He was giving nothing away. In fact, he changed the subject all together. "Hungry?"

"A little," she said uneasily.

"Good. I've decided that we're going to have lunch in your room."

"Okay." She actually wouldn't mind putting her foot up again. The ache had returned.

He nodded. "I'll meet you there in ten minutes. I'm going to shower first."

Tess paused, and for the first time since Damien had found her at his desk, she really looked at him. From shoes to spiky hair. He had gunk all over him, all over his hands and clothes, probably a mixture of tile adhesive and grout. Her mouth twitched as she remembered him looking like this many a time. He was a man of labor once again.

He stared at her. "What?"

"What?" she returned innocently.

"What's with the face? The grin?"

Was she grinning? That wasn't good. "You just reminded me of this guy I knew a long time ago."

"Really," Damien said in a surly tone.

She nodded. "Yep. He'd always come to pick me up with his hands and face caked with paint or something equally gross."

"Yeah, I remember that guy," Damien said, sticking his hands in his pockets. "He used to be so damn excited to see you he'd forget to clean up before driving over to your house."

"I let him use my shower, didn't I?" Tess said, grinning.

Damien's lips twitched with a faint smile. "You did more than that."

Heat rushed into Tess's cheeks, and she laughed. "Come on."

He walked toward her, his gaze eating her up. "You were damn good at getting paint off and out of the most intimate of places."

"I was a dedicated worker even then."

"I'll say." Without a warning, he scooped her up. "Too bad you've got that bandage on. I could use a little help in the shower today."

For one second she felt the urge to fight him, fight being in his arms. But the feeling quickly dissipated. She didn't have to fight him or fear him. No matter what his motives were in making her come to Tribute and fix up the house, she knew in her heart, in her gut, that Damien Sauer would never make her feel like a frightened, trapped animal.

They were nearing the door to the library when Tess called out, "Wait. My crutches."

"Nope. No crutches, no more getting out of bed."

"Fine. I'll just get Olin to swipe them for me. We're like this now." She crossed her fingers.

"Yeah, right." Damien shifted her in his arms and kept right on walking. "Come on Tess, I need you healthy and walking and back on the job."

Tess laughed as they headed down the hallway. "Manual labor getting to you already?"

"Tiling was never something I enjoyed. I liked the actual building, though." He walked into the guest room and placed her on the bed. "You might find it hard to believe, but on my jobs in California I get in there from time to time and put walls up."

"You're right. I'd find that hard to believe."

He narrowed his eyes with mock severity. "I'll be back in ten minutes."

"I can hardly wait," she said sarcastically, fighting a smile.

"I know—but you'll just have to."

For the first time in a long, long time, Tess watched a man walk away, fully enjoying the view of his lean, hard backside as he went.

The last time they'd eaten in bed, they hadn't made it past the salad.

Damien stared. And if Tess's robe crept open any further, exposing the gentle slope of her breast any more, they weren't going to make it very far today, either.

Lying on the bed, her hair loose and her face free of makeup, Tess held up her sandwich and announced, "This rivals Olivia's Croque Monsieur."

Damien grinned. "High praise?"

"The highest. This cream sauce is insane. And the ham… And these French fries," she continued, lounging back against the dense pillows. "How are they made? They're as light as a leaf."

"If you really want to know, I'll ask Marilynn."

Tess paused, stared at him, her mass of red hair falling about her face. "I can't believe you have a chef."

"Is it that you can't believe I have a chef or that I made enough money to afford one?"

She stopped eating, even put down her fry. Her eyes blazed with sincerity as she said, "I never doubted you'd be successful, Damien."

"Hmm." Why did he find that so hard to believe?

"It's true. I never thought for one second you wouldn't accomplish your goals and make a million."

"Too bad a million wasn't enough." He knew he sounded like a spoiled ass, yet he didn't attempt to apologize or take it back.

"You have the wrong idea about all of this," she said, her food forgotten as her eyes filled with melancholy. "I didn't care about money—I don't care about it now. You know my history, Damien. Losing my parents so young, and having no other family to hang on to. It was brutal. I wasn't ever looking for money. All I wanted was family, a comfortable life, a—"

"A safe life," he finished for her.

"Yes. Safe was the ultimate prize to me, it's what I felt I needed to be happy."

"I wasn't safe."

"No, you weren't. You were all about risk back then. Taking risks. And for you it paid off big-time, and I'm glad."

He didn't need her to be glad for him. He didn't want her to be glad for him. "So you made your choice based on safety."

"Yes."

"And did that make you happy? Were you happy with him?"

The expression that passed over her face was quick but very telling. Pure, unadulterated revulsion.

Damien's eyes narrowed. What the hell? What had happened when she'd left Minneapolis, when she'd left him? What had happened with the safe choice, Henry?

He was about to probe further when they were interrupted by a knock at the door.

Annoyed, he fairly shouted, "Come in."

It was Olin, looking appropriately sheepish. "Sir?"

"What is it?"

"I'm sorry, sir, but there's a problem with the house down the hill."

"What it is?"

"There's been a break-in."

"What? At one in the afternoon?"

"The workmen had gone to lunch, and when they got back the door had been knocked in."

Damien cursed. "By who?"

"A young lady," Olin supplied.

He felt Tess's gaze on him and he turned. A smile tugged at her full mouth and she lifted a brow at him. "Someone you know?"

"Doubtful," Damien said testily. "The women I know would never follow me up here and break into one of my properties."

"You sure about that?"

"Actually, Miss York," Olin said quickly, not meeting her gaze. "The woman says she's a friend of yours."

Tess looked shocked. "What?"

Olin nodded. "She was brought here. She's downstairs in the foyer. Shall I bring her up?"

Damien answered first. "Absolutely."

Eight

"You know this is insane, right?"

As she sat on the bed, in the very spot that Damien had occupied not more than sixty seconds ago, Ms. Olivia Winston's large brown eyes were filled with concern.

Tess's business partner, chef extraordinaire and, after today, nearly a class-C felon, made no bones about what was to be done. "I'm taking you home right now."

"I can't go now," Tess told her.

Olivia frowned. "Can't? Is this guy keeping you here against your—"

"No, no, no. I hurt my foot during the renovation and he's…helping me out." She wondered where Damien was now. He'd been very polite to Olivia, the woman who had broken down his door, before leaving the room.

Olivia took a deep breath and blew it out. "Jeez, Tess. When the hospital called looking for you, I completely freaked out—"

"Wait…the hospital called you?"

"Called the office. It was the number you gave on the form in the *emergency room*." She said the last two words with real feeling.

Tess leaned back against the pillows, cocked her head to one side. "I'm sorry you got scared. It's just a cut. I had a few stitches, and I should be up and moving by tomorrow."

Olivia took a moment to process the information, then seeming somewhat pacified, she asked, "So, are you okay here—I mean, barring the foot. This guy is cool?"

"He's fine."

"Yeah, he is fine," Olivia said dryly, "gorgeous even—but is he treating you well?"

Tess laughed. "Very well. Don't worry."

"Come on, Tess. You're in a client's house, a guy who's basically a stranger. It's not right. I really think you should pack it in and come home."

Tess chewed her lip. She didn't want to go there, didn't want to tell her partner the truth. But Olivia looked as though she wasn't about to let up on the subject. "Listen, Liv, Damien Sauer isn't just a client, and he's definitely not a stranger."

Olivia's brows knit together. "Oh?"

"We used to be an item, back in my college days."

Her brows relaxed. "Oh."

"Yeah, he wanted me to renovate the house. It was the first house he bought back in the day when we were dating, and we spent a lot of time there… So I really know the ins and outs of the place."

She shrugged. "Well then, it makes sense that he'd want to hire you."

Tess gave Olivia a tight smile.

But Olivia wasn't done with the questions. "Why didn't you tell me?"

The reason was right there, on the tip of her tongue, and that's where it remained. She shook her head. "I don't know."

The three partners of No Ring Required had secrets in their past and in their present, and each had done her very best to keep those secrets hidden. But as Tess knew, and Olivia and Mary as well, eventually those secrets had a way of coming out. Maybe knowledge of that was what kept Olivia from prying and pressing Tess for more. Whatever it was, Tess was thankful.

"So," Olivia said, "do you at least want me to stay and help you finish the house?"

Tess kind of did, but she knew that Damien would never allow Olivia to stay and help her. He wanted Tess, and only Tess, to make the house into a home. She smiled at Olivia. "No. Thanks though. It's something…I have to do myself. You understand."

"Not really, but I'll take your word for it."

Tess pointed at her. "Hey, aren't you the only one at the office right now?"

"Yep."

"Well then, we need you there." Tess paused, thought of something that had the nerves in her stomach dancing. "You didn't call Mary when the hospital called you, did you?"

Olivia shook her head. "No. I thought I'd wait and see what was going on here before I interrupted her honeymoon."

"Good." Things had really changed with her partners. Five years ago they hardly spoke unless it was work related. And look at them now.

A bashful grin curved Tess's mouth as she looked at Olivia. "I can't believe you came here."

"Why?"

"We're business partners—"

Olivia leaned in and took a fry from Tess's plate. "If you say we're not friends I'm going to slap you—which would incidentally not be the greatest thing for your recovery."

Tess laughed. "No. It wouldn't."

Nibbling on the cold fry, Olivia said, "Listen, Tess, the three of us—you and Mary and I—we might've started out as 'just business partners,' but I think we're way more than that now. I think we've all been through a lot together. We've all come from something…maybe something not so great, something we want to continue to run from, but I think maybe it binds us."

Tess nodded. "Maybe."

"I believe we got together for a reason. And I hope we're friends now." She gave Tess a coy smile. "You know, I'm thinking that maybe it's not such a bad thing to have each other to lean on."

Olivia's words were passionate and truthful, and hard for Tess to ingest. Right now, anyway. Too much was happening with Damien and the ghosts of the past that he had brought with him. For now, Tess could only nod at her partner, but she hoped that Olivia would understand her small gesture, take it as a sign, a first step toward a future, a friendship.

And in Olivia's way, she did. Smiling, she pointed to Tess's plate and the Croque Monsieur. "Can I have a bite of that?"

"Of course." Tess handed her the uneaten half.

After taking a bite, Olivia sighed. "So good."

"I know, right?" Tess said, laughing.

"I can't believe you're supplying my food here. I left the office too quickly to make anything—you know how much I hate going anywhere without a food offering."

Tess nodded, said with mock seriousness, "I do. You're freakish that way."

Olivia narrowed her eyes. "Watch it, or you won't get any of the truffles I brought. I had them stashed in the freezer, so I could grab them quickly."

"You're such a sugar tease, Liv."

"So I've heard." She reached into her purse and

pulled out a square Tupperware, then she handed it to Tess. "Go nuts, Miz York."

Smiling, Tess settled back against the pillow, a Tupperware full of chocolate truffles against her chest. "So, how many clients are you juggling right now?"

"Three."

"Oh, man. You should get back."

"Not until I know you're all right."

"I'm fine."

Again Olivia narrowed her eyes. "You like being with this guy, don't you?"

Tess heard the question, but was too busy dealing with the shot of awareness that was rolling through her body to answer right away.

Olivia just sighed. "All three of us are raving lunatics when it comes to men. No common sense, no thinking things through—just allowing the beautiful man to sweep us away into a fantasy—"

"So, how is Mac, by the way?" Tess asked dryly.

"Wonderful. But he's such a guy. Did I tell you about his obsession with this portable driving range I bought him?"

"It's winter."

Olivia sighed. "He has it set up in the house. Three broken windows so far…"

For the first time since he'd been back in Minnesota, Damien felt a wave of apprehension move through him. Tess had a good friend in Olivia Winston, and he wouldn't be surprised if the dark-haired beauty had already convinced her to return to Minneapolis.

He sat at his desk in the library, staring at the photograph of Tess and Henry on their wedding day. Damien had gotten so close to finding out the truth about their marriage. The look that had crossed Tess's face. Pretty damn close to horror.

Damien gritted his teeth. Well, she deserved it, didn't she? To be unhappy in her marriage? She'd walked away from Damien for a safe, carefree life, and he was willing to bet that it had been anything but. Time would tell…

Damien thought about ripping up the picture and tossing it in the trash. He didn't need it anymore. He had her, had access to her memories, the real story. That would fuel his fire and the need for payback. But when he tried to rip the photograph in two, he couldn't do it.

"Dammit," he muttered to himself. Why did he need the thing? Was it that he had to look at them, her in that dress and him with that persuasive grin, to keep going, keep punishing her?

He sighed, thrust his hands through his hair.

Whatever the reason, he dropped the picture back in his desk and slammed it shut. Then he grabbed his coat and walked out into the hall. He heard them, Tess and her partner, laughing in the guest room. The sound filled him with lust and he forced himself to turn away and go downstairs. He wanted to be in there, in that room. He wanted to be the one who made her laugh, see her gray eyes sparkle and fill with happiness.

Olin met him at the base of the stairs.

"I'm heading over to the red house," Damien told him. "I'll be back around six."

"Yes, sir."

"If Ms. York asks…"

Olin nodded. "Yes, sir. I'll tell her."

Only for a guy who had donated millions for a new emergency room, Tess thought as she watched Tribute Memorial's chief of staff change the bandage on her foot, all from the comfort of her bed in Damien's guest room. Doctor Keith Leeds had descended on Damien's home twenty minutes ago, medical bag in hand, ready to give Tess a thorough checkup and see how she was healing.

This was an odd occurrence, to say the least, Tess thought. After all, it took a good month for her to get an appointment with her regular doctor—forget her ever-vacationing gynecologist.

"So, what do you think?" she asked him when he'd finished dressing her foot.

Dr. Leeds was short, kind and hovering around fifty. He had a full head of gray hair and liked to fiddle with his glasses when he talked. "Looks good. Really good. But more important, how does it feel?"

"Sore. But the intense pain is gone."

"I'd take things slow. No more than a few hours on it at a time."

"So, I could walk on it?"

He nodded. "Tomorrow, you should be able to get around quite well without the crutches. Just listen to your body. If the pain graduates from sore to more—"

"Nice rhyme."

He laughed. "Thank you. Sore to more, take a break, okay?"

She nodded. "Got it."

It was at that moment that Damien walked into the room. He was dressed in jeans and a black shirt and looked as though he'd just showered, his dark hair wet and spiky. Heat moved through Tess's body at the sight of him, and she turned her attention back to the doctor.

"I'll make sure she takes it easy," Damien said, holding out his hand. "Thanks for coming by, Keith. I know house calls aren't your thing."

The man shook his hand and granted him a smile. "No problem, Damien. It's on my way home."

"So, did I hear you say Tess could walk on her foot tomorrow?"

"I did."

Tess smiled broadly at Damien. "That's right, sir. Back to work."

Doctor Leeds's brow went up, and he said to Damien, "Interesting situation you have here."

Damien chuckled. "You have no idea." He walked the doctor to the door, then said, "Olin is waiting downstairs. He'll see you out."

Dr. Leeds waved at Tess. "Take care, now."

"Will do." She smiled. "Thanks again."

When he was gone, Tess settled under the covers, then proceeded to ask Damien about the new tile. "Is it all in and grouted?"

"Yes." Damien sat on the edge of the bed. "Looks good. The stone you picked out is perfect. Modern, yet warm enough for a cottage."

"Good." With large, excited eyes, she pressed a button on the remote control that was half hidden in the comforter and watched the television slowly rise out of the chest at the end of the bed. "This is the just the coolest thing." When she looked up, she caught Damien staring at her, his eyes heavy with amusement. She heaved a dramatic sigh. "Don't worry, Mr. Sauer, I'm not getting too comfortable."

"What does that mean?"

"Just because I'm fascinated with the elevator television thing doesn't mean I don't understand what happens tomorrow."

"What happens tomorrow?"

"I go back to work, and back to living in the red house."

"Back to work, maybe," he said. "For short bursts. But you're not living in that house."

"Yes, I am."

"No." He crossed his arms over his chest and waited for her to acquiesce.

She didn't. "I think it's best."

"Not for me. You've had one accident there. I'm not taking any risks with a second."

"Not taking any risks, huh?" she said slyly.

"Not with you." A wicked glint appeared in his blue eyes.

A jolt of heat flashed into her belly. Great, she thought. Twice in five minutes.

It was back—the lust—back with a vengeance. She wanted him to kiss her again, touch her, taste her.

Fear gripped her heart, went to war with the sparks of desire heating her blood. What would he think if he saw her scar, that disgusting reminder of a past they both wanted to put behind them?

But as it was, she didn't need to worry. At that moment Damien was thinking about something completely different. "If you go back to the red house and something worse happens," he was saying, "you could sue me."

He was thinking about business.

"Right." Feeling like a jerk, she turned back to the television and started flipping through the channels. "Can't have that."

They were silent for a moment. Then Damien pointed at something on the TV. "Hey, what's that?"

"What's what?"

"Go back two stations."

Curious, she did, but once there, she shook her head vehemently. "Oh, no."

"Oh, yes."

"Hey, we're not dating anymore. I don't have to pretend I like this movie."

He turned away from *Dirty Harry* and tossed her a sardonic look. "How many times did I have endure

Meg Ryan and that Barrymore girl? *French Kiss* was not about what I thought it was going to be about…"

She laughed. "Are you saying I owe you?"

"Yeah."

"You know, you could watch it in another room—you have a media room, for God's sake."

"And not see your horrified face when Clint Eastwood says that, 'Do you feel lucky? Do yah, punk?' line? What fun is that?"

"You're a sadist."

He didn't answer, just leaned over and pressed the intercom on the table by the bed.

"Yes, Miss York?"

"We need popcorn, Olin."

The man was silent for a moment, then he said quickly, "Ah, yes, sir."

Damien looked over at Tess, raised a brow. "Butter?"

She snorted. "Are you kidding? Not that much has changed in six years."

He laughed. "Extra butter, Olin."

"Very good, sir."

Damien kicked off his shoes and got in bed beside her. Not all that close, but close enough for Tess to breathe in the clean scent of his hair and skin. Close enough for her skin to tighten and feel prickly, feel desperate for his touch.

"Can you turn it up?"

She turned back to the screen and pressed the volume button. "Just so you know," she began, "*Last of the Mohicans* is on after this."

He groaned. "No way. That's not just a chick flick, that's a period chick flick."

She laughed. "After this classic here, you're gonna owe *me*."

"Fine." He reached over to press the intercom again. "But we're going to need a few beers to go with that popcorn."

He was screwed.

It was midnight, the movies were over, the beer and popcorn consumed, the room was lit by a full moon, and Damien was still in bed with Tess. She wasn't naked and sitting on top of him, but he felt as though he might explode just the same.

Halfway through the *Mohicans* movie, she'd fallen asleep, rolled in his direction and now here they were: Damien on his back and Tess curled up beside him, her arm around his waist, her head on his chest.

He was no sap, but tonight had been fun, sexy in an odd, sweet way—like old times. And he didn't want it to end. Maybe it didn't have to.

Could he just close his eyes, fall asleep and wake up with her next to him? Could he? He dropped his chin and kissed the top of her head, the soft, red curls that were scented with apples from her shampoo. He grinned. It was the same shampoo she'd used in college.

She stirred then, her knee escaping the confines of her robe and sliding up his thigh. An inch higher, he mused, and she'd feel every hard inch of him.

She moved again, her head lifting, her eyes, groggy and heavy, opening and trying to focus.

"Damien?"

He ran his thumb over her bottom lip. "Yes, sweetheart?"

"I wanted you." She spoke softly and slowly as though she was still in a dream state. Then her eyes closed again and she shook her head. "I wanted you so much."

His body went still. His fingers went under her chin and he lifted her face to his once more. "What did you say?"

Her eyes opened again and she looked like she was trying to focus.

"What did you just say, Tess?"

She licked her lips. "I want you."

Disappointment roared through him, but he dismissed the feeling. It wasn't what she'd originally said, that was for sure, but it was enough—enough to put flame to sun-dried brushwood.

He dipped his head and kissed her, gentle and slow, trying to coax a response from her. She was cautious at first, her kisses guarded and quick. But as he rubbed the back of her neck, nuzzled her lips with his own, her body relaxed and she opened for him, lapping at his tongue, matching his speed and the pressure of his mouth.

It took every ounce of self-control for Damien not to pull her on top of him and have his way with her. Every nerve ending, every muscle was alive, inside and out, and when she slid her hand up his chest, to his neck and around his head, he allowed himself to take her.

Like a possessed animal, he rolled, sending her to her back and settling himself above her. For a moment he just looked at her, watched her eyes glisten, her lips part and her chest rise and fall with every breath.

She belonged to him.

He would have to let her go soon, but for now, right now, she was his.

He bent and kissed her, her mouth, her chin, then down, his lips searing a path from her neck to her collarbone. He wanted to feel every part of her, taste every inch, make love to her until they were both too exhausted to speak about the past or even think about it.

Maybe then she'd be out of his system and he could go back to California and breathe again.

His hands moved over her collarbone and he pushed aside the white terry cloth robe, revealing her pale chest and her heavy, full breasts. She arched her back, thrusting her breasts and tight, pink nipples forward. Damien cupped them firmly, then rolled one taut nipple between his thumb and forefinger. He dipped his head and took the other into his mouth, rolled the tight peak against his tongue, lapped and suckled, then ever so gently bit down on the tip.

"Damien," she moaned, her head thrashing from side to side against the pillow, her hips thrusting, trying to meet his.

But Damien couldn't keep things slow and relaxed. He needed to be inside her body, needed to consume her. He cursed his frustration and reached down for the knot that held her robe together. But just as he'd gotten it undone, Tess put a hand over his and squeezed.

"Damien. Please. No more. I can't." She sounded like an injured bird, and Damien watched as she covered herself back up with the robe.

Like a hammer, the blood in Damien's veins pounded inside his head and chest and groin. But he wouldn't make demands or beg her to put him out of his misery. That wasn't his style.

Instead he moved off her, off the bed, stood there with his erection pressed against the zipper of his jeans.

Tess stared at the comforter. She wanted to die.

She sat there in the bright light of the round moon, not looking at Damien, not wanting to face what was coming next. She had allowed things to go too far. Again. What was wrong with her? Did she have no self-control when it came to this man?

She grabbed for the comforter and pulled it over her legs. What a fool she was. Damien had been unbelievably close to touching her scar.

"Tess?"

"Yes."

"Look at me."

Cowardice was not a part of her makeup, and she lifted her chin and looked at him. Her stomach clenched. Never had a man looked so sexy, his hair tousled, his eyes heavy, his cheeks flushed.

"What's wrong?" he asked darkly.

"This can't happen."

"It is happening."

He was right. They'd started something, and how was either of them supposed to go back? "I was half-asleep, Damien, too comfortable…"

"Don't try and pretend you didn't want this, Tess, because—"

"I'm not." She shook her head. "I did want it, but now…"

His eyes were devil-black and menacing. "And now? What?"

She stared at him, trying to think of what to say next. If she lied, was cruel, would it stop him from wanting her? Would it stop the flirtation and fun and frivolous moments?

Is that what she wanted?

No, but she couldn't have him find out her secret. And she would protect herself at all costs.

"Now I know that it's not fair to you to continue this," she said evenly.

He lifted a brow. "Oh? How so?"

She squared her jaw. "Because when I was kissing you, I was thinking about…" She stopped. She couldn't.

He looked ready to kill as he ground out, "Finish your sentence, Tess."

"No."

He stared at her for a moment, then he turned to leave.

Her heart pounded against her rib cage. This was

ridiculous, insane and juvenile. She was a grown woman, for God's sake.

His hand was on the door when she called, "Stop. Wait, Damien."

He glanced over his shoulder, said with a bored tone to his voice, "What?"

"It's not true."

He said nothing.

She continued, "It's not true." She released a breath. "I needed you to stop touching me, so I lied. You were right. So right. I loved it, every second that you were kissing me and touching me. I haven't felt that good in a long time. But I needed you to stop."

His jaw hard, he leaned back against the door. "Why?"

She shook her head. "I can't tell you."

His fist shot back, pounded the door. "Dammit! Come on, Tess. This is bull."

"Maybe. But to me it's my life."

He cursed.

"Damien, I'm going back to the red house tomorrow."

"You're not going anywhere," he said in a dangerous voice, his gaze fierce. "And I'm warning you, don't push me on that again."

He said nothing more as he turned, gripped the door handle and threw it wide. He was gone in seconds.

Tess dropped back against he pillow, feeling miserable and lonely. And what made it worse was that the faint scent of him lingered on her pillow.

Nine

As the first week of renovations drew to a close, the little red house had taken on a whole new look. New windows, new tile, new tub and toilet, new cabinets and new light fixtures had been installed. Tess had worked hard with some help from Damien and of course the labor of several subcontractors.

Today the beautiful vintage floors that Tess had ordered were being put in. Normally a house was painted before the floors went down, but with her injury things had gotten a bit turned around.

After an hour or so at the red house, making sure everything was going as planned, Tess had asked Damien to drive her into Jackson to pick out the new kitchen countertops. Though her foot was much better, driving was still an issue.

They hadn't spoken a word about last night, not at the red house, not on the drive to Jackson and not as they walked through Hubbard's Tile and Stone. Tess figured it was just as well. Best to get the job done and get on with it. No entanglements, no regrets and no secrets revealed.

But then again, she missed the intimacy they'd shared last night, the fun they'd shared—and the heat of his mouth when he kissed her senseless.

As the salesman hovered at her side, Tess rubbed her hand over the honed black granite she had picked out. She sighed. "This is gorgeous." Then she pointed to the clean, white Corian. "But this is practical."

Damien finished a call on his cell phone, then stated dryly, "You know my opinion on practical."

"I do."

"Well then, you know which one to get."

Tess asked the salesman to excuse them for a moment, then she turned to Damien. "Are you like this with every project?"

"Like what?"

"Impractical. I can't see you making much money if that's the case."

His gaze turned intense and personal. "This isn't every project."

She didn't want to go there, and didn't acknowledge the look. "If you're just going to sell the place, what's the point of such personal taste?"

He lifted a brow. "Who says I'm going to sell it?" His cell rang again. He checked the number, then let the call go to voicemail.

"So, what are you going to do with it, Damien?" she asked with perhaps too much interest. "Keep it as an investment property?"

"I don't know."

"Pass it down to the next generation of Sauers?" she pressed.

He shrugged. "Perhaps. But that could be a while. I'd have to get married first."

"You don't have to get married…"

"If I'm going to make little Sauers, I do."

Tess stopped talking, stopped asking questions she didn't want the answers to. The thought of Damien having children with anyone else made her feel physically ill. Not just the act that it would take to create them, but the thought of him sharing a life, a day-to-day life with a woman and their children… she couldn't conceive of it.

Oddly enough, she'd never been able to. It was one of the things that had gotten her through the past six years, settled her with Henry—believing that Damien Sauer would never get married and have babies.

And now, here he was talking about it as though it could actually happen.

Tess turned back to the granite. "I just don't see it. You and a family. No, don't see it."

"I'm an old-fashioned guy, Tess."

"Sure." She laughed, but it was a heavy, sad sound. "The millionaire jet-setter with a glass compound and a penchant for making women pay for their mistakes."

"Just one woman," he said, his gaze intense.

"Right."

He added, "And when did you decide that leaving me was a mistake?"

She opened her mouth to deny it, then stopped, ran through what she'd just said—what had accidentally popped out. How she felt that leaving him was a mistake…

She sighed inwardly. It was a truth she hated to look at, much less admit out loud, and she pressed on, changed the subject. "Are you going to tell me what you plan to do with the house or not?"

He frowned. "I'll decide what to do with it when the work's completed."

Frustrated, she shrugged. "Fine."

"So, do you want the granite?"

"Yes, I want the granite."

Damien gestured to the salesman. "She'll take the granite." Then he walked off, his cell phone to his ear.

He couldn't sleep.

Again.

Damien glanced at the clock. Midnight. What was up with midnight? His body just couldn't seem to shut down, and his mind couldn't seem to shut off. All he could think about was her. The fact that she was down the hall, sleeping, and he wanted to be next to her again, feel the warmth of her body, her arm draped over his chest.

He rolled off the bed and threw on a T-shirt and sweats. He was a jackass, thinking he could go to her and she would welcome him into her bed as though nothing had happened, as if it was six years ago and she was waiting up for him.

But he was out his door and down the hall and knocking on her door before he could talk himself out of it.

When she didn't answer, he knocked again, even said her name. When there was still no answer, he contemplated going back to his room. But then he got a strange feeling, a worried feeling, that maybe something was wrong, and he decided to go in— deal with her ire if he had to.

He opened the door silently. It wasn't terribly dark in the room. The shades were pulled back and the moon was brilliant and nearly full, illuminating the furniture. He walked over to the bed, blinked to make sure he was seeing things clearly. Then he leaned down and flipped on the bedside lamp.

His gut clenched. The bed was made, and all of Tess's things were gone.

He muttered a curse, stalked out of the room and went to find Olin.

With a large hoop of painter's tape circling her wrist like a bracelet, Tess moved on to the next window. Tomorrow was priming and painting day, and she'd wanted to get a head start.

Well, that was mostly true.

Staying in Damien's guest room was starting to feel a little too comfortable, and kind of uncomfortable at the same time. Lying in that bed, she'd wanted him beside her, watching a movie, feeling his warmth….

She ran the tape over the window molding and snapped it off. The paint colors she chose were going to be amazing, especially with the new floors.

Oh, the floors.

They were so beautiful that when she'd gotten there tonight, she had actually sat in the middle of the living room and stared at them for a full thirty minutes. If she ever won the lottery, the beige carpet in her apartment was going into the trash and these floors were going in.

Suddenly the front door burst open and Damien stood there, looking diabolically sexy and ready to do battle.

"Holy…Jeez!" Tess gripped her chest, felt her heart slamming against her ribs.

"Get your things, we're going," Damien said, his voice low and menacing.

She glared at him. "You scared the hell out of me."

He closed the door and walked into the room, his long, wool coat trailing behind him like a villain's cape. "As if you didn't know I'd come after you."

"Well, sure I did. But I thought it would be in the morning." She was starting to believe that there was no escaping this man. "How did you even know I was gone?"

"Doesn't matter."

"Olin squealed on me, didn't he?"

Damien lifted his chin. "His loyalty should be to me."

She sighed. The poor guy. She shouldn't have put him in such an awkward position. "Don't be mad at him. I begged him to drive me, told him it was sort of a life-and-death thing."

"Whatever the reason, he made a mistake and he's fired."

Damien bent and pulled back the tarp covering the floors. Tess bent next to him, her sore foot aching a little with the movement. He looked at her. "Floors are beautiful."

Awareness moved through her, sent chills to the outside of her body and heat to the inside. Her voice was easy and intimate as she said, "You're not really going to fire him, right?"

His blue eyes softened, and he gave a small shrug. "No. But I should."

"Thanks." She sat on her backside.

Damien followed suit, looking far too handsome and put together to be sitting amongst drop cloths and paint buckets. "You don't just disappear, Tess. I told you to stay in—"

"Please, Damien," she said, putting up her hand to stop him from saying anything further. "I am not your prisoner and you are not my warden."

"This isn't about keeping you captive, Tess."

"What's it about, then?"

"Keeping you safe, dammit!"

She sighed. "That was one freak accident. It's not going to happen again."

His eyes glimmered with heat. "You're right it's not, because you're coming back with me."

"No," she said firmly.

"No?"

He looked so shocked, so vexed, she couldn't help but laugh. "I know that's hard for you to hear," she said, sobering slightly. "I'm sure you don't hear it very often."

"Tess—"

"I like this house. I feel comfortable here."

"You don't feel comfortable in my house?" he demanded darkly.

She sighed. Didn't he get it? "Damien, I can't stay there…with you."

His mouth curved into a wicked grin. "Afraid I'm going to finish what I started last night?"

"Frankly, yes."

He reached over and took her hand, then bent and kissed the inside of her wrist. "Sweetheart, it doesn't matter where we are. In that house or in this one."

"So why fight it, is that what you're saying?" The heat from his mouth had branded the skin on her wrist and she felt weak. Clearly he still remembered where her most sensitive spots were.

"Why not go with your instincts, Tess?"

She forced herself to return to reality, to remember the past and what it had taught her about instincts. "I did that once before, and it didn't turn out…it didn't turn out as I'd planned."

His brows knit together. "What are we talking about? You and Henry?"

She nodded.

"Do you want to tell me what happened?"

"You only want to know so you can use it against me."

He said nothing. Didn't agree, didn't deny it.

She pulled her hand away and shook her head. "I'm right, aren't I? There's something in you that wants to really hurt me?"

Silence met her query. Damien stared at her for a good long time before he finally said, "If I'm honest with you, will you be honest with me?"

A shot of panic went through her. How honest did he want her to be? How honest would she allow herself to be?

But even as the questions circled her mind, she looked at him and nodded.

"Yes, I want to hurt you," he said softly. "I want you to feel just a fraction of what I felt when you left. And even after we're together, after we make love—because you and I both know that's going to happen—I'll still want you to hurt because I'm an ass, a miscreant." He reached out and touched her face, his fingertips brushing gently over her cheek. "When you left, I became someone else, a machine, a man with no soul."

His words cut deeply into her, fisted around her heart. Six years ago she left the man she loved for a promise of what she'd always believed would make her happy. The mistake had cost her in so many ways.

It was her turn, and he was waiting. She knew she wouldn't go all the way with the truth, but Damien deserved to hear as much as she could give him. "My marriage was a lie." She saw the surprise register on his face, but just kept going. "I wanted the perfect little life, the perfect family. Henry promised me that, and I believed him. When we knew each other in college, he was uncomplicated and sweet, but one week after we got married he showed me who he really was."

"And who was that?" Damien asked softly.

She swallowed the knot in her throat. "A mean, manipulative, controlling monster."

Damien said nothing, just stared at her, expressionless.

She said shakily, "You think I got what I deserved, right?"

He stood, held out his hand for her. "Come on, Tess."

"Henry took away my faith and my hope." She felt so tired all of a sudden. She put her hand in Damien's and let him pull her to her feet.

"You think I deserved it…" she started weakly.

But Damien was clearly done with the conversation. "Get your things," he said. "We're going back to the house."

* * *

Damien sat on a stool at the minidiner inside Wanda's store. It was hours past closing time, but when he'd shown up on Wanda's doorstep a few minutes ago, she hadn't turned him away.

With wild graying hair and a robe so thick it could double as a winter coat, Wanda poured them each a cup of coffee, then took the seat beside him at the Christmas-festooned counter. "Well, well, well…"

"I know. It's late."

"Never mind that," she said. "Are you going to tell me what the problem is or do I have to guess?"

The problem. He wasn't exactly sure himself. He just knew that after dropping Tess off at the house and getting her settled—then tossing out some threats to Olin regarding the penalties given if he ever offered Tess a ride to the red house in the middle of the night again—he'd needed to get out of his house.

Wanda grunted at him. "Fine. I'll guess. Business?"

"No."

"Must be personal, then. Not my favorite thing to discuss, but I'll do it. Spill."

The cat clock above the griddle meowed twice. Two o'clock in the morning. Damien shoved his hands through his hair. "You know how I got so successful, Wanda?"

She grinned at him. "Fine brain, fine man."

He chuckled halfheartedly. "No. Try follow through and a killer instinct."

"My second guess."

"I made a plan and I followed it through to the letter. No second thoughts, no kindness, no compassion."

"And?"

"And I'm having second thoughts about my plan."

She stood, reached over the counter and grabbed a small bottle. "Why?"

"I don't know." But he did, actually. After hearing Tess's confession about her bogus marriage and Henry being a monster, he was having second thoughts about his plans to hurt her. If she'd been hurt already, how could he…

"Come on, Damien," Wanda said, pouring the liquid from the small bottle into each mug of coffee, which, knowing Wanda, was probably whiskey. "You just don't want to admit the reason because it'll make you feel like less of a man."

Damien grinned at her over his hootch-laced coffee cup. She never let him get away with anything. He'd been parentless for more than fifteen years now, and had done just fine on his own. Then he'd met Wanda, and she'd offered her friendship and sage advice and over the years had become a motherly figure to him.

"It's the woman you met—the redhead," he admitted darkly.

Wanda nodded. "Thought so. But, Damien, hon, you can't let love influence your decisions."

"You're the only woman I know who'd say that."

Wanda just smiled and sipped her coffee.

"And incidentally," he added, "this isn't about love."

"No?"

"No." Then he amended the statement. "Well, not love now. There was love in the past and it was thrown back in my face, and you know how well a man takes something like that."

"I do. So use it. Use the anger and pain and stomped-on pride. Use that to regain your momentum and stop those second thoughts."

"Why aren't you trying to talk me out of my plan and into the flowery world of forgiveness?"

Wanda poured the rest of whatever alcohol had been in the bottle into her empty coffee cup. "Hell, Damien, if I advise you to forgive and move on, then I've got to do it myself."

"Who are you talking about?" Wanda had been seeing her produce supplier for a few months now. Damien didn't know the guy all that well. But he did know the man's name. "Is it Paulo? Did you two have a fight, because I will break him in two if he hurts you—"

"No, no." She shook her head. "This is way before Paulo."

"Well, who was it then?"

"You don't know him, my first husband—"

"You were married before?"

"That's enough now. My past is my own and I don't like 'sharing time.'" She drained her cup, then stood. "I need my beauty sleep and you need to get back to your life." She leaned in and kissed him on the cheek. "Lock up when you go, all right?"

"Sure."

Damien drank the rest of his coffee, but didn't move from the counter. Wanda was right. Every time he felt connected to Tess, felt sorry for her, he needed to go back in time and remember how she'd walked away without giving a damn about how he felt.

He needed to revise his plan. He needed to remember that he hadn't come back to Minnesota to rekindle a romance, but to get close to Tess again, make her love him, then make her pay.

And as soon as her foot had totally healed, that's just what he was going to do.

Ten

Stitches out and foot feeling good.

Tess walked out of the doctor's office, sans crutches and Band-Aid free. The doctor, who, even after Tess had assured him that it had been no trouble getting there, had insisted that he could've come to Damien's house for the final checkup.

But Tess wasn't an invalid anymore and she didn't want to act like one. She could walk and work and drive again. And Damien, thank goodness, hadn't given her any trouble, even when she'd told him that she was going to take a cab to the doctor's office and not his town car.

In fact, Tess mused as she walked out of the building and down the sidewalk toward the waiting cab, Damien hadn't made any trouble or made any passes at her in the past few days.

After coming home from painting the red house, he'd basically checked in on her, then disappeared. Could the reason stem from all those things she'd told him about Henry and her marriage?

As she sat in the back of the taxi, she wondered if Damien had given up on her, didn't want to deal with her baggage and had his sights set on someone else. The thought of him even looking at another woman made her lungs feel as though they were having the air squeezed out of them.

When her cab pulled into the driveway of the little red house, the first thing Tess saw was Damien, looking very sexy under the December sun. He had shoveled the snow off of a large patch of grass and had put down a tarp. On top of the tarp were the kitchen cabinets. Damien had work clothes on, and he didn't look up when she got out of the car.

Not until she was practically upon him.

"Hey," she called as she walked toward him.

He glanced up, over his shoulder. "Hey, there." Even with the slight warmth of the sun, the cold, clear morning had brought color to his cheeks, and his blue eyes glittered like sapphires.

"What are you doing?" she asked him.

"Sanding the cabinets."

"They look good."

"They're a work in progress."

"Well, I just came from the doctor and he said I'm good to go."

"What does that mean?" he asked.

"That means you don't have to do this anymore. Go home, get back to your regular life, and I'll take over here."

He paused, thought about this, then said, "I don't think so."

"Excuse me?"

He stood, looked down at her with a resolute expression. "I've decided that we're going to finish this house together."

Her heart started to pump faster. "You have?"

"Yes."

"Why?"

"Could be fun."

"Yeah, but doesn't that defeat the purpose?"

He cocked his head. "What purpose is that?"

"Making me suffer, making me work my backside off as punishment for my sins."

A wicked smile tugged at his lips. "I think your backside is pretty perfect the way it is."

Heat swirled in her belly and her legs felt shaky and weak. She tried not to smile too broadly.

"The truth is," he began evenly. "I need to get back to California sooner than I expected."

"Oh." She tried to mask the disappointment she felt, but she wasn't sure if she'd pulled it off.

"I need everything done by Wednesday."

Her jaw dropped. "That's two days away."

"That's right."

He seemed so blasé about the whole thing, but Tess just wasn't up for pretending she was, too. "I'd better get on the phone and see if we can have the countertops and furniture delivered ASAP."

As she walked toward the house, Damien called after her. "Throw money at the problem. That always works for me."

Tess didn't get it. Who was this guy? This chameleon? Warm and vulnerable one moment, then cold and demanding the next.

She went inside and took out her cell phone, dialed the number for Hubbard's Tile and Stone. As she spoke with the manager about changing their delivery date, she tried not to think about how in just two days Damien would be out of her life for good.

It had been a long, dusty day, but much had been accomplished. The cabinets were sanded, stained and affixed to the newly painted kitchen walls. The bathroom was completely done, the bedroom, too. The only things that needed to be done were the countertops, moldings, outlet covers, a few fixtures and the furniture. Tess had already brought back the three pieces she'd bought from Mr. Opp, and the other two delivery companies had jumped at the extra cash, and were going to be at the red house tomorrow before noon.

Tess stood in the living room and sighed. She hadn't expected to fall in love with the house all over again. It had always been cute, but now it was modern and charming. It was how she would redo her home if she had the funds. It was perfect, and no doubt some perfect little family would stumble upon it and make it theirs.

Just moments ago Damien had gone out for pizza, and Tess decided to get cleaned up and get off her feet at the same time. She headed into the bathroom. The soapstone spa tub she'd picked out looked inviting. Would it be so wrong if she tried it out?

She sat on the edge of the tub and turned the knobs. Water gushed from the tap. Hot, steamy water. Just the sight of it made her muscles relax.

Ten minutes later, she was up to her neck in bubbles, daydreaming about a man with dark hair and blue eyes, who was hovering over her, ready to explore every inch of her body. Just as she was about to let him, there was a knock on the bathroom door.

"Tess?"

Damien's booming voice brought her instantly back to reality and she sat up, sloshing water over the sides of the tub. "Yes. What?"

"You okay in there?"

"Yeah. Of course. Just cleaning up."

"In the new bathtub?" She heard the amusement in his voice.

"I had to make sure it was…"

"Seaworthy?" he supplied.

"Comfortable."

"I have the pizza, and I got those garlic knots you like."

She smiled at the thoughtfulness of his gesture. She called out, "You can go ahead and eat if you want."

"No, I'll wait. Take your time."

Yeah, as if she could just lie back and relax with him out there waiting for her. Not possible.

"I'm done," she called, standing and stepping out of the water. But in her rush, she knocked the bar of soap she'd just used off the holder and onto the floor. It made a loud thud of a sound. She called out a rather terse, "Dammit," as she leaned over to retrieve it.

She knew her mistake the minute she stood up again.

She heard his footsteps, then the door opened before she could even grab a towel. Her heart slammed against her ribs and a silent scream escaped her throat as she realized that he was going to see— her leg. The scar on her leg.

No, no. She couldn't let him.

But it was too late. He was coming through the door. "What was that? Are you okay?"

"Damien get out!" she shouted, full on panic in her tone. "Out. Please."

But like anyone with a disaster in their sites, Damien couldn't look away. "Tess?"

She felt weightless, out of her body.

He cocked his head to one side and his eyes narrowed, he stared at her inner thigh, at the massive burn scar that had eaten up her smooth, beautiful skin five years ago. "What the hell happened to you?"

Misery gripped her and she shook her head. "Please go."

His gaze found hers. "Was that an accident?"

"No. Now please go."

"Someone did this to you? He looked horrified. "Who—" He took a few steps closer. "Holy sh—"

"Damien, please don't." She grabbed the towel off the hook and wrapped it around herself.

"Why didn't you tell me?" he demanded, going to her, pulling her into his arms. "Oh, my God, why didn't you come to me?"

She shook her head. "I couldn't."

"You could have."

Her towel slipped, and she tried to retrieve it, but Damien stopped her.

Her eyes implored him. "I need it."

"Screw the towel." He looked into her eyes, his own so stormy, so intense and she saw the man, the boy from long ago. And he was thoroughly pissed off. "I'm going to kill him."

"Too late."

He wrapped his arms around her and held her close, kissed her hair, her neck, her mouth. Against her lips, he uttered miserably, "You should've come to me."

Wearing nothing, the air hitting her scar, she felt so vulnerable. "And what would you have done, Damien? Tell me I deserved it?"

He tipped her face so she could see him, see the passion in his eyes. "Never, do you hear me? Never." Before she could respond, he slipped an arm under her legs and lifted her up, then he headed out of the bathroom.

She wrapped her arms around his neck. "Where are you taking me?"

"Somewhere where I can kiss you properly," he said, leaving the bathroom.

"You *were* kissing me."

He paused at the bedroom door, his gaze moving over her mouth. "I need you on your back for this kind of kissing."

Excitement warred with the panic in her belly. She'd dreamed about him touching her, kissing her, spreading her legs apart and using his tongue to drive her mad. But in every fantasy, her leg was unblemished, smooth and perfect.

She didn't want him to see her, touch that part of her….

He placed her on the bed and bent his head, applying soft, teasing kisses over her toes, then little nibbles at her ankles. Up he went, suckling her calves and the soft spot over her knee. Tess wanted to enjoy it, but she couldn't allow herself to let go. He was so close to seeing it, feeling— So close to her scar.

"No, Damien, please." She put her hand over the rough skin on her inner thigh.

"Sweetheart, let me touch you, please." His warm hand moved up her leg, gently forcing her hand off her scar.

Tess could barely breathe. "I'm not…can't…it's ugly…"

"No, sweetheart. You're beautiful."

And then he was there, applying soft kisses to the rough, sensitive surface of her scar, and Tess loved it and hated it at the same time. While her mind roared with thoughts and fears from her past, Damien kept talking to her, whispering sweet, erotic words as he soothed her with his hands.

So many nights she had dreamed of this, wondered if she'd ever feel sexual, if she'd feel desired by a man. On a hungry groan, Damien moved upward to the wet curls between her legs. She could feel his breath on her, and she released a tense, excited sigh.

"My Tess," he uttered as he reached beneath her and cupped her buttocks, squeezed the round flesh until she lifted her hips. Then he lowered his head.

Tess stared at him, at his head between her legs, electric heat flickering inside of her at the erotic sight.

And then he touched her with his tongue, soft, slow circles over the hard bud that she'd thought for so long was dead.

"Damien, please…" She didn't know what she was asking for.

But Damien responded to the ache of desperation in her voice by nuzzling her, lapping at the tender bud with his deliciously rough tongue, suckling it deep until she wriggled beneath him, called his name again.

Tess pumped her hips, feeling as though she could cry, it felt so good. She wanted the incredible heat and pressure to last forever.

As she fisted the white comforter, pointed her toes and mewled like animal in pain, Damien's mouth teased and twisted. Beads of sweat broke out on her forehead as his hands gripped her buttocks. No matter how desperately she wanted to, Tess couldn't hold on to the sweet feeling for much longer.

It had been so long, and the pressure was building and had to be released. And then she called out, thrust her hands in his hair and spread her legs as wide as she could.

Damien gave a guttural sound of approval, then sank his tongue deeply inside her. Blinding heat surged through her as she shook with climax. Her body was out of control and on fire and she pressed against his mouth, taking his tongue into her body, then out again. Over and over until the pressure eased, then subsided.

When it did, Damien sat up. His gaze was thunderstorm dark, and he looked ready to pounce. Quick as a jungle cat, he pulled off his clothes, grabbed a condom from his pocket then sheathed himself.

Unable to breathe, to think clearly, Tess watched every move he made, watched his hand glide over his thick, hard erection, watched the muscles in his chest and abdomen tighten when he did.

The muscles between her legs quivered with anticipation. She remembered how well their bodies fit together, and the wait was torture. She'd waited too long. They both had. She wanted him on top of her, his shaft inside of her.

When Damien was poised above her, the long, hard length of him bobbing sensually against her belly, she licked her lips. She had been starved for so long.

Not anymore.

Her legs were weak and shaky, but her body craved more and she opened for him, no longer self-conscious about her scar. The slick evidence of her need dripped from the center of her onto the bed sheets, and as Damien watched, his eyes glittering with need, he reached out and touched her, played with the damp curls above until he found the wet folds beneath. Tess's breath caught in her throat as his fingertip circled the entrance to her body with slow, torturous strokes.

Panting and dizzy, Tess let her head fall to one side as she pressed herself into his hand. "Damien, please. I want you."

Damien was over her in seconds, the hard tip of his erection poised at the entrance to her body. And then he entered her, slowly, one delicious inch at a time, stretching her, giving her body what it craved, what it remembered.

When he was all the way inside of her, he hovered there, his gaze locked to hers. "Hey."

Her arms went around him and she smiled. "Hey."

As she stared up into his eyes, their breath mingling, their bodies joined, she knew she had fallen in love with him. Or was it *back* in love with him?

Maybe she had never stopped.

The heat inside of her continued to build, demanding that she take it and release it. She wrapped her legs around his waist, and he starting moving, slowly pumping inside of her until she caught his rhythm, the perfect rhythm. Her hands drifted down his back and over his buttocks. She loved the way his muscles flexed as he thrust deeper and deeper inside of her.

Damien bent his head and kissed her, nuzzled at the entrance to her mouth until she opened for him. His tongue lapped at hers, mimicking the movement of their bodies.

Tess was growing restless again as the building pressure of orgasm was upon her. Heat and pleasure swirled through her, and when Damien slipped his hand between them and spread her wide, pressed himself against her and rode her hard, she felt her mind slipping away and the slow, booming fire of climax returning, taking over every muscle, every limb, every inch of her hot skin.

Damien must have felt it, too, because his thrusts turned from tame to wild, his forehead glistened with sweat and he reached underneath her buttocks and lifted her higher.

His erection slammed against the sweet spot inside of her, the core of nerves that had only ever been turned on by this man.

"Oh, yes, Damien," she called, thrusting her hips upward in a wild, jerky motion as he thrust into her. Her skin was slick, hot and she ached for release. Damien gave it to her with one hard thrust against that soft, aching spot deep within her and she cried out, gripping his back, thrusting her hips.

Damien shuddered, his body racked with the spasms of climax. Saying her name over and over, he lifted up and plunged back down, burying himself as deep as he could go. Then his body gave one last tremor and he collapsed on top of her.

Tess held him close, breathing heavily, her eyes closed tightly as she felt small aftershocks of her release play through her. Feeling so close to Damien, Tess stroked his back and buttocks, even lifted her hips to feel him deep inside of her again as their bodies cooled.

After a few minutes Damien tried to roll to one side, but she held him there.

"I'm going to smother you," he said softly, gently.

She shook her head and held tight. "No, I love it."

This man's weight on her was pure heaven and she just wanted to feel him for as long as she could have him. But after a few minutes his prediction was correct and her chest started to grow weary from the pressure.

She let him roll to his back, and smiled when he took her with him. He held her possessively, curled her against him, and as they started to breath normally again, he played with her long red hair, his fingers dancing in her curls.

"Damien?"

"Hmm?"

"There's something I have to say."

He paused, then said softly, "Okay."

She closed her eyes, snuggled deep into his arm. "Back then, six years ago, when we were together, I had so much passion for you, so much love. I thought that such a deep love, such an intense attraction couldn't last. Honestly, I thought a real, committed relationship, the kind that went on for fifty years, had to be something tamer and more sensible."

"Oh, Tess. That's silly."

"I know. I was an idiot."

"You were young."

"Yes, I was a young idiot."

He chuckled softly. "Doesn't matter."

"Sure it does."

"No, sweetheart. All that matters is what you believe now."

She'd never felt so safe, so happy. She knew the feeling was probably a temporary one, but she didn't care. She was going to enjoy it for as long as possible.

She ran a hand over his chest, played in the sprinkling of damp hair. "I believe that love is the most important gift. I believe in second chances and that being afraid of your feelings can only lead you down the path of unhappiness and regret. And I'm done with regret."

Damien pulled her even closer and kissed her hair.

Tess nuzzled his chest. "You know, I was leaving him when he got in the accident. It was the day after he gave me the scar. He was following me. He swore he'd always follow me. That's when he got into the car accident."

"Oh, Tess." Damien kissed her hair softly. "Don't think about it. It's done."

She rose up on her elbow and looked at him, deep into the dark-blue fire of his eyes. "What about us, Damien? Are we done?"

Damien's eyes turned hungry and his jaw clenched, but before he could say anything, Tess put her fingers over his mouth, his full sexy mouth, which just minutes ago had made her body ache with pleasure. "Don't answer that. Not tonight, not now."

On a growl he pulled her to him and kissed her hungrily.

"Stay here with me," she whispered against his mouth. "Don't go back to the house tonight."

He nipped at her bottom lip, uttered hoarsely, "I'm not going anywhere."

She smiled, then dropped her head back down and snuggled into the crook of his arm. "We'll work together, be together…for now."

He held her tightly and she closed her eyes, let her heart relax and her heartbeat slow, until finally she gave in to sleep.

It was close to dawn when Tess climbed on top of Damien and eased herself down on his thick, hard, shaft. Outside the bedroom window, snow fell to the ground, blanketing the earth, the glistening white color illuminating the walls of the room and the naked skin of the two people making love in it.

His back to the warm sheets, Damien stared up at her. His body rigid with need, he watched her eyes dance with hunger, her breasts rise and fall and her hips sway back and forth. He had been here a hundred times in his mind, had planned this moment, but nothing could compare with the reality.

She brought her legs forward, bracketing his shoulders, and settled her hands back on his thighs, giving Damien perfect access to her swollen cleft. As he watched her move his erection in and out of her body, the perfect connection that he would die before breaking, he placed his thumbs on either side of her wet folds. Gently, he opened her and began to circle the tender bud.

Tess sucked air between her teeth and dropped her head back, moaning with pleasure. The light played off her skin, turned her hard nipples into a ghostly pink and the scar on her thigh to a blatant reminder of a horrible past she wanted so desperately to leave behind and never revisit.

And he was planning on hurting her again....

He was a monster.

Her thrusts quickened and Damien's mind turned off. She was close, so close, and as he flicked the sensitive, white-hot bud back and forth, over and over, she let go, arched her back and called out.

The sound and the heat were too much for Damien. As she pumped and moaned, her muscles fisting around his erection, he finally allowed himself to go, fly, follow her over the edge into the sweet ecstasy of climax.

Eleven

It was nearly nine in the morning. Damien and Tess stood in the newly remodeled kitchen, wearing next to nothing. As they waited for the coffeepot to do its thing, they jovially debated some of Tess's choices in her purchases for the home.

Grinning, Tess wrapped her arms around Damien's neck and tried to help him remember their initial deal regarding the furniture-buying decisions. "I seem to recall you saying—many times, in fact—that I should consider this my house when I do the design."

His hands went around her waist. "That was before I saw the pot rack."

"What's wrong with the pot rack?" she asked,

mystified. "It's stainless steel. Who doesn't like stainless steel?"

"I hit my head on it this morning when I was getting a glass of water."

She laughed. "You are very tall."

"Hey, you're supposed to be sympathetic."

"I am?"

"You're my wife, after all."

"Wife for hire," she corrected.

He shrugged. "Technicality."

Her heart tugged at his words, and she rolled onto her toes and gave him a quick kiss. "I can have the pot rack taken up—"

"You mean taken down?"

"No," she said, giving hive a playful swat.

"And then there's the sink."

She turned her head and stared at the white porcelain farm sink. "What's wrong with the sink?"

"It's a bathtub."

"It's beautiful."

"You could get two kids in here!"

"Well, maybe I'll have two kids, then," she teased.

But the teasing part was lost on Damien. His smile died instantly, and a cloud moved over the brightness of his eyes.

"I just meant someday," she said lightly, noting the stiffness in his arms as he held her. "Someday I'll have a sink of my own like this, and maybe someday I'll have a couple kids to stick in it."

Not much better, Tess.

Damien's blue eyes narrowed. "Who are you planning on having kids with?"

She didn't know what to say. "I don't know. I was just playing—"

"Yeah." He released her, walked over to the sink. "I don't like it."

Neither did she. She didn't want to think about him being with someone else either or having kids…. But this was their last full day together and he hadn't given her any indication that he wanted the relationship to continue after he went back to California tomorrow.

"Coffee's ready," she said, trying to force a light tone into her voice. "Counters should be here in a few hours." She glanced around. "This place is so great, so fresh. You know, you could rent it out if you wanted to. Hang on to the property, if you wanted to. Someone might like it for a getaway. Tribute's got that cute, charming, small-town feel."

"We'll see," he grumbled, his dark, irritated gaze raking over her.

"Why are you looking at me like that?"

"I can't get the thought of you and another guy and kids out of my head."

Sighing, she put her arms around him and pressed herself against him. "You know what? I'm a little tired from last night. How about you?"

"No."

She smiled to herself. "I think you are. I think you could do with a nap."

When she glanced up, his eyes were changing from frustrated to ferocious as he got her meaning. With a hungry growl, he lifted her up and held her in his arms possessively. "I'm taking you to bed."

"Good."

His brow lifted wickedly. "But just so we're clear, there'll be no napping going on."

By the time the sun went down that day, the house was complete. From soup to nuts. And Tess had never felt so proud yet so cheerless in her life. Not that she was going to let Damien see how sad she was. In fact, she had planned a lovely night for them. Dinner by the fire, then a repeat performance of that morning.

Tess heard the shower running as she put the water on the stove to boil. In her mind's eye, she could see Damien, naked and wet, the water sluicing over his skin.

One thing was certain, a night or two of sleeping with him, making love with him, wasn't going to be enough, and she imagined that after he left for California her life would return to that empty shell it had once been.

She turned into the cutting board and set to work chopping tomatoes for sauce. She wished she knew how Damien felt. But he didn't give her much. Sure, he didn't want to think of her with another man or having another life, but he'd been tight-lipped about the future and what he wanted.

Was it possible that he might want to continue seeing her? Long distance? Or maybe moving to Minnesota part-time?

She stopped chopping. One thing she did know for certain was that being here together, in Tribute, had changed them both. And the red house represented that change. From something that was broken-down, messed up and battle-scarred, the little red house had been transformed into a clean, warm, safe, happy place. And Tess and Damien had been transformed along with it.

Tess turned off the burner and left the kitchen. She needed to see Damien, feel him, feel his arms around her again.

The shower was still running, and as she entered the bathroom, she was engulfed in hot, wet steam. Her heart pounding with need, Tess stripped off her clothes, then pulled back the shower curtain.

Damien looked even better than she could possibly imagine, every inch of his hard, muscled body dripping with water.

He grinned at her and offered his hand. "Dirty mind or just plain dirty?"

She took his hand and stepped inside. "A little of both."

"Good answer," he said, turning her so her back was to his front. He pulled her against him, against his already-hard shaft, then took the soap in his hand and began to wash her. Down her neck and over her collarbone.

"You let me know when you're clean," he whispered in her ear.

She smiled.

He moved the slippery bar over her breasts, over each tight, hard nipple. "How about now?"

She shook her head and uttered a shaky, "No."

He slipped the soap over her stomach, down over her hip bones, then between the wet curls at her core. "Here? Is this where you need my help?"

She nodded, unable to speak as he stroked her with the slippery soap, as he washed away the feelings of sadness and uncertainty, as he sent her to the moon again and again...

The phrase *eating in bed* had taken on a whole new meaning for Damien tonight. Like the perfect wife, Tess had served him spaghetti and champagne, pausing every so often to kiss him, nuzzle him and tell him she couldn't stop thinking about what he had done to her in the shower.

It was pure hell.

And total heaven.

He was leaving for California tomorrow night and everything inside of him was screaming to stay, to forgive her, let it go and try to be happy for once in his miserable life. But there was a force stronger than his feelings for Tess at work here, something that had been six years in the making, an undeniable force.

Damien downed his glass of champagne, then

turned to look at Tess. He had never seen her look more beautiful. Happiness and the glow of great sex radiated on her face.

The sucker, the fool inside of him could only think how great it would be to see her look like that every day, every morning when he opened his eyes.

He inhaled deeply, trying to quell the sudden feeling of being pissed off. "Hey, Tess, can I ask you something."

"Sure."

"Do you have any regrets?"

She laughed. "Tons."

"No, I mean, about coming here."

"I didn't have much choice, if you recall." She smiled over her glass of champagne. "But no, I'm glad I came here." She shrugged. "Maybe this started out as payback for you, maybe it still is, but whether you like it or not it's ending up being the best thing that could ever happen to me."

His brow creased. "How's that?"

She looked up for a moment. "I feel free, for the first time in six years…even longer, maybe."

He stared at her. Dammit! He had a plan in motion already, an anvil poised and ready to crush the dreams they'd built over the past two weeks. But what? She had made her peace with him already, with being here? She'd found freedom by being here and he was responsible for that?

What the hell? Did she deserve to feel free after what she'd put him through? And did he still have a right to want to make her pay? After everything he knew and had seen.

He didn't know. But as she put her glass down and slid the sheet off of his body, as she kissed his ear, then his neck and his chest, he decided he didn't need an answer tonight.

What he did need was her, her heart, her eyes locked with his as she scattered kisses over his chest, down his belly, down to where he ached for her with granitelike hardness....

Twelve

Tess woke to bright sunshine streaming through the bedroom window, and a Damien-less bed. At first, she panicked, thinking he had already left for California, but as she read the note on his pillow, her tension eased.

He had a meeting, and he'd be back by one.

Five hours…what could she do? The house was done, furniture in, appliances up and running. Sure she could pack, but what fun was that?

Then an idea popped into her head. A Christmas gift for Damien. The perfect gift.

With her pulse pounding, she jumped out of bed and headed into the bathroom. She just hoped she could find someone with enough skill to make it, to create the perfect representation of what had happened here in this house, between the two of them.

She knew that trying to find that perfect gift in such a short amount of time was a long shot, but it was something she had to do.

It was just business.

He would tell himself that until the day he died.

Damien pulled his sleek, black car into the driveway and shut off the engine. Before he got out, he stared at the little red house, testing himself. Did the place evoke any feelings that were useless to him now? Warmth, caring, vulnerability, comfort?

Of course they did, and Damien instantly hardened himself.

From day one, his plan had been to make Tess love him, make Tess love the house, then sell it without a thought. He had been a cold bastard then. And over the past two weeks, he had surprised himself by allowing Tess to get under his skin and melt his icy heart.

But the truth remained; she had hurt him once, screwed him over big-time. What guarantee did he have that she wouldn't do it again?

Better to cut things off here, cut her loose, and if it had to be in a blatantly obvious and hurtful way, so be it.

He stepped out of the car into the freezing air and walked to the front door. The offer that had just been made to him was highly lucrative, and needed to be acted on immediately.

When he came through the door, everything that was Tess cried out to him. The happy fire in the fireplace; the peaceful furniture in the living room; the quiet, sensual paint colors on the wall; and that damn sink in the kitchen.

Then he heard her. She was in the bedroom, talking on the phone in a merry voice. He stepped into the doorway and lifted his chin in a silent hello.

Sitting cross-legged on the bed, her hair loose about her shoulders, Tess caught sight of him and waved. Her gray eyes were bright, and she was clearly happy to see him.

"No, the foot is fine," she was saying to whoever was on the other end of the line. "I'm so much better, Liv. All healed." She looked up at Damien then, a smile tugging at her perfect mouth. "He's been wonderful." Her smile widened and she winked. "I do. Even more. Honestly, I've never felt this way before."

Damien's gut twisted as he realized what she was saying. She loved him.

Damn her. She loved him. Now. And she had said it out loud, to his face.

She'd never felt this way before.

Anger bubbled inside of Damien and he walked out of the room. He went into the living room and stood by the fire. He *had* felt this way before and look where that had gotten him.

It played like a broken record in his head. He had loved her and she had walked out on him, and even though he'd tried to bury it these past few weeks, those wounds were still fresh.

Maybe selling the house, tearing this little world to bits right in front of her would help heal him—maybe not.

But it was done, the deal was done.

He heard her walk up behind him, felt her hand on the small of his back. "That was Olivia."

"I guessed."

Her arms went around him. "How was your meeting?"

"Fruitful." Unlike the crackling fire beside him, Damien's voice lacked warmth, and was completely emotionless.

"Well, that's good," she said, sounding a little confused by his tone. "Was it about a house?"

"Yes, this one."

"Oh." And that's all it took. She released him.

He turned to face her. It killed him to see the disappointment and worry in her gray eyes, but there was nothing for it. "There was an offer made on it."

Her brows went up. "Wow. Without even seeing the place?"

"They didn't need to see it."

"Seriously, with all the work we've done. That sounds odd."

"They don't care about the renovations," he said, being careful to keep his voice casual.

"Then they're idiots because—"

"Tess." He stopped her right there. "They don't want the house."

Her eyes narrowed and she shook her head. "I'm sorry, you've lost me."

"They want the land."

"Well, the house is on the land, so—"

"They want to build a motel here, and they've offered me a considerable amount of money."

The doubtful, sad look she'd worn just moments ago was now replaced with the glare of a woman who understood what it was like to be hurt and was ready for it to happen again. "They have to tear down the house to do that, don't they?"

He nodded. "Yes."

She released a weighty breath and crossed her arms over her chest. "So what did you tell them?"

"I told them nothing," Damien said evenly. "I asked them where I should sign."

Tess stared at him. She felt numb, except for the scar on her inner thigh. For some reason, the skin there burned like the devil.

Maybe because she was dealing with the devil.

She left Damien standing beside the fire and walked to the couch to sit. She felt like the world's biggest fool. Her happy mood, her trusting spirit—the gift she'd spent hours designing for him. But mostly, for even thinking that there might be a future for them.

Clearly, it wasn't in the cards, never had been.

His back to the fire, Damien attempted to explain. "It's business. A great deal."

"I'm sure it is."

"And I know you worked hard on the property, so there will be a substantial compensation—"

"I don't want your money, Damien," she said, her gaze and tone reflecting the insulting offer he'd just made.

But Damien didn't get it. "Why the hell not? You could use it for your business or—"

"Or nothing," she uttered, disgusted.

But, for whatever reason, he wouldn't let up. "Take the money, Tess."

She stood and stalked over to him, faced him with her jaw tight and her lower lip quivering. "What is wrong with you?"

His blue eyes were almost lifeless in their apathy. "What do you mean?"

"A few hours ago you were nuzzling my neck."

"Things change," he said coldly.

"What exactly changed for you?" She lifted her brows. "Come on, I can take it. I'm no schoolgirl anymore, as we both know."

His gaze dropped and he turned to the door. "I have to get back to the house. But you should be aware that the bulldozers are coming tomorrow. Eight a.m."

"What?" she called after him.

"Eight a.m." he repeated, then walked outside.

She followed him out, into the cold afternoon air. "I heard the time part, Damien."

"They wanted to move fast, Tess."

She watched him walk away as her socks grew damp from the snow on the walkway. Then it finally dawned on her. Stupid, silly Tess, who had allowed herself to be whisked off into a fairy tale, minus the happily-ever-after part.

Tearing down the house had been his goal from day one. Have her build her dream, her perfect family home, then tear it down—while tearing the girl who'd hurt him to shreds in the process.

Damien was nearly at his car when she shouted, "Stop right there!"

He did, then turned and stared coldly at her as she walked toward him. "You're going to freeze. Go back inside."

She was in his face, feeling nothing but a burning desire to punch him. "You knew from the beginning that there was a good possibility that this house was going to be torn down, didn't you?"

"There were many possibilities."

"And you had me picking out the most beautiful materials…" She shook her head. "My fantasy materials."

He leaned against the open door. "I wanted you to feel what it was like to have something you loved ripped from you."

She just stared at him, not believing what she was hearing. "Oh, Damien. You really think I'd be emotionally destroyed because this house is gone?"

He didn't answer, but his jaw went hard as steel.

"You don't get it, do you?" she said, her warm breath making small clouds in the cold afternoon air.

"Get what?" he muttered.

"What the true payback is. You did hurt me, Damien. Make no mistake about that—you succeeded there. The true payback is that I actually thought we had something…real. I thought we'd both grown up enough to get over the past and start something that was so amazing." Her throat felt tight, but she refused to cry. Not in front of him, she wouldn't give him that. "Remember how I told you that with Henry the last bits of my faith and hope were gone?" When he didn't answer, she continued, "These weeks, I found it again. I had some faith—in us."

She smiled self-deprecatingly. "And, fool that am, I was ready to give my heart to the wrong man again."

She didn't give him time to respond. She said, "I hope you can finally leave the past in the past and move on at some point. I really do. Maybe when this house is nothing more than concrete ash…I don't know. But I'm done. I'm going home."

And with that, she turned around and went inside, to pack her things and to leave the red house and its sweet memories and unfulfilled wishes behind.

For good.

Thirteen

Christmas was supposed to be the happiest time of the year, and for most people it was. Presents and trees and Santa, happy couples and baby's first holiday bibs. How could anyone not smile at a neighbor and hum the chorus of "Jingle Bells." But for Tess, she just wanted to run out of NRR's office every day after work, get in her car and head home—hide under her bed until the whole holiday blew over.

It wasn't that she was a Scrooge or anything. She wanted to smile and sing, but it just wasn't in her.

Four days ago she'd left Tribute and the little red house and the man she had come to love once again. Today was Christmas Eve and that house had probably been bulldozed to the ground and that man was

probably having a snowless holiday season in sunny
California.

With a folder of new client information tucked
under her arm, Tess walked by Mary's office.

When Mary spotted her, she called out, "Hey,
Tess. Come here a sec."

Mary and Ethan had returned from their honeymoon a few days before, and Mary had been walking around the office like she was on cloud nine
ever since.

Tess went in and sat across from her partner.
There was a two-foot grinning Santa on the
woman's desk, and Tess had to stop herself from
knocking it to the ground. "What's up? I have
someone waiting…"

"Oh, it won't take long." Mary flipped her blond
hair over her shoulder and smiled. "I have something
I want you to think about."

"Okay."

"You like kids, right?"

Tess laughed. "Of course I do. Mary what's this
about?"

"I want you to be my baby's godmother."

A strange sadness moved over Tess. She was
flattered, and incredibly honored by the offer—so
pleased that Mary deemed her that close a friend.
But right now the suggestion just served as a
reminder of the family that she herself was never
going to have.

She gave Mary her best smile. "Thank you for

thinking of me. It's an honor and a great responsibility. I need to think about it, okay?"

"Of course." Mary returned her smile. "After the holidays we'll talk."

Tess nodded. "After the holidays would be perfect."

She was just about to leave when Olivia walked in to Mary's office.

"Oh, good, Tess, just the person I wanted to see."

If Olivia was pregnant and wanting a godparent, too, Tess thought inanely, she was going to pretty much lose it right there.

But pregnancy was not what the pretty brunette wanted to see her about. "Your...client," she said with a half smile, "sent payment for service, but not a return address to send the receipt."

Tess asked, "Which client is that?"

"Mr. Sauer."

Her heart dropped. "He sent payment?"

"A rather large one."

Mary eyed her. "Have you upped your fee without telling us?"

"No." She turned to Olivia. "Listen, I don't want that money. Send it back."

"I can't."

"Then rip it up."

Mary came around her desk and touched her arm. "Tess, what's wrong. What's this about?"

"I knew he wasn't cool," Olivia said, staring at Tess's face. Then she looked at Mary and explained,

"Her client was also a past boyfriend, who obviously jerked her around."

Mary took Tess's hand but nodded at Olivia. "Rip up the check, Olivia."

"You bet," Olivia said quickly.

Tess looked up and gave her friend a thankful smile.

Olivia nodded. "Whatever you need, girl, okay?"

Tess took a deep breath. "Thanks, but I'm going to be fine." And she meant it. It might take a while to get there, maybe next month or next year, but she was going to be happy again.

"I'd better get going," she told the women. "I have a client waiting."

Mary squeezed her hand before releasing it. "Then go, we'll talk later."

Tess went into her office and sat at her desk. The man across from her was handsome, she noted. But in a boyish way. The man across from her had blue eyes, but there was no anger there, no arrogance there, no passion.

She was almost thankful for it.

She stuck out her hand. "Mr. Sumner, I'm Tess York. How can I help you today?"

The man looked grim and said, "I promised my mother I'd be married by New Year's Eve."

"And I take it you're not."

He shook his head. "Not yet."

"Do you have a girlfriend? Someone you're thinking about asking?"

He shook his head.

"And how would you like my help?

"Can you be my pretend fiancée?"

She smiled. "No, but I'll help you find the courage to tell your mother the truth."

He blanched. "How much is that going to cost me?"

Tess laughed, and it felt good. "Not a cent. This one's on the house."

He'd put it off another day. Soon they were going to give up on him and back out of the deal altogether.

Maybe that's what he wanted.

It was near midday, and Damien sat in front of the red house like a protester without a sign, staring at the bulldozers that were unmanned and stuck in the snow. They had been sitting there for days, and he had not allowed them to get any closer. He didn't know what was wrong with him. He should've been in California, back to work and on the road to recovery. Not sitting with his ass in the snow and his head on a cloud.

Damn Tess York. She'd ruined him again.

A car pulled into the icy driveway—a pickup truck, actually—and came to a skidding stop right in front of the walkway.

Damien had known it was only a matter of time before she would show up.

Dressed like Mrs. Claus, which she did every year for the kids who came into the store, Wanda got out of her truck and bellowed at him, "I don't have time for this, Damien. It's Christmas Eve."

"I know," Damien called dryly. "Shouldn't you be helping someone get dressed and on his sleigh right about now?"

Her eyes narrowed as she walked over to him and sat on the stoop. "Don't get smart with me, Damien Sauer."

"I'm sorry."

"Good. Now, what the hell are you doing?"

He shook his head. "Acting like an ass."

"I'll say. Four days of stopping that truck from doing its job…"

"Yeah…" He plowed his hands through his hair.

Her voice dropped, even softened a touch. "Do the deal, Damien."

"Can't."

"Why not?" she asked. "End it. Get it, and her, out of your system."

"The problem with that is I have a sneaking suspicion that taking down this house will not get her out of my system."

"What will, then?"

"I have no idea."

"It's freezing out here." She clicked her tongue. "This deal is sweet. It's a helluva lot of money—"

"I have enough money."

She snorted. "Please don't say, 'But I don't have her.'"

He threw her a sideways glance. "You are one sarcastic broad, Wanda."

"Damn right." She looked at him, studied him.

"Tell me you weren't foolish enough to fall in love with her again."

"I don't think I ever stopped loving her." It was the first time he'd admitted it, out loud and to himself, and it cut deeply.

Beside him, Wanda cursed like a race car driver.

"What are you going on about?" he asked her.

"I have to give you something," she said, thrusting a medium-size brown box at him. "Here."

"What's this?"

"Present."

"Wanda, you didn't have to—"

"I didn't. It's from the girl. Christmas present she ordered a few days ago at Remi's place." She frowned. "He asked me to get it to you."

Damien's heart twisted, and he felt like ramming his fist through a wall. After all they'd been through, after all he'd said, she'd gotten him a Christmas present.

He opened the package and his heart sank. It was a handmade snow globe with a model of the red house inside of it. Lights glowed from the inside and there was a Christmas tree and presents and two people by the fire.

He looked at the card. It read: "So you'll always know where you began, where you ended up and where you are always loved. Tess."

A muscle twitched in Damien's jaw, and he turned away.

"You could use it to knock out the window," Wanda said beside him. "Get the ball rolling.

Damien turned and stared at her. "What are you so angry about? Always expecting the worst, hoping for the worst. What is it? Did someone leave you heartbroken and pissed off, too?"

"Yes."

Her mouth was thin and hard, but her eyes held the sadness and pain of a lost love. Damien knew what she was feeling, and for the first time he saw what life, what his future, would be like if he remained as bitter as Wanda.

It wasn't a pretty picture.

He wanted what was in the snow globe.

He wanted her.

He dropped an arm around Wanda's shoulders. "What are we going to do, huh?"

"Not we." She faced him, lifted her chin and pretended her eyes didn't sparkle with tears. "I'm too old for forgiveness, but you're not."

He turned back and faced the bulldozers for the last time. "No. I'm not."

The word on the street was that Christmas day was to be spent with family. The women of No Ring Required might have started out as just partners, but in the past few months they had grown into so much more—friends. And if you asked any one of them, as they sat around the Christmas tree in the NRR office, family as well.

It was midmorning and all three women had left their homes, cats and sleeping fiancés, and had come to the office to eat Olivia's challah French toast and open their secret Santa gifts. A few days ago they had drawn names telling them which partner they would be picking out a present for.

Olivia had drawn Mary's name, and she went first. "Here you go, Mama."

Like an excited little kid, Mary took the small box and ripped it open. She squealed when she saw the pearl-and-diamond earrings inside.

"I love them, Liv," Mary said, giving her friend a huge grin. "Thank you."

"Pearl is the baby's birthstone," Olivia explained. "The diamonds are for you."

"As they should be." Mary laughed. "Thank you so much!"

"Okay. I drew your name, Olivia." Tess got up and pushed an enormous box toward the excited-looking brunette. "For you."

"Wow, thanks. Is someone going to pop out of here?"

"Yeah, Mac would just love that," Tess joked.

Grinning, Olivia tore at the Santa wrapping paper, then stopped and stared at what was inside—twelve bottles of what Olivia had always deemed the best Sicilian Olive Oil ever made. "Oh, my goodness, how did you find it?

As Olivia leaned over and hugged her, Tess said, "One of my clients this year is an Italian importer."

"I can't believe it," Olivia began, her eyes dancing with excitement. "A dozen bottles. Where to begin? Well, first thing I'm going to make will be Panzanella salad, then a basic tomato sauce, then of course—"

"Ease up there, Chef," Mary said on a laugh. "The culinary masterpieces can wait for five minutes. It's Tess's turn."

Olivia's cheeks turned pink. "Of course, sorry, Tess."

"No problem, Liv," Tess said with a smile as she took the box Mary held out in her direction. "We all know how deep your obsession runs."

"I hope I got the size right," Mary muttered.

The wrapping paper came off easily, and Tess knew right away that Mary had gotten her shoes. But when she opened the box and saw the rich red Jimmy Choo pumps she nearly fell over. They were beautiful. Something she'd never buy for herself, but always craved.

She looked up. "Thank you, Mary. They're stunning. And my size."

"They're supposed to be ruby slippers," Mary said with a little shrug. "My version."

"Like in the *Wizard of Oz?*" Olivia asked, confused.

Mary nodded, her eyes on Tess. "'No place like home,' you know? I just want you to always feel that way about this place and us. Whatever happened before, whoever came before, me, you and Olivia— we'll always be a family."

Heat shot into Tess's throat. She didn't want to get emotional in front of them, but it was too late. She swiped the tears from her eyes and shook her head. "Damn you both for making me cry," she said, laughing. "And thank you. Five years ago when I got into this business, I never would've thought I'd gain two best friends in the process."

Olivia grabbed her hand. "Me, neither."

"I say we make this a tradition," Mary said, her blue eyes brimming with emotion. "Every Christmas morning."

Tess nodded. "I second that suggestion."

"I'm in, too," Olivia said, picking up the torn wrapping paper to stick it in the trash. But as she passed by the tree, she paused. "Hey, there's something else here." She reached down and came up with a long envelope. "This has your name on it, Tess."

"Who's it from?" Tess looked at Mary.

She shook her head. "Not me."

Olivia shook her head, too. "Not me." She then looked down at the envelope again. "It says, 'Tess, keep the faith. Love, Santa.'" Olivia glanced up again. "What does that mean?"

A mixed bag of fear and warmth and wonder churned in Tess's belly. She knew exactly who the envelope was from. What she didn't know was what was inside and she was scared to find out. But both women were pushing her.

"Open it," Mary urged.

Olivia thrust the envelope into her hand. "Yeah, Tess. Come on."

Tess swallowed the hard lump in her throat and tore

open the envelope. There was a group of papers inside and she slipped them out, uncurled them and read the first page. Her pulse picked up speed and her head felt heavy, dizzy. It was the deed to the little red house. Damien had put it in her name. He had given it to her. He hadn't destroyed it.

"What is it?" Olivia asked softly.

I don't know, Tess thought wildly, tears building. What was it? An apology? Forgiveness? A final farewell. Tess looked up at them both and smiled. "I think it's a peace offering."

Olivia's brows lifted. "From a certain ex-client/ex-boyfriend?"

Tess nodded.

Mary looked from one to the other. "Okay, no more snippets of information. Someone better fill me in with the whole story."

Olivia laughed. "I will. But I think Tess has some-where she needs to be right now."

With a quick smile at both of them, Tess grabbed her coat and purse and, as she was heading out the door, heard Olivia explain, "Remember that superhot guy with the blue eyes from your engagement party? Not that you should have, because you were only supposed to be looking at Ethan, but this man was hard to miss. Turns out he and Tess used to date…"

Traffic was light, just a few cars out on the road, heading for grandma's house or the airport or the 7-Eleven to pick up another carton of eggnog.

Tess made it to Tribute in two and a half hours. Her heart beat frantically as she got off the freeway and sped into town. But as she turned onto Main Street, then onto oh-so-familiar Yarr Lane, a sudden fear gripped her. What would she find when she got there? Would the house be just as she had left it, or had the bulldozers gotten to any of it? What about the inside?

And, God help her, what about Damien?

The answers to some of her questions came quickly as she pulled into the driveway and saw her sweet little cottage perfectly intact. There were even twinkle lights hanging from the rooflines and railings. The nerves in her belly eased, and she turned off the engine and got out of the car.

The wistful scent of turkey met her at the door. Not knowing what was inside, she decided to knock.

Damien opened the door, and his blue eyes glittered when he saw her. "Hey."

She nodded. "Hey."

"Welcome home."

His words, and the warm way he said them snaked through her. But she was too afraid to hope, to wonder what he was thinking and feeling.

She walked in, past him. He looked too good in jeans and a black sweater, his jaw clean shaven and his black hair thicker than usual.

"Merry Christmas," she said, noticing everything inside the house was just as she'd left it, and designed it—except for the blue spruce tree in the corner, heavily and oddly decorated with bubble lights, blue bulbs, paper ring ornaments and garland that was made out of pine cones and strawberries.

It was a mess, a homemade mess, but it made Tess smile. Clearly, Damien had done this.

She faced him. "I thought you'd be in California by now."

"And miss snow on Christmas? Not a chance. By the way, thank you for the snow globe. It was…perfect, exactly what I needed." He stared at her, his gaze heavy with longing. "You look good in this house."

She smiled tentatively. "So do you."

"You got the deed?"

"Yes." Her pulse jumped. She didn't want to ask, but she had to. "Was it another way of putting me and the past behind you?"

His eyes searched hers. "The past, yes. You, never." He reached for her hand, and when she gave it to him, he brought it to his mouth and kissed her palm. "I'm so sorry, Tess. I was such an idiot."

His touch made her weak, and all she could do was look at him, wait for him to say everything he needed to say.

"Fear makes people do crazy things," he said, lacing her fingers with his. "I thought I needed to hurt you to make myself hurt less. And that's just a load of bs— yet it's what I had to tell myself to stop myself from wanting you." His sincere gaze remained locked on her. "What I did was so wrong, Tess, and I almost lost you a second time because of it." A muscle twitched in his jaw and his voice dropped with emotion. "Tell me I have another chance to make it right."

His apology, his understanding of what had happened and why, stunned and amazed her. But she was still afraid to believe…. "Damien, I can never take back what I did—"

"Oh, sweetheart, I'm not asking you to. That's over, done. Doesn't matter. What matters is right now. What matters is that I love you."

She stared at him, her lips parted. "You love me?"

He nodded and pulled her into his arms. "Then, now and always." He kissed her neck, whispered in her ear, "Tell me you love me, too, before I go completely insane."

She smiled against his shoulder. "I love you, Damien. More than you'll ever know."

"I want to know." He pulled back so he could look at her. "Be my wife, Tess? Marry me and have my children. Let me give you the family you've always wanted."

Her heart soared with happiness. She couldn't believe what she was hearing. Never in a million years did she think this man would come to love her this much. She nodded, kept nodding.

"Is that a yes?" he said, laughing.

She stood on her tiptoes and kissed him squarely on the mouth. "That's a 'in a heartbeat.' That's a 'how about right now!'" She grinned. "Yes, Damien Sauer, I'll marry you."

He pulled her to him, his mouth covering hers

tenderly. When he eased back, he took her hand. "Come open your presents."

"I already have everything I could ever want. You and our little red house."

"Darling, there's so much more for you to enjoy." He led her over to the tree. "As you may have noticed, I'm not great with decorations. But there is one thing, right there in front of you that I am pretty proud of."

Tess looked at the branch sticking out in front of her, and her breath caught in her throat. Hanging on a thin length of pine was the most beautiful diamond ring she had ever seen.

Damien slipped it off the branch, then slipped it on her finger.

Tess stared at her hand. "It's so beautiful."

"You're so beautiful."

She looked up, felt as if she were floating on a cloud. She couldn't believe this day, this perfect Christmas day.

A holiday that had started off without a hope had turned into a season of true blessings.

Damien held her close as they stood by the tree. "Anything you want, it's yours."

"All I want is your love," she uttered with rich emotion.

"You have that, Tess."

And then he kissed her again. Not a soft sweet kiss this time, but a deep, heart-tugging, gut-clenching, knee-weakening full-mouth kiss.

"Damien," she uttered against his lips.

"Hmm?"

"You said I could have anything I want…."

He nuzzled her mouth, nipped at her lower lip. "Yes, my love. Of course. What is it?"

"That family you were talking about," she whispered.

"Yes?"

She grinned, brushed her lips teasingly against his. "Can we start making it right now?"

Damien slipped his hands beneath her and lifted her up. "Yes, my love," he said carrying her toward the bedroom. "Right now."

Epilogue

Dressed in a slightly over-the-top pink maternity bridesmaid gown, Mary glanced around the room. "Hearts, flowers and chocolate."

"Oh, my," Olivia finished, laughing.

The NRR threesome sat at one of the round reception tables, watching the wedding guests boogie on the white marble dance floor. The ballroom at Le Grande Hotel in downtown Minneapolis looked as though it had gone through a pink-and-red-and-white froufrou machine with all the ribbons, roses, hearts and toile. The wedding planner Tess hired had gone a little overboard with the *love* theme, but Tess didn't care. It was Valentine's Day. She had a beautiful white dress, great friends around her, a wonderful man who loved her and, for the first time in her life, a genuine enthusiasm about her future.

"This is one crazy wedding, Tess," Olivia remarked, pointing to the cupid ice sculpture.

"I think I like crazy," Tess said, grinning.

"You know you could've waited until the slow season, and Mary and I would have been happy to plan everything."

As the warm and familiar tune "We Are Family" blasted out of the speakers, Tess smiled widely at her girls. "Nope, I really couldn't wait."

"What do you mean?" Mary asked, confused.

Tess touched her stomach and shouted over the music. "Bun in the oven. I mean, a little Sauer in the oven."

Olivia squealed and hugged Tess. Mary smiled and shook her head. "Sorry, I'm just too big and uncomfortable to lean over."

"You're only six months pregnant, Mary," Olivia said, laughing.

Mary glared at her. "Just wait."

Olivia grinned, her brown eyes sparkling. "We are waiting. For a little while, anyway. I want my man all to myself."

"I hear that." Tess laughed. "Speaking of your man…and ours, too…"

"What?" Olivia said, her dark brows drawing together.

"Here they come."

All three women turned. Walking across the dance

floor toward them, looking tall, handsome and oh so wicked in the strange light cast by the red and pink decorations, were Ethan, Mac and Damien.

Mary gave a low wolf whistle.

Olivia muttered a dry, "Wow."

"Did we land some seriously good-looking man flesh or what?" Mary remarked dryly. "How lucky are we?"

"Very." Tess laughed. "But then again, they got pretty lucky, too."

The three women turned back to each other and smiled, They understood now that, through this newly found friendship and the stories of the past that they had shared with each other, they were forever linked. They had an unspoken promise. They were family, partners and there for each another always.

For Tess, it was not just a happy wedding day, it was a hopeful one—for all of them.

The future looked very bright indeed.

* * * * *

MILLS & BOON
Desire 2-in-1

On sale 17th October 2008

Captured by the Billionaire *by Maureen Child*

Trapped on an island resort with the man she'd once jilted, she knew her sexy billionaire captor would like to teach her a lesson…

Sold Into Marriage *by Ann Major*

Can a wealthy Texan stick to his end of the bargain when he takes the very woman he vowed to blackmail to bed?

∞

Secrets of the Tycoon's Bride *by Emilie Rose*

This playboy needs a wife and thinks his accountant the perfect bride-to-be…until she says no and her scandalous past is revealed.

The Executive's Surprise Baby *by Catherine Mann*

The father of her child-to-be is also her family's arch enemy, and Jordan Jeffries is determined to claim his baby and make Brooke his wife!

Series – The Garrisons

∞

The Desert Bride of Al Zayed *by Tessa Radley*

She decided that her secret marriage to the sheikh must end… just as he declared the time had come to produce his heir.

Best Man's Conquest *by Michelle Celmer*

She had agreed to be a bridesmaid at her cousin's wedding…until she discovered that the best man was her gorgeous ex-husband!

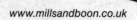

Celebrate 100 years of pure reading pleasure with Mills & Boon®

To mark our centenary, each month we're publishing a special 100th Birthday Edition. These celebratory editions are packed with extra features and include a FREE bonus story.

Plus, you have the chance to enter a fabulous monthly prize draw. See 100th Birthday Edition books for details.

Now that's worth celebrating!

September 2008
Crazy about her Spanish Boss by Rebecca Winters
Includes FREE bonus story
Rafael's Convenient Proposal

November 2008
**The Rancher's Christmas Baby
by Cathy Gillen Thacker**
Includes FREE bonus story *Baby's First Christmas*

December 2008
One Magical Christmas by Carol Marinelli
Includes FREE bonus story *Emergency at Bayside*

Look for Mills & Boon® 100th Birthday Editions at your favourite bookseller or visit
www.millsandboon.co.uk

2 FREE

BOOKS AND A SURPRISE GIFT!

We would like to take this opportunity to thank you for reading this Mills & Boon® book by offering you the chance to take TWO more specially selected titles from the Desire™ series absolutely FREE! We're also making this offer to introduce you to the benefits of the Mills & Boon® Book Club—

- ★ **FREE home delivery**
- ★ **FREE gifts and competitions**
- ★ **FREE monthly Newsletter**
- ★ **Exclusive Mills & Boon® Book Club offers**
- ★ **Books available before they're in the shops**

Accepting these FREE books and gift places you under no obligation to buy, you may cancel at any time, even after receiving your free shipment. Simply complete your details below and return the entire page to the address below. You don't even need a stamp!

YES! Please send me 2 free Desire volumes and a surprise gift. I understand that unless you hear from me, I will receive 3 superb new titles every month for just £4.99 each, postage and packing free. I am under no obligation to purchase any books and may cancel my subscription at any time. The free books and gift will be mine to keep in any case.

D8ZED

Ms/Mrs/Miss/Mr ....Initials ....
BLOCK CAPITALS PLEASE

Surname ....

Address ....

....

....Postcode....................

Send this whole page to:
UK: FREEPOST CN81, Croydon, CR9 3WZ